IN HIM WAS LIFE

IN HIM WAS LIFE

Caroline Glyn

*With a Foreword by
the Bishop of Lincoln
and illustrations by the author*

THE WESTMINSTER PRESS
Philadelphia

© Caroline Glyn 1976

Published by The Westminster Press ®
Philadelphia, Pennsylvania

PRINTED IN THE UNITED STATES OF AMERICA

Library of Congress Cataloging in Publication Data

Glyn, Caroline.
    In Him was life.

    1. Jesus Christ — Fiction. I. Title.
PZ4.G568In [PR6057.L98]   823'.9'14   76-26492
ISBN 0-664-24118-2

CONTENTS

FOREWORD

CAROLINE GLYN HAS written a book which will be much
valued and enjoyed especially by those who are beginning to have
some valid and personal experience of Jesus Christ as a reality.
Her book will widen, warm and colour that experience. Though
she uses her imagination vividly, there is, in the background, a
real faithfulness to the Gospel narrative and structure. The
imagination she brings to bear upon her subject is unusually
varied. She writes, for instance, with true poetic insight into
human feeling and human situation. But she also writes with a
deep spiritual understanding, and is able to identify herself, in a
penetrating way, with human spiritual responses and a whole
kaleidoscope of people. Since she is a poet, a novelist and a
Religious, it is, perhaps, not surprising that her different gifts all
play their part in what she has written. But it makes an unwonted
combination and will thereby deepen in varied directions the
experience of those who read her book.

SIMON LINCOLN

INTRODUCTION

SINCE 1967 I have been a member of a monastic community dedicated to living out the life of Christ by prayer, liturgy and study. Out of this intensity these stories have arisen spontaneously. They are therefore the overflowing of joy, but not only that. The contemplative life is in the first place a stripping of complacency, and it has forced me to ask painful questions: "Who was Jesus Christ? Why was he crucified? What have I to do with him?" And (since he is inseparable from them), "Who were and are the Jews?"

These stories are part of the asking. They are my attempts to see him, because if I cannot "see him clearly" I cannot "love him dearly", let alone "follow him nearly". A pictorial mind like mine cannot study in the abstract. The scholars tell me nothing until I can picture it. My stories are therefore the pictures of all the study I have done for the past seven years.

They are, nevertheless, fiction, not documentary, and must not be taken too seriously. However, I am sure that fiction has its own way into truth. To use a novelist's craft to imagine how anything happened is in one way inevitably to falsify it, but in another way it is to honour the very reality of it. Perhaps it was like this—it was like *something*. To say, "We do not know how it was", and to say, "Suppose it were like this", are both ways of asserting that it was. Naturally, I have done my best to find out and keep closely to what *is* known, but even where I am guessing, I am affirming that it *was*.

As to the form of these stories: I am only one of a long line of authors of apocryphal gospels to find first-person narration the easiest. (The canonical authors did not need such props.) In my own case, however, it came particularly naturally, since I began using this form of story to get inside the Bible when I was eleven years old.

"What do *you* think?" Christ was always asking that, but he seldom told anyone what to think. I am no luckier: the only answer I get to my questioning is that in him was life, and if I understood that I might also know who he was, why he had to die, and why I cannot live without him. Meanwhile, there can be the trying to understand.

I should like to thank all who came to my rescue in various ways, above all the Rev. Neville B. Cryer of the British and and Foreign Bible Society for his unstinted help in checking the background detail.

Finally, I must admit with an evangelist before me that "there is much else that Jesus did. If it were all to be written down, I suppose the world itself would not hold the books that should be written."

C. G.

1
A NEW THING

THE DARKNESS OF the years lay over the land, and the power of the oppressor. Our cry, "Israel is God's people for everlasting", grew fainter and fainter, weaker and weaker, against the triumphant shout of the heathen, "Rome is eternal". God has turned away his face from us, people moaned, he has forgotten us. And yet we waited and hoped.

And I was as barren as a dry tree, childless as a stone, shamed among the women. "God has hardened himself against Elisabeth, the wife of Zacharias the priest," it was murmured. "Is the time coming when he will loathe us altogether, and none of our women bear children any more? Is he soon to destroy Israel from off the earth? For Elisabeth is blameless, and her husband is upright." And all the young girls of our neighbourhood began to go in fear that they, too, would be stricken barren.

"The light is failing, have you not seen?" people asked. "The sun is growing dim. The nights are longer than they were. Is the end of all things upon us? Is this the dawning of the day of the Lord, in gloom and great darkness? And will he condemn us to darkness?" But I answered all who spoke to me in this way, "As for me, I will look for the Lord my God, and trust in him, though he hide himself in darkness and smite us with affliction; for what hope have I but the Lord?"

In the fortieth year of my husband's priestly service, when fulfilling his turn to offer the evening incense in the Temple, and when the Days of Affliction of the Soul were past, a tablet of wax was brought to me from him where he was, at Jerusalem, and he had written on it:

"Rejoice, O barren that never bore a child! For God shall deal with you as with Sarah, and have mercy on you as on Hannah; and at this time next year you shall bear a son, and call his name John. The mouth of the Lord has spoken it."

Then I knew that an angel had visited my husband in the Temple, and that salvation was upon us. I went up into the hills behind our town, to pray and give thanks to God, and there a vision was shown me. I looked northwards, where God has ever dealt us his hand of anger, and I seemed to see the smoke of armies riding down like locusts to destroy; I cried aloud to see the kingdom of Israel falling, the proud hill of Samaria brought low, the kingdom of Judah invaded and the violence of war seething even to the gates of Jerusalem, the city of peace. I looked east, to the insolent Edomites, our brother nation that has always longed to see us cast into the sea, and saw its mountain strongholds hanging over us like eagles' nests in their pride. I looked southwards, and saw the smoke of the abominable sacrifices of the heathen rising from Mount Zion; westwards, and I beheld all the arrogant, God-insulting power of Rome, the last and worst.

And as I looked, my ears were filled with the howls of prisoners and the shrieks of women, with the groans of those dying in famine and the barking of jackals, from far ago, from long back: all the ages of grief of our land. Those oppressed generations seemed all to be with me now, for not once, and not twice, has God humbled his people, but from age to age we have drunk our own tears. Wherever I looked, my hand shading my eyes, I saw the stumbling, fleeing multitude, little shapes against the brown hills, stumbling, fleeing and falling. All who had ever feared and fled in Israel were there. But as I watched, it seemed to me that the tiny figures grew black, and long shadows raced out before them, outstripping them, as a great light slowly dawned behind them. "The Kingdom!" I cried. "The Kingdom of God is at hand!"

I saw it rising, its brightness behind them, illuminating them all, overtaking them all; not one of those children of Israel from so far back but was caught and lit by the glory rising in the east, on the edge of the world and the edge of time. And I wept with joy because the Lord was giving us our youth back like the eagle's: my youth, and not mine only, but sinful, weary Israel's: all would be made new. "Surely," I said, and caught my breath, "surely it is time for Elijah to come and set all to rights." And

it seemed to me that a voice answered in me, "It is time." Can it
be he, I thought, can it be he, my own child, who shall be conceived by the power of God?

And I cried aloud and spoke to all whom I had seen in my
vision: "Blessed are you who have suffered; blessed am I who
was cursed; for it is to his poor and afflicted that God has sent
his salvation, and to those that were outcast that he has said 'You
shall be mine'."

But when my husband returned, he was dumb, for he had
dared to argue with the angel of the Lord who had spoken to him;
but he wrote a second time on a wax tablet, commanding me,
"See that he is named John: because he shall be a sign of grace."
(John means "God is gracious".)

And I conceived, and purified myself, rejoicing more than a
young bride, and I ate nothing unclean, nor drank wine, so that
my son should be holy to the Lord, a Nazirite; and as a Nazirite,
his hair should never be cut, as a sign that the Lord's power was
in him. "For surely," I said, "God has raised him up to be a mighty
one in Israel, and he shall begin to deliver us out of the hand
of our enemies." But to myself I thought, He shall be greater
still. He shall be a prophet clothed in the spirit and power of Elijah.

All the women of the tribe of Levi were glad with me, when
they saw me great with child. "God will show us his mercy too!"
they said. So I lived apart, blessing and praising the Lord. But
fear was among us as well as joy, for everyone knew the
angel of the Lord had visited us as once he visited Abraham and
Sarah; and they asked, "What can it mean? What shall this child
be? Will there be a new covenant, a new promise? Will God set
his love on us once more, as he did of old?"

But I knew that his love has never been turned from us, that
he had loved us always, before ever he called Abraham out of
Ur of the Chaldees; and I prayed, "Blessed art thou, O Lord
our God, Shield of Abraham, and our exceeding great reward!
Blessed art thou, who raisest the dead, and makest salvation
spring forth like the morning! Blessed art though who redeemest
Israel, and healest their backslidings; who blessest the years and
fillest us with peace!"

Then in my sixth month my cousin Mary of Nazareth came to me, who was only a young betrothed girl. When I saw her running up the hill towards me, she who had been only a child herself when I saw her last year, I knew that in her God was doing a new thing, new as a little baby, and in her all things were new, all restored; all that had been old grown young and all that had been soiled made sweet. And seeing her there my heart was knit to her and I loved her as my own soul; and I knew that she who came after me would be a greater mother than I. And when I heard her calling as she came up the slope, "Peace, peace be with you, Elisabeth, dear mother!" the baby leapt in my womb for joy, and I exclaimed, "O blessed of the Lord, have you come to me? For I know that if my child shall be Grace, yours shall be Salvation." Then she fell into my arms crying out, "I thank God, I thank God with all my heart, for he has truly filled me with his whole salvation!"

And so her child was indeed named when he was circumcised. And she was honoured above all mothers, for a great star with a tail to the horizon shone in the months of her childbearing; I saw it from my own hilltop, and later it was told me that the Chaldeans had interpreted it to mean a birth. And more, they say that after its appearing, strangers from the East came to Judaea who were sages and kings in their own lands, all to pay homage to my cousin and her baby son Yeshua: God's salvation. For God had put forth his arm to save us when he sent those two children to us; but it was his ancient and abiding love that was working new salvation, and his purpose from of old that had brought us new grace. For in our creation he set his heart on our redemption, and in every destruction that has come on us he has planted the seed of all things made new; and it was not the end that was at hand, but the beginning.

2

DEAD SEA FRUIT

THESE ARE EVIL days. The power of the nations goes from one heathen emperor to another, each proclaiming himself God, as though any of them knew what that name meant. The inhabitants of the earth live in their filth. They grub in ungodliness and never except in mockery lift up their eyes to Zion. And why? Why are the prophecies not being fulfilled? Why are the Gentiles not kneeling at our feet and learning our ways? Because the greatest filth of all is in Zion herself. And that is why we of Qumran have withdrawn ourselves to the desert.

Corruption in the state; corruption in the palace; corruption in the Temple, stinking corruption in the Temple. For into the Holy of Holies year after year goes a High Priest who is no High Priest, who is called so by violence and fraud: to such a pass are we come, the men of Jewry believe their God could be bribed. But his pure eyes do not even look on their iniquity. In vain does the foul smoke of their sacrifices rise! The Temple is an abomination. Israel is apostate. Only the pure and faithful remnant shall live in his sight. So we strive for purity, and keep ourselves far from the defiled and misled multitude, not for our own sakes but so that at his coming there shall be a people prepared for the Lord. We are prepared for him! Though all Israel and all the world be sunk in evil and darkness, the Children of the Light are prepared for his coming. All clothed in white, washed clean, we study his Law and honour him in our lives, hidden away from unclean eyes among the rocks and on the shores of this separated sea, our own sea, called by some Dead. Our enemies say that our life is a living death, and if holiness is only to be had so, they will remain unholy. Fools and mockers! They will laugh differently on the day of Judgment, the Last Separating! And it is very soon!

Ah! How the moon will fall in blood on that day. How their

sinks of rivers will rise up and overwhelm them, sweeping away all their uncleanness, and how the Lord will blow away those polluted rivers with the breath of his mouth! How the people shall mourn! How the oppressors of his Holy Ones shall lament, and all who oppressed the Children of Light! Then shall all of us who followed in the way of the Teacher of Righteousness shine as the sun in our white robes, and all the apostate shall groan to see us, when God himself shall crown us. Ah, but bitter is the suffering before that day shall come.

And then we shall see too whose baptism washed clean, the baptism of our holy community or of the renegade priest John. Ah, then we shall know!

When he first came to us[1] I saw by the wild red light in his eyes that here was a proud, scornful boy who would soon forsake the way of holiness. How right I was! I was never so glad to see a novice go. The whole place felt cleaner for his departure. But if I'd guessed what madness and power would come on him I should not have rejoiced so. Yet after all, I had plenty of opportunity to know, when I think how he could capture the minds of our young brethren. . . . How he and Matthias used to walk together in the lakeside hills all day long, talking of the new world. . . . How it was impossible not to be moved, even shaken, by his glowing eyes fixed on one—how strangely it stirred me, when on first interrogating him on why he had come to us, he answered in a shout: "To prepare the way of the Lord!" How could I know then that he would later be calling *us* to repentance —that our departing neophyte's last words to us would be, "The axe is laid to your roots! Beware!" This was more than a young man's arrogance. This was God-insulting pride. But even then I did not guess he would be back here, ten years later, in business as a prophet, out to denounce our sins—and take away our best brothers: Matthias—well, that's hardly surprising; Nathan, Jonathan—all had their heads turned and have gone off to help him baptize in the Jordan.

[1] There is, of course, no evidence that John the Baptist was associated with Qumran or the Essenes; the Gospels state merely that "he was in the deserts".

Sins were always his favourite subject. I remember when he tried to convert me, long ago when he was a novice. He took me out over the salt pans and up into the burnt salt rocks, shouting to me and to the sky that the wrath of God searched the secret places of the heart and burnt it like brimstone and scoured it like sand. I was glad, then, of such fervour in a boy. Then he turned to me in quite a different way, suddenly so young and anxious, and said, "Tell me, by your reading of the holy books, will the time be long?"

"To the Day of the Lord?"

"Yes, yes! Isn't it coming soon?"

"We have been told," I said: "A time, two times, and half a time. Our Teacher of Righteousness expounded it thus. . . ." He listened like thirsty ground, exclaiming, "But who will be ready? Who will be ready? Will Israel repent in time?" He almost made me afraid that day: the rocks had never looked so arid, the sea so dead; somehow his urgency caught me, and his alarm. Meditating on the Day as much as we do, the impact does become lessened perhaps; he certainly had the gift of renewing it. But what's the use of that? It's madness that has seized him, out there in the desert, baptizing the people by the hundreds and thousands, sinners of every kind—tax collectors, whores, the unclean. . . . Is that how he thinks to purify Israel for the Coming of the Lord? Is that all his sense of God's holiness has come down to? No, no, it is possession. I saw it coming long ago. The lying spirit of false prophecy. The people, of course, would not know the difference. Ah, the days are evil indeed, and Israel is far astray. False teaching is everywhere. But who will hear the true? Truth is not heard, it is rebuked, as the Holy Community suffers rebuke. But God shall rebuke our rebukers. And it will be soon, soon enough even for you, John. . . . Then we shall see whose baptism avails.

3

THE SHOUT

So HE HAS died a martyr in Israel—a witness to the truth and holiness of God. As he preached it in his life, he proclaimed it by his death, John the righteous, the last prophet; and he suffered like all the prophets. What evil would we stop short at? Can any voice make us repent if his could not? And even now they will not hear him, those who refused him: the Pharisees, the "Holy Ones", the priesthood.

How he came sweeping into that barren community of Qumran like the desert wind itself, crying out to them to turn, turn before it was too late: to wash their lives and not only their bodies. And how many heard? How many recognized God in him? Five or six of us followed him. I was the only one who had known him ten years before, when we were in the novitiate together.[1] I had never known such excitement, such a sense of the living God, as in those weeks with my wild companion John. If ever there was a man called apart to holiness, it was he. That anthill of white-robed figures could not hold him. It was judgment enough on them that he could not be one of them, if they had but seen it. And now I know that what he said is true: the axe shall fall on them, fall on their roots; the time shall come, and soon, when the very place of the holy community is forgotten, because they could not repent of a pride harder than Jerusalem's own.

But it was the beginning of all joy in my life when John of the deserts came back to us, thinner, browner, and wilder than before, a man now and more than that, a prophet filled with the spirit of the Lord. He stood on the hill over the writing-rooms and cried down on us to repent or die, and when I looked up from my copying and saw who it was my heart leapt within me, knowing now that all I had sensed about him long ago was true:

[1] See note on *Dead Sea Fruit*, page 18.

God was behind this man, it was God himself coming to us in the dust-storm of desert fire which was John son of Zacharias. There was purity, there was holiness, in that gaunt and skin-clad figure from the rocks, not in all our robes and hourly lustrations. I was with him as soon as I could scramble up there, and fell on his neck, weeping with gladness, not only to have found my friend again, but for the sudden burst of hope that was flooding up in me. I cried out "It's beginning, isn't it? The salvation is beginning?" and he answered in a great voice, "Yes!"

The common people felt it—not the proud, not the rich, but the poor and despised. They knew what his appearing meant. All Judaea and Jerusalem came out to him, and from the farthest north of Galilee to the coasts of Egypt they came, like the old days: from Dan to Beersheba the country was roused and came to him. He stood there by Jordan with the barren mountains behind him and thundered and pleaded with the voice of God, and though the people bowed themselves and wept, the deep joy was running like an undercurrent. As we—his disciples and assistants—went to and fro through the crowds, we heard everywhere: "It is the word of the Lord! The Lord is speaking to us again! He has remembered us! God our Saviour has remembered us!"

The joy was in John too, sombre as he was. He knew that the Lord had never forgotten his people and had turned to them again, to smite and to heal. It was his certainty that was spreading through all his baptized until the excitement seemed to be speaking of itself:

"The Kingdom of Heaven is at hand!"

Then at last it had been said; but they all knew it.

"Turn again! Turn again! Come back to the Lord your God! For he is standing ready over his threshing-floor. The last great harvest of Israel is about to begin. Turn again to the Lord your God, for he is among you!" And the cries of fear and contrition that arose were all of them at the same time cries of longing.

"See where his Kingdom is dawning in fire!"

And when we looked, we saw indeed the evening horizon ringed in fire, and John below it, with the thick Jordan undergrowth black behind him; and where he stood against it, the sunset was reflecting in his eyes, so that it seemed as though they were piercing through to the fire behind the blackness, as though he were possessed by fire, filled with it.

Even the uninhabited river-bank seemed too domestic for John. He was like some fiercely shy animal from the deserts which he loved, the wastes and barren uplands where he had lived with the animals and with God, the silent and almighty God of the desert. We knew that he would not stay long among us, because he could not bear to. He himself spoke always as though he were soon to pass away: imagining himself, it seemed, consumed in the evening brightness. The people, who loved him, could see how impatient he already was for it. We used to see him, in the late evening or first dawn, running over the rocky hillsides above the river gorge to some place where he could exult alone in the breaking glory that he felt so certainly. "You will see," people said to one another. "The chariot will come for him again, and carry him up into heaven—for isn't he Elijah returned?"

But when they asked him, "Master, aren't you the Last Prophet —he whom Moses spoke of?" he would cry out in distress, almost in anger, "Don't ask who I am! I am nobody! I am a voice shouting in the desert! I am the Lord's road-maker! When the mighty One, the Holy One, comes to gather in his harvest, I shall have gone my way. I am nothing but the crier of his coming. He has no need of me, and I am not worthy to be the slave who ties his sandal. All my reward will be to be wholly burnt up in his fire."

I remember when John stood on the rock he used to preach from, and gazing across the river into the eastern mountains of Moab cried: "Behold, I look from afar, and see the Power of God coming, and a cloud covering the whole land! When he comes go out to meet him, and say to him, 'Tell us if you are he that shall rule over God's people Israel?' Let the everlasting gates be opened wide for the King of Glory to come in: for is this he that shall rule over God's people Israel?"

And if he seared them for their sins, the people loved him all the more, for he was like the fierce southern wind blowing from the desert, free with God's own freedom, into their stifled, baffled lives. To his weeping, broken penitents, after they had confessed, as he helped them struggle out of the water with his strong brown arm, he would say: "I have baptized you with water for repentance. But the Holy One who is coming after me shall baptize you with God's Holy Spirit and with fire!" They knew it was true, that the mighty wind of the creation was blowing again already, that John's sternness was the same sternness that had stood round Israel always: God's ancient truth and righteousness.

There were strange scenes by the Jordan in those days, where people camped wherever the thickets gave way to patches of scrub or stone; their fires lined the rocky banks of the river. All Judaea and Jerusalem seemed to be coming out to John, and many from remoter parts as well. All who came were desperate in one way or another: desperate for health of mind or body, desperate for hope, desperate for forgiveness. Indeed if they were not desperate, if they came from curiosity, or to be sure they were in on a good thing (as was the case with many of the Pharisees who bothered to come), John would not baptize them, but sent them away with a rebuke.

The devils feared John, and at night the crowds shivered as the cries of lunatics hollered through the bushes; and there were often struggles in the water as the possessing demon tried to throw John away from its human victim. But John was afraid of nothing, though many people were afraid of him.

Most who came were too awed to press forward for baptism the first day, but stayed watching and listening, some longer, some shorter, some remaining indefinitely as his disciples. They forgot their affairs, their money-grubbing, their lending and borrowing, for an urgency of another kind burnt through us all from John and nothing else seemed to matter, any more than it did for him.

For now his message was changing again:

"He is standing among you, God's Holy One, he is among you now, and you do not know him!"

"Master, master, tell us how to recognize him."

"No. I cannot. Neither do I know him. But soon, soon he will be revealed, and all flesh shall cry: Verily thou art a God that hidest thyself, O God of Israel, the Saviour!"

And the people began to look at each other in great wonder and fear.

"He is standing among you, the unknown one!"

I was the only one of his disciples who ever followed him into the mountains when he slipped away alone. Even I did not always dare to, but sometimes I needed the solitude as much as he did. On one burning Sabbath day we climbed to a high point at the edge of the plain and sat and rested there looking down towards Jericho, with the heat-haze rising like mist. I said to him: "Master, do you truly not know who God's Holy One is to be? Although the day of his revelation is so near?"

His dark face seemed to grow sad, and he said, "I truly do not know, Matthias. It is hidden from me. I think the time of his glory will not be for me. Once I used to dream that I would be his servant when he came. But it's not going to be like that. My service is to vanish away at his coming."

Then the glow came back into his eyes, and he said, "But I shall see him, Matthias! The Lord has told me that I shall see and know him before my work is over. I shall see the Spirit come mightily upon him, and shall know that this is he in whom Israel hoped!"

I was full of grief for him at his words. "The Spirit is mighty in you, too, John son of Zacharias," I said. "Will it then leave you and alight on him?"

"I shall be nothing, and he shall be everything!" he cried. "And that shall be my very joy and the fulfilling of my joy."

When I saw him in prison I knew that he had foreseen truly. There was no power or prophecy in him any more. But when I tried to say something to comfort him, he silenced me abruptly: "A man can have only what God gives him. Don't you remember what I said?" But that still lay months ahead. On that Sabbath in the hills I made him promise, "If it is permitted, and if there is time, will you point him out to me when you have seen him?"

"What need? God will reveal him at the right time."

"But you must play your part in the revelation."

"That's true," and he promised.

It was soon after this when he came towards me through the crowds one evening and caught at me with a hand that I thought was shaking. "We must go from here," he said. "My time is nearly ended. I have seen him—the one on whom the spirit has alighted."

"And you didn't tell me!"

"It was not permitted. The Spirit came terribly upon him and heaven was opened. I was as one dead. Then the spirit drove him out into the wilderness. When he returns, it will be to claim his own. If my work is not done I must leave it. Oh that I may truly have prepared his way! For heaven and earth shall be shaken by the tread of his feet."

I saw that he was changed already. The light, the fire, were diminished. We moved upstream next morning to a much more sparsely populated region, and he no longer spoke much in public. He spent more and more time away from us. But still the penitents came.

A few weeks after that, one morning early as we were ending the dawn Shema', John suddenly stopped dead and his hands fell by his sides. I looked where he was looking. I could hardly make out what John could see (he had the vision of an eagle), but thought I could distinguish a tiny figure coming down the mountainside, from the heart of the Judaean wilderness, it seemed, where no man can live. A great fear seized me and I looked at John, my throat dry and choking. John was muttering, "Do you see him, do you see him now? God's Holy One?" Then his voice began to rise: "Look at him now, look well at the chosen and beloved of God, the firstling of the new flock of Israel, God's lamb! Look at the unblemished ram through whom the whole flock shall be sanctified! For I could do nothing but baptize for repentance. It is he who brings forgiveness. O Israel, see your salvation, who shall take away your sin at last!"

And as the figure strode down the goat-path to the riverside and stood there unmoving, a little distance from us, John fell on his face and spread out his hands; and the rest of us followed him. When we looked up the stranger was gone.

We were in a village at the edge of the desert at that time. The only accessible place on the banks was likewise the communal watering spot, and so the baptisms were going on amid flocks coming to drink, women singing at evening as they filled their jars, travellers fording the river. I think John was glad of that village. He was a tired man.

The day after we saw the strange figure coming out of the wilderness, when the flocks came down to be watered in the afternoon, there seemed to be one more man with them than we had been used to greeting: and then I saw John's face and understood. The stranger was mixing with the goatherds like one of them, a casual hand helping out, unrecognized by any but John. John did not bow this time, but helped with the watering; his flair with animals was almost uncanny, learnt during his long companionship with them in the desert. As the herdsmen, laughing and chatting, were rounding up their flocks again to drive them up, John said to the two of us who were there—Andrew and myself —"Go and follow him, God's chosen lamb. Talk to him. Don't be afraid. You see the power is quiet in him now. The heavens will not open again."

So we went. Andrew and his brother Simon were both fishermen from Galilee who had come with all their friends and relatives, thirty or forty of them, on pilgrimage to be baptized, and falling under John's spell had remained behind after the others had gone north again. I had become fond of them both; it was our loss, at Qumran, never to meet rough, rugged, illiterate folk like these. But I was as awkward and inarticulate as Andrew when the new "hand", rounding up the stragglers, suddenly turned as though he knew we were following and demanded, "Do you want something?"

"Master," we stammered, and I blurted, "Where are you staying?"

He had to smile at the ineptitude of it, but said quite gently, "Come and see." So we did go and see, and spent an evening among tents and shepherds, until it was too late to go back to John (but John had known that would happen). I was thinking all the time: "Is it true? Can this be the Messiah?" The contrast was so great between those images of fire and thunder and the heavenly Son of Man, and this quiet evening among the tents, with the lean brown man in dusty clothes, listening to the herdsmen spinning tales. Where, now, was the breath that would destroy God's enemies and the glory that would blast the heathen?

Presently, relaxing with supper and rest, one of the men asked him, "You worked at shepherding before, up in Galilee, then? Shepherd, are you? You got them stragglers up nice."

I looked sharply at him to see what account he would give of himself. He said, "Yes . . . Yes, I am a shepherd." Then he looked up at me, aware of my gaze, and I knew where the fire and thunder were. It was the same fire I had seen in John's eyes: the same fire, the same spirit. But he was greater than John.

The only thing I remember that he said was when he asked, "What do you think? Does God care for sinners?" The men chorused indignantly. "Oh, no. We know the answer to that one. God hates sinners and will not hear their prayer."

"And what of yourselves?" he asked. "If you lose a sheep do you write if off as a loss and leave it to die? Or do you go out to search for it? Which of you would be content to lie down until he had searched the whole mountain over and found it, and brought it safely back?"

It was the first time I saw the stupefaction on human faces, as they began to guess his meaning, that I was later to see so often, wherever he went. But it didn't go further than that, that night. He was listening to them, rather than they to him. And next morning we went back to John.

I couldn't leave him. All my love and allegiance belonged to him. But it was different for the others, Andrew and Simon, Nathanael and the rest. They knew their time with him was over. Apologetically, awkwardly, they left to go home to Galilee. When I next saw them it was as leading disciples of the "new Rabbi", as he tended to be called. (But I always think of him by John's name, the Lamb of God, the ram without blemish, the Passover-victim of deliverance.) When and how they became explicit followers of his I don't know; presumably there was some encounter in Galilee. But I wasn't with them at this time.

I treasure the memory of every day of those last weeks of John's ministry. It was true that he was consumed with happiness. When we were told that Jesus was baptizing more people now than he was, he said, "Of course, it is his baptism. I was only baptizing till he came. It is the bridegroom who has the bride; but the bridegroom's friend has his own joy in hearing the bridegroom's voice. That's my joy now."

I can't remember it without emotion: how he seemed to be fading into light, and then what great suffering seized him. He thought he was going to be allowed to return to the deserts. Instead, he spent his last months confined in Herod's grim fortress beside the Dead Sea, he who had not slept under a roof since his boyhood—almost as though Qumran were taking its revenge on him. But he didn't seem to foresee it, when he went to Caesarea to denounce Herod's new incestuous and adulterous marriage. There was always a kind of innocence in him. He could not understand my hinted warnings. He saw only the clear horror and scandal of such evil in the high places of Israel. And though the spirit of prophecy left him, the spirit of courage and upright-ness never did. So he went, and preached against the king in the palace gate; and so he was arrested. They put him in Machaerus to isolate him from his followers, but plenty of us managed to camp outside all the same, and so terrified of his prisoner was Herod, that we were allowed access to him. In fact we were prepared to carry on baptizing, but he wanted no more of that. His time was over. The old vehemence and anger still came out, I heard, when-ever Herod sent for him (for that contradictory man, coward as he was, enjoyed being frightened; John's denunciations gave him a thrill, though he did nothing about repenting). But with us John was a broken reed, a guttering wick. That dark prison cell slowly crushed him. I heard him through the casement crying aloud: "Why hast thou cast me into the pit, O Lord, and into the darkest depths? The waters of bitterness have come up to my throat, Lord, they are up to my throat." But more often we only heard him groaning.

I tried to comfort him by reminding him of his role, saying, "You can no longer deny who you are now. For who else suffered so at the hands of a wicked queen? Who but Elijah at the hands of Jezebel?" But he cried out in anguish, "I am not Elijah! I am no-one! I know nothing! I was a voice shouting down the wind, and now the wind has changed."

I did not then understand fully what was in his cry, "I know nothing"—though indeed it did remind me of his words long before, when he kept telling us, "The unknown one in our midst —I don't know who he is any more than you do." But I understood at last the terrible restlessness of John in prison when he sent for me privately one day and asked me if I would make a journey for him. I was struck by his haggardness, his staring roving gaze. I was surprised, too, that he should even ask; by his furtiveness, as though he were ashamed. Then he said, "Go for me to Jesus of Nazareth and ask him if he is indeed the one who should come, or are we to expect some other? Ask him in the name of God to tell me the truth." And he turned away from me to the wall.

My heart was breaking with the pity of it, and I travelled cross-country with young Jonas faster than I ever had in my life. Jesus moved about so much, it was hard to catch up with him. I was even afraid in a way of doing so. What sort of answer could John expect? His question made me love him more than ever. It was like his ingenuous bluntness to expect a straight answer to a straight enquiry, clearing all up. He had not really changed. But Jonas and I journeyed speaking little, thinking, "That John should doubt! John!" Yet I'd known a similar hesitation already, the hesitation of too peaceful an evening among the flocks, the wonder: "Can *this* be the redemption? Can *this* be the redeemer? Where is all the glory?" But still! That John should doubt! John! And I prayed, "Let him know. Let Jesus answer so that he knows, yes or no. Deliver him from the suffering of not-knowing."

We found Jesus at last by means of the crowd gathered round him: we saw the gaily-dressed multitude from a hilltop village, swarming by the lake-shore beneath. We could scarcely push our way through, when we had hurried down, for all the invalids and their beds—the invalids were not *on* their beds; they were dancing and clapping and singing and hugging their families, while the harassed disciples tried to fend off the crush of the grateful, the impatient, the beseeching, the curious, so that Jesus could get through. I noticed that he, however, seemed quite unconcerned. When he wanted to teach them something he simply raised his voice and said "Listen! The kingdom of heaven is like this. . . ." or "Listen! A sower once went out to sow his seed. . . ." There was an immediate hush for him, though not for dear Simon and Andrew. They recognized me coming, but only gave me a distracted wave. Jesus, however, sensed our trouble, and turned to us, silencing the immediate hubbub with his hand, saying, "Welcome, friends of John. Is all well with him?"

I said, "All is not well, Master." Then I gathered courage and got it out: "He asks you to tell him this in God's name: Are you the one who is to come, or should we expect some other?"

For a long moment there seemed to be no answer. I looked up at last and saw his eyes were not on me, but roving over the tumultuous scene, like a great festival—Tabernacles in Jerusalem is something like it—or an enormous wedding. I found my gaze going where his did. I could almost have forgotten John for the amazing spectacle. Then Jesus' voice broke in on me: "Go and tell John what you see and hear: the blind receive their sight, the lame walk, the lepers are cleansed, and the deaf hear; the dead are raised up—and the Good News is preached to the poor. And blessed is he who can take me as I am."

As we went away the words of Isaiah were ringing in my ears: "Then the lame man shall leap like a stag, and the tongue of the dumb shall sing. . . . The Spirit of the Lord is upon me, because he has anointed me to preach the good news to the poor. . . ." I had only to say to John, "He is fulfilling the prophecies of Messiah! He is entering on the work of the anointed one. . . ." And then the other words would come back to mind, the stern warning: "Take me as I am"; and my heart would sink again. What if John could not—or I could not?

Climbing back into the hills, I looked down on the scene once more, and could not help comparing it with the scenes of John's baptisms: the same people perhaps, but how different the crowds. Here were none of the rows of bowed bare backs, no forests of upflung lamenting hands—and beside Jordan you would never have seen whole groups of people breaking into dances, three or four families of healed sick joining hands and leaping on the spot. People wanted to run and jump in this crowd, the children especially, because perhaps they hadn't done so for years. Later, I heard that Jesus himself said the two followings, his and John's, were like children playing weddings and funerals (his point was that the Pharisees would not play either, therefore it was not the game that was at fault). I thought, "I'll say to John, 'It's like a great feast. Who but the one that was to come has the right to hold God's feast?' "

Jonas and I delivered the first part of the message together, describing all we had seen. It took some time. John listened eagerly but wistfully, longing to be convinced. I told him Jesus was holding God's feast, but he only sighed. But when at last I told him Jesus' concluding words I saw that they had gone home as nothing else I said had. He stiffened as though struck by a blow, then a strange light came into his eyes—something of the old fire—and he turned away from us. We left him then, but the next time I talked with him I said hesitantly, "There is a word he keeps repeating. He says, 'If you have ears to hear with, then hear!' " And John said quietly, "I have ears and I hear."

Jesus' harsh and cryptic words to him had brought him back to life as no lofty assertion, "I am the one", could have done, as though their very abrasiveness had had power to rouse his courage —and his faith. It's something I've seen on several occasions since, when a rough or abrupt answer from Jesus has only served to strengthen.

But John could not live in prison. He would have died of confinement if of nothing else. I found myself even wishing that he might die, since there was no hope of freedom for him while Herodias had any power. Young Jonas brought him wild rock honey which he had gone out and found; but he grew thinner every day. Yet at least he was at peace now. He would sit or lie very still, gazing up at the crack of sky he could see, no longer speaking much to any of us. I think we would have spoken more if we had known that by the end of the summer Herodias would have succeeded in getting him murdered. She trapped Herod in his words when he was drunk and inflamed, and John was beheaded and his head served up on a dish at the banquet. It was Herod's birthday. One may ask why he held the feast at Machaerus at all, if he had not meant to torment John at it? But I don't believe he would have murdered him willingly, afraid as he was of him, if he had not been even more afraid of his terrible queen.

Herodias knew that John had to die. She was sensitive to the living judgment that he was on her, to God's own holiness which was in him, standing against her. It was for the sake of the righteousness of God that he died more foully than any of the prophets. They say that his head came alive and denounced them at the banquet. That's their way of admitting that God's living, holy anger is burning them now and for ever, and that John had been a word to them which they rejected.

After we had buried his body—and head—I did something which seems foolish now. I was half crazed with grief and horror. I travelled down the sandy coast to Qumran and told the news to the community there, thinking obscurely that though they too had rejected him living, they would listen to him dead. I was not granted admittance, being considered an apostate from them, but Asuel and some others came and talked with me through the gate. And the response was pure stone. Though they were shocked, they were not entirely sorry; indeed Asuel's eyes gleamed, I thought. As for receiving John's call, did I not know that the Teacher of Righteousness had taught them all truth? Nor did they need another baptism.

Desperate, I said, "Will you not then at least send someone to hear the words of him of whom John prophesied? For all that John said is being fulfilled, and the one that should come is among us."

"When the Messiah comes," replied Asuel, "he will come here."

There was no more to be said. Their hardness of heart was impossible even to chip. I came away thinking, will the Pharisees be any different, or the priesthood and Levites? Has Israel changed since Isaiah complained of it, "Who is blind and deaf, as the Lord's servant?"

I slept among the rocks above the settlement that night, those same rocks where John and I used to wander long ago, and all night my mind was full of images of the lithe, free ardour and grace of him. Above me was the ridge where he had stood once and cried, "See him coming in the brightness of the light, and his glory streaming behind him! My flesh trembles, my bones are rotten for the beauty of the Lord and the terror of his majesty! For it shall be my destruction when he comes, yet he knows I have desired the day."

Slowly during that night I began to understand that John had all he had desired, and needed no pity, for God's fire had taken him at last. "And he shall live for evermore," I said to myself. Yet it was still true, as he had said, that the time of the redemption was not for him. In his own image, he was the bridegroom's friend, happy to stand at the door of the wedding-chamber and keep watch. He had insisted that it was his very joy and the service he desired to give, yet I could not help grieving a little; he was like Moses dying in sight of the promised land he had led the people towards but might not enter; I wept bitterly for him that night, yet in the morning I rose and blessed the God of heaven for his prophet and martyr John. Then I went in all haste to Galilee, as I should perhaps have done at first, and brought the news to Jesus.

I could see he was deeply moved, though all he said was, "So they have had their way with him, as it was written that they would." Then he began dismissing the crowds, and would not teach them any more that day. "Prophet and more than a prophet; he had to suffer," I overheard him say. Then he called to the departing crowds, "No greater man than John has ever lived; yet the least in the kingdom of heaven is greater than he. Think well what that means!" He turned away saying half to himself, "Yes, such a prophet had to suffer. And now shall the kingdom itself escape violence? Or shall it not suffer at the hands of violent men?"

B

I was suddenly afraid. I did not understand. I thought with a thud, is worse still to come after all? Was it only grief and shock that were making Jesus so sad?

"Let's go away somewhere," he was saying to his disciples. "Let's go somewhere we can be quiet and alone for a little." Then he looked at me: "You come too," he said.

And so I crossed the threshold where John stands, faithful and patient, keeping watch. His claim to be the bridegroom's truest friend was no vain one. It was reciprocal too. We gradually came to realize how much Jesus respected John, and how much he is in his thoughts, by the frequency of his allusions to him: often veiled, often with both sorrow and foreboding. "John was a burning and a shining light, but you did not let him shine on you for long!"

Yet if Jesus has outshone him now, his light has not been put out for all that. Israel—the whole world—will never be able to forget him. For Herod, he is undying, unkillable condemnation. He is even rumoured to have said that Jesus must be John risen from the dead. So men send themselves mad with terror of their own guilt. But for us he is now, as he always was, unquenchable hope, the sign of hope, the first who told us that God was turning again to show us the light of his face, who brought us the good, good news of God's anger, for God is only angry with those whom he has chosen to be his own; his anger is the hot blood of his love. And wherever that love comes now the great shout that is John still rings ahead of it.

4

THE DARK ROOM

UP, OLD JOANNA! Up and repent! Arise, Israel, and repent!
To the very ends of the land the trumpet of terror has sounded:
the true and burning terror of the Majesty of God. I know God
is with him because of the terror. He knows of judgment. John
knows what God's judgment is. Ah, that in my days a true
prophet of the Lord should arise. There is burning darkness
behind him. There is burning darkness coming. Flesh shrinks
and quails from the terror of the Lord and his prophet. Old bones
would hide and stay at home. But flesh must arise and lament
before the glory of his wrath. Oh, but his words sting like
scorpions. And my tears sting. Old eyes have shed too many
tears. The shedding burns them now. But the lion is roaring,
and who shall not shake? The doom is coming, and who shall
lie in peace? Arise, sinful Israel, bow and weep before the terrible
words of John. Up, old Joanna, sinner and the wife of a sinner,
up! Shall old flesh be spared? Up and humble yourself under the
mighty hand of God, where it wields its great scourge over
faithless Israel's back. Ah, the terror, the glory of him!

The old woman seemed to stumble and keen to herself as she
trudged through the sun-dazzling dust, with the thin boy silently
clinging to her. It was as though she were forcing herself on, and
every now and then she stopped, swaying, and covered her face
with her hands; then she would cry, "Oh Lord, holy and just art
thou! Yet smite not thy servant utterly into the grave!" The other
pilgrims overtook her all day, and many looked at her and would
have had her join them, but she would not speak to any but the
child beside her.

For Joanna had to tear each foot from the ground, each step
of the way, because of the holy anger that was awaiting her under
the harsh hills of Judah. She looked at the other travellers pressing
eagerly on, straining their eyes into the distance where the hard

line of the mountains hung against a blue-black sky, and thought, "You do not understand. None of you understands." These mountains were not like the graceful peak of Mount Hermon, which had stood over her life in Galilee. These were a cruel, horizontal mass of rock, blazing under a barren sky. No life was in them, no place or pity for mankind. But they were John's mountains. Though she had never seen him, but only heard his preaching repeated, she knew him as she knew herself, as she knew the voice of God.

She heard footsteps coming the other way—towards her—and a voice called, "The peace of the Lord be with you."

But Joanna did not answer. She looked up and saw two men and a woman, members, she thought, of the caravan that had just passed her, singing soft lamentations, the whole of one of the rambling lakeside families turned penitent: twenty or thirty blood-relations, on their way to John. These people had turned back to speak to her. She said grudgingly at last, "The Lord keep you."

"Mother, will you not travel with us? We have donkeys and tents. It will be less weary for you."

"I will walk alone and weep," she said. "Do not try to snare the lonely bird."

"Widow in Israel, who was your husband? Where do you come from?" asked the woman.

"In my youth I was given to Chuza of Damascus. Alas, that ever I was!" She saw the men start and exclaim at the name, but did not let them speak. "Woe to the father who gives his daughter for a bride price of gold, and the child of his heart for silver! Woe to the father who sells his daughter to a Gentile, and who cuts his maid child out from the inheritance of Israel! And now shall old Joanna find favour with the Lord?"

"You may, but you may!" said the woman eagerly. "For he is pitiful and gracious, and rejects none who turn to him."

"Fool!" shouted Joanna. "Fools all! Do you desire the day of the Lord? What good do you think you shall have from it? Do you not know it will dawn in darkness, that great and terrible day? Are God's ways as our ways? Leave me and do not trouble me! Your songs and tambourines are a weariness to me, I hate the sound of your dirges!"

So all day she walked alone, and the child whimpered, and the uplands lowered close above them, till the merciful dusk began to hide them. But at last, long after nightfall, turning a bend in the road, she saw suddenly ahead of her a fire, an awning stretched between the olives, and heard soft laughter, and gripping her child till he yelped, she pulled him stealthily after her. "Come," she whispered to him. "They are good people. They will care for you."

"But you, mother, where will you lie?"

"Alone. Not with them. But you, poor little one, why should you suffer? Come, we'll go to them."

But before they had broken into the circle of firelight Joanna stiffened, hearing:

"Surely she is a prophetess!"

"But I still don't understand why she wears widow's mourning. Chuza, Herod's steward, was alive last week. I sold him some fish for the palace in Tiberias."

"She may be the wife of his father Chuza. She said she was old."

"She is not old!" came the woman's voice suddenly. "That is her son with her! She is scarcely older than I am. It's sorrow, not age, in her face!"

Then Joanna broke in amongst them, and stood and cried, "My husband is dead to the Lord! He has cut himself off from the congregation of Israel. For he swore to serve the Lord when he and I were wed. He was circumcised! And now he bows to the gods of the nations. He has been seen in their temples. He sports naked before Herod with the young men like a Greek. Therefore I am a widow!"

There was silence after she had spoken: only the cicadas sang and behind them in the darkness Jordan ran. Then she said, "Good friends, will you take my child? I have no food to give him."

She saw one of the men opening his arms to him, and then she turned away into the darkness.

For two days she stayed under the rocks of the river cleft, watching the crowds spilling on the hot stretch of shale down to the river, where John was baptizing on a sandy spit. Twice she had forced herself down to bear a scourging from the words of this holy, holy man, but still she had shrunk from baptism: each time John had looked at her she had found herself crying out: "Turn away thine anger, O Lord, and destroy not!" and fleeing away, with her skirt gathered up, to the shelter of the rocks.

There she knelt and prostrated herself alternately, and prayed. "Two things I ask of thee: take thy hand away from me, lay it not upon me; and let not thy terror make me afraid." But the more she prayed, the heavier lay the hand and the terror. "He will not hear me," she moaned, "there is no mercy for me. Am I not defiled in his sight? Am I not as the heathen? Have I not brought forth a child of iniquity? Yet let my sorrow make atonement for him." For since Ishmael was born she had fasted to save him from wrath. "Though he shall never be called Isaac," she had said, "yet the Lord did hear Abraham when he cried for his son Ishmael." "And I am like Hagar, driven from the presence of Abraham," she would have added now, "for who shall show mercy to the rejected of the Lord?" And she would watch the distant, fierce figure of John with reverent eyes, and then bow and lament again.

"Holy John, righteous prophet, man dear to God! Save me!" Ishmael hung about her fearfully, glad when she gave him permission to go. Then she watched him running straight and fast to the camp of the fishing family from Capernaum: watched almost hungrily. He ate with them always now, but she would only eat the crusts of the bread she had brought from Galilee, smiting her breast as she ate and crying: "Thou knowest, O Lord, I have eaten my bread alone in bitterness of soul!"

On the third day the Capernaum family was baptized, and she watched them coming back; even from here she could see the radiance of their faces, and how the children were dancing. And still she hung back, but that night she followed Ishmael down to his friends' fire, hardly knowing why. "I will ask them to take him to John," she thought. "For they are clean now, and I am defiled. O my little one, may the Lord our God spare you the punishment, for my sins and your father's sins! O may the children's teeth not be set on edge! May he be forgiven, for thou seest my weeping!"

But once again, on the edge of the circle of firelight she stopped, knowing that she could not enter it. "Heavy is thy hand upon me, O Lord," she groaned, "who make me sit solitary, and drive my companions from me. Heavy is thy hand . . ." But she sat on in the shadows, huddled there, watching her son, who was her only contact with that warmth and friendship. They had not seen her, for they were talking too excitedly about the holy baptizer John.

"Isn't he the Messiah?"

"He says he is not."

"But he's no ordinary man. Is he Elijah?"

"He says he's not Elijah."

"He won't say who he is. I believe he is Elijah and doesn't know it."

"There was a prophecy about him," an older woman's voice broke in, "spoken over him when he was an infant. You're too young to remember how the tale spread, of miraculous speech and words from God given to his father. But there are some of us who have been waiting a long time to see what the child of that prophecy would become. . . . It went like this:

'Child, you shall be called the Prophet of the Highest, for you shall go before him to make ready his way, to bring the news of salvation to his people, the news of their forgiveness;
to speak to them of his mercy, of the sun rising on them
that shall be light to those that sit in darkness and the shadow of death
and shall guide our feet into the way of peace.' "

The silence was broken by the younger woman crying out in fright to her husband, "Simon! What is that—there—now, in that shadow?"

"I can't see anything," he muttered, staring into the bushes and lumbering to his feet. But Joanna was no longer there to be seen. She was fleeing away through the night to her pitch by the rocks, moaning: "Shall a light rise on those that sit in darkness and shall it not be a greater darkness, O Lord our God?"

She thought for a moment that someone was following her. She stopped for breath and heard nothing. But when she moved she again thought it. "It's Ishmael," she said, and at the rock called "Ishmael!" There was no answer, no-one there. She lay down alone. Why should Ishmael leave his friends and his fire? He had not slept at her side since they left Galilee.

But all night in her dreams she saw the figure of Simon standing up from the fire to come to her, and this time she was helpless to run; she could only turn and shrink away, crying, "No! No!" Sometimes it was not Simon but John, sometimes the mountains moving in on her; until in the end she slept deeply and knew it certainly—the terror and darkness of the Day of the Lord, coming at last, standing over her, falling on her. . . . She awoke in half-daylight and for an instant's waking certainty knew someone was standing there. But by the time she had dragged herself up he was gone. Even so, she found herself crying under her breath, "No! No! No!"

"Even so, Lord!" she prayed. "Let the day of evil come! I will bow myself under the baptism of thy judgment. I will go today! Though thou destroy me utterly, yet thou art righteous, O Lord!"

When the sun had full risen she went down towards the Jordan. "Ishmael," she called softly, as she passed the other family's camp. They were awake, breakfasting on bread and olives. The boy came reluctantly when he saw her. "Come, we're going to John," she said. As she went on she heard one of the men saying behind her, "I think *she*'ll baptize John. . . ."

Already there were people there ahead of her. Joanna knelt down and bowed herself to the ground, awaiting her turn; Ishmael did the same, still covertly chewing. But a scream from the water made them both jerk upright. A woman was fighting and thrashing with John as he tried to hold her under, screaming and jerking uncontrollably. The murmur began to go round: "She has a devil." And over the murmur Joanna's laughter began to compete with the screams.

"She hasn't a devil, she has seven! It is I who cursed her with them! Don't I know her, that whore? That Ammonite? That woman who first took my husband away from me? That daughter of Amalek who estranged him from Israel? Ah, I cursed her! And see the devils! Seven devils! She can't be baptized! Hah, she can't be baptized! The water's burning her—look at her, it's burning her!"

The woman was indeed writhing and shrieking as though in pain from every drop. Joanna laughed and laughed, but now John was turning on her with eyes blazing like red coals—just as they said, he had fire in his eyes.

"Get out of here, you poisonous snake! There's no baptism for you while you can laugh like that. Go and repent!"

Joanna was already going, stumbling, shaking with hysterical laughter, until under the shade of the osier bushes she fell on her face, clawing the ground, and wept.

She did not know how long she lay there, or where Ishmael went. The cackling laughter and tears—her own? the other woman's?—went on and on in her ears. She could feel the sun's rays on her legs: the sunrise of utter darkness.

And yet through it all she was listening to the voices from the river, to John shouting the glory of God, to the broken voices of the penitents, because now she heard, almost as though she had been waiting for it, the change in John's tone, the gasp and breaking voice, the sudden silence in the splashing.

"Is it you? Have you come? Are you coming—to me?"

Then with a greater ugency, almost with fear: "No! How can I baptize you? No! I need rather to be baptized by you!"

She did not hear the answer, but John's voice again, much lower, "Then in God's name I baptize you into newness of life."

Joanna did not move, she could not see, yet now, as John reluctantly performed this baptism, there came knowing clearer than any sight. Someone was coming. The sky was falling. The darkness, her darkness, was being broken into, invaded. Strength to shake the heavens was bowing itself, coming, entering, rending open; God himself was kneeling on the vault where she was buried alive, and it was breaking, crumbling, under him; there was light pouring in, terrible light. . . . Screaming "No! No! No!" Joanna had scrambled to her feet and fled from the terror of that light bursting in, of that bowing glory, fled from the mighty one who was shattering his way into her world. All the way to Galilee, he seemed to be following her, in a pillar of fire by night and a pillar of smoke by day, and not until she had crossed Samaria dared she believe she had left him behind.

Ishmael did not come for some weeks, for the Capernaum brothers remained till after Passover as disciples of John. If they had not brought him in the end, loneliness and longing might have driven her out to seek for him, but when they came with him in the spring she gave a shriek of joy, pulled him inside and quickly slammed and fastened the door. Since she had come back, she had never dared to uncover her window or open her door, except quickly to go out, when she must, to fetch water, and always in the late dusk.

Now she had Ishmael with her; silent, glowering, he sat with long pale legs showing in the guttering lamplight of the house, while she served him with might and main and wept on his hair.

In her dreams and in all her thoughts she was never free from the shaking of that coming, the descent of that strength into the valley where she sat in darkness, clutching herself into the last dark corner, while the shadows shrank about her as the brightness approached.

The only place where her thoughts could shelter was the memory of how the other woman had been burnt by the water at her baptizing; when Joanna thought of that fresh chuckles of mirth came rising.

Towards the end of the summer, Ishmael came in from working (he had been apprenticed as a tanner to Jacob Hannas, who was also the synagogue scribe), he said to her, "Mother, do you know what has happened to the prophet John?"

"Are you telling me . . ."

"Herod has had him beheaded in prison. They say his head was brought into the banquet in a dish."

"Holy John! The man so dear to God! Will the iniquity of

Israel never be complete?" And then a greater horror struck her, and a kind of satisfaction too.

"And now who is accursed in Israel but Herod the king and Chuza, Herod's steward, who fatten themselves on the blood of the Lord's saints and count the head of a prophet a delicacy for a feast?"

Joanna knew what she must do now, though she lacked immediate courage. Through brooding, she gathered it. Though John had dealt her God's judgment of rejection, this she could do for him, and this she could do against her husband. She could curse him.

So on the eve of Sabbath she stood up in her house in the prayer-mantle, so long disused, which she had woven for her husband in the time of their betrothal, and she prayed: "O Lord God, that seest the right, and sparest not: behold now and smite. Let his name be blotted out, and darkness cover him. Remember thou his sin for all generations; have no mercy on his child. Let me become a widow, and let all who loved him forsake him. Let him be condemned in thy presence, and his prayer be turned into sin. Let his lands fail and his portion cease, let his bones become as oil, let his flesh be covered with rottenness. Destroy thou all that he has, and burn him with everlasting fire, O Lord our God."

Before she had finished, her voice was breaking with tears, but she forced herself to stand upright and go on. "So your blood is avenged, O holy John!" she cried. When she ended, she fell gasping on her bed, no longer even able to weep, breathing heavily and dryly. On the day following, the Sabbath, Ishmael fell feverishly ill.

"Blessed be thou, who hast heard my prayer, O Lord," she said, and then: "Yet perhaps he will relent now and spare the child's life." She neither ate nor drank, but sat by his head, in the shuttered and darkened house, nursing him with all her skill and all her desperation. She lost count of time; she thought she could see the boy wasting as she watched. Her eyes were burning with tears that would not flow. It seemed to her she was bleeding through her eyes, so that soon all the room was turning in circles of blood, round and round her. "It is the end," she thought, "the

Day I have dreaded, and the sun and moon are turned to blood, and the rivers; as when the Lord plagued the Egyptians for Moses' sake, so he is plaguing us now for John." In lucid moments, she knew that both Ishmael and she were dying. Still the blood and fire spun, all the heavens and earth dissolving into them. "Yet there was light," she thought. "I saw brightness descending, and the hosts of heaven hiding their faces, as I hid mine." Lying with her head on Ishmael's wet breast, she prayed, "If there is any help, let it come now." Then she could not even remember words to pray, but thought she was reaching out to brightness, as though it were something solid she could have caught, but because of the terrible shaking, she could not touch it, but only reach and reach, blind with darkness and blood.

. . . What was John doing, battering at her door? Had he forgotten that he had told her there was no baptism for her? She knew he was there, and heard his voice saying once again, "Is it you? Have you come to me?" Or was it her own voice?

"*Is it you, at last? Is it really you?*"

John was breaking down the door. Cracks of light were appearing and widening. The whole house and all her body were being shaken by his battering.

"*Then in God's name I baptize you into newness of life.*"

She knew he must be performing the baptism now, his hand on the other's head, pressing him down under the water. Then the door burst open and the white-hot harvest sun blazed in, sending pillars of light across the floor towards her. She cried out against the figure standing in the door, "What have I to do with you, you man of God? Have you come to bring my sins to remembrance?" For the merciless light was striking on her with an anger that was all the more terrible because it was silent. But the figure came forward into the room, still full of all the fierceness of the light, and it was not John, it was greater yet than John, surely the angel of the Lord himself bringing death. She heard her own screams as she threw herself on Ishmael, and then felt the hand: the hand laid on her, that she had tried all her life to shake free of, the hand of the Lord, and it seemed to be holding her so still she could not struggle any more. And a voice spoke easily over her shrieks, "Away with you, Satan! You have no place here any more."

She felt Ishmael stirring under her, and rolled aside, all the blood and beating fading away. But the hand did not release her. The angel of the Lord was sitting on the bed speaking gently to Ishmael and holding her down. Then he addressed her, "Mother, give me that. Give me what you are carrying."

All the darkness, all the fear, all the cursing—

"Give it to me."

The cursing—but she remembered suddenly: "But he is an apostate! He bows in the temples! He runs races with Greeks! He was steward of the feast when John's head was served up! He married me and forsook me, he dispossessed me and murdered that dear and holy man!"

"No, mother, let me have it. Let go."

And all at once it came to mind how the right tuft of Chuza's beard would curl quaintly sideways whether he would or no—the day when she and he had tried to straighten it together, and had ended in tears of laughter. Tears came at last again now, and laughter.

"But he is still Herod's filthy slaver—he will still go to harlots——"

"No, mother, I've got it now. Let go."

The limpness, the rest, the healing, the fever ebbing; tears and laughter. The cypress tree Chuza had planted and named after her. The white Arab colt he had brought from Damascus and tamed. She remembered him wrestling with it, both of them rearing together, glorying in the battle of wits and strength. He and the horse were alike in their pride and beauty and innocence. And remembering and knowing that innocence Joanna turned to the figure beside her and wept on to the skirt of his robe. "Bless him for me, my Lord," she sobbed, "bless him in the name of your God, for I have cursed him."

"Very gladly, I will."

"And that woman, Mary, whom I cursed with seven devils— you surely have power to free her. I don't know where she lives now. She used to practise her trade at Magdala."

"I'll find her. For my work is not ended till I have taken away all burdens."

Joanna was half aware of others in the room, pulling up blinds, bringing in food; of Ishmael bouncing in the middle of the room shouting, "Jesus, can't I follow you? I want to follow you now!" The one at her side, angel or prophet, was rising to go, saying laughingly, "Why not?" Some of Joanna's old cunning returned, and she caught at him, saying, "The curse, what has happened to the curse?"

"I've taken it. Don't think about it any more. And I have honoured John too, more than by any vengeance, by fulfilling his words, that the one God sent should take away the sin of the world."

He went out at last, followed by his crowding, happy disciples, and by Ishmael hopping and calling, "We'll both come! Soon as Mother's well! We're both coming!" And as they passed through the door all the darkness in the room seemed to go out with them, as though that, too, had been taken away.

5

BURDENS

You will never understand what his coming was to us, a whole family of tax-gatherers, you who have a right to respect and a name and a face that is not living shame to you. You will never understand, I dare say, what his coming was at all, who he was at all. Not till you have sat in darkness as we have sat in darkness and the shadow of God's anger, that is worse than the shadow of death, the weight of the darkness of his displeasure and his face turned from us. You who have never been a sinner in Israel, you cannot know that night, there is no escape from it. Once a family has begun to sin how can it stop? How can the children be free when the parents have fallen into slavery? Or shall they not eat the sour figs on which their parents fed?

My father's father was in the service of the Temple in the days of Antigonus the high priest, and what deceit he practised there I do not know, but his son, inheriting his riches, could only live by lending them on usury; already the shadow of sin had trapped us. I was the heir to those same riches, doubly cursed now, and fit for one use only. I bid high and secured the post of toll-receiver for Capernaum and its villages. Thus I did better for myself than either my father or my grandfather; and all that I had was triply cursed now; for how can I say that I was the one just tax-collector in Galilee? How can a man serve in that post and not be a swindler, not extort? What uprightness would he need to refuse to use his chances? I am an old sinner and I know it. Yet I never forgot I was of the priestly tribe of Levi, that my ancestors had indeed served as Levites, and I named my son Levi, in hope and sorrow, knowing even as we circumcised him ("holy to the Lord"), that he was doomed to follow me.

Of course he did follow me. It was easy enough to pass him on my post. But what of his sisters, his innocent sisters, whom no one would marry but men already defiled by their trades?

One went to the toll receiver of Magdala, one to a magician at Herod's court, the third to a herdsman of the hills who was in fact a robber on the highways. Did my daughters want to be married to such men? And what will their children become? Or what of my other son James, receiver and seller for his brother-in-law's stolen goods in Capernaum, assisted by his brother Levi at the customs, because no law-keeping man will employ him, knowing him to be a son of Alphaeus?

I've seen what I've brought on my children and I've seen the darkness growing, and no hope, no hope, for generation unto generation. "And so," I said, "the Lord is holy and we have proved it by our sorrows. But he will destroy us in the end."

And, brooding, I began to believe what some were saying since John the Baptist arose, that the end was soon. "A little longer," I thought, "and fire and everlasting night shall fall on all my family," and I dandled the little son of Levi, my firstborn grandchild, on my knee and wept.

Yes, it was in that darkness we were sitting, all of us, when Jesus of Nazareth walked past my son Levi as he sat in the seat of shame, and called him away, out of it, to follow him and not me, and set him free. He was the first of us to be delivered. How he came running home that first night, bursting in as though he were a boy again, and fell on my neck crying "Father! Oh Father!" I held him from me in amazement and saw that he was weeping, and in his face was the light of the glory of God, the brightness you may sometimes see on the face of a true Israelite; never had it been seen in our family, never.

"My son!" I exclaimed. "What's happened to you?"

"The mercy of God, Father," he said; "the mercy and love of God." And he told me how the holy Teacher of Nazareth had stopped by his seat at the customs, stopped there where every righteous man would normally hurry past, had spoken to him in friendship, and called him to be his disciple.

I drew back from him. He seemed a stranger suddenly. "So, my son," I said. "You have joined the Pharisees. Then don't defile yourself by coming here!"

"Oh, no, no, Father," he said. "It is to us he has come, to us as we are, don't you understand?"

"He would not come here," I said.

Levi answered, slowly, "He would. He would."

I spoke harshly to force away the hope that he had begun to infect me with. "Then bring him here!" I cried. "If he thinks we are of the stuff of which Pharisees are made, if he thinks there is any good in the house of Alphaeus, then let him come here and eat with us!"

They were savage words, the words of a man tortured by what might have been; for of course a Rabbi would never come to eat in the house of Alphaeus the old swindler and his brood; who were, nevertheless, the sons of Israel and Levi.

Levi straightened up and looked towards the door, where the sun was pouring in; and he said, "He will come."

"Then what sort of Rabbi can he be?" I asked in amazement. "Doesn't he care how he compromises himself?"

Levi smiled at that and said, "No. No, he doesn't. He cares nothing for his reputation or for any man's opinion. Else would he have chosen me?"

"But I thought you said this was a holy man."

Levi turned on me and said, "There is such holiness in him that it consumes and burns away all evil wherever he goes. He has no need to be afraid for it, he fears contact with nothing, however accursed, but he seeks out the unclean most of all. For the love of God is in him."

There was a silence, and I said roughly to hide my longing and hope, "Well, I should like to see him. It is a long time since I spoke of God with a Rabbi."

But my son would have it that I must come and hear his new teacher first, "and then you'll understand. We must not ask him to our house to put him to the test, but out of friendship." So I came with him next morning to the waterside, and there he was preaching from a boat, because the quay was crowded with his eager hearers. I had no need to ask Levi who he was. His voice came clearly over the water, raised, lilting, half singing, in the words of the prophecy:

"The spirit of the Lord is upon me
    because he has anointed me;
He has sent me with good news to the poor,
    amnesty for prisoners, sight and light to the blind,
to heal the broken victims and to set them free,
    for this is the Lord's year of grace.
And now is the time, and yours are the eyes that see it,
    yours are the ears that hear the good news come true!"

A murmur like a shiver ran through the crowd, and I fell on my face to the ground.

"Master," cried someone, "why to us? Who are we? We keep the law as we can but we have not kept pure, we are not Pharisees, we are not ready for the coming of the Lord!"

Jesus answered:

"The last shall be first,
    and the first last.
How blessed are you who are poor before God!
    The kingdom of God is for you.
How blessed are you who are hungry now!
    You shall be filled full.
How blessed are you, the lowly and meek!
    The whole earth is your inheritance.
How blessed are you who weep now!
    You shall laugh.

"Is there a smaller, more insignificant seed than mustard? Yet from it grows a spreading shrub that can shelter birds from the sun. Or think how tiny a piece of leavened dough is enough for a woman making her household's bread. She breaks up her little piece and mixes it into a great quantity of dough, and yet all of it is leavened. So it shall be with the kingdom of God."

"Ah, Rabbi, don't deceive us!" cried a man. "Does God want wretches like us in his kingdom? Does he?"

"It's those he wants most of all," answered the Teacher.

"Amen, I tell you, it is not given to the wise and proud; but
  to the very children, who have never read the Law.
For how could it be my Father's will
  that one of his little ones should be lost?"

The people were murmuring, "How does he know? How can
he speak like that? Yet he does know. Where does he get his
authority?"

But I knew by now, and did not need Levi to tell me. I was
listening on my knees, keening to myself and rocking gently to
and fro, and tears were running into my beard.

He stood up then in the boat and cried, or sang:

"Come to me, all of you
  whose labour is hard, whose burden is too heavy to bear!
Come to me and I will give you rest.
  Take my own yoke on you instead, and learn humility of
  me; that's the only load a man can carry."

I had carried such a weight for so long! I had laboured for so
long! How did he know? How could he know? He had come
right into the land of those who sat in darkness, he had not merely
proclaimed amnesty for the prisoners but had come himself into
the prison-house and taken our chains from us. And there was
never a teacher before him who knew what it was like to be one
of us, to be Alphaeus or Levi, but he knew. And so I knew that
God knew too, and did not condemn us.

I said to Levi, my son, "Bid the Rabbi to dine with us at our
house. Tell him that all we have is his."

"Why don't you ask him, Father?"

But that I could not do.

We prepared the best we had for him, knowing that all of it
was paid for by extortion and misery over so many years. Thinking of it, my heart sank anew. "How can we ever be forgiven
this?" I asked myself. "How can we ever be free of it?" And now
I waited in fear for the Rabbi to come, for his entering here would
be judgment upon us as much as the year of grace. The little

house seemed dark, the air heavy, for we never dared to unshutter in case stones were thrown in; my wife seemed a shrunken, withered thing. My hands trembled as I helped her make ready, while Sulamith, Levi's wife, kneaded and baked. All the family were there, all had heard and come. I tried to set the tallow candles and knocked them over again and again. But it was still in a shaking trust that I set them in honour of him who knew what house he was coming to, who knew what our life was and that we could not bear it.

At last the door was flung open, my son's voice outside called "Enter, Rabbi!" and, stooping a little under the lintel, Jesus came in, his warm voice ringing through the room, "Peace be to you and to your house." And I ran through the house of our shame and threw myself at his feet, clasping his knees, because my heart and bones were turned to water within me at his entering and greeting. But he took me in his arms and raised me up, saying softly, "Old father, don't grieve; see, I have brought you peace."

And it was so. He sat there at table amongst us with the spirit of the Lord upon him, anointed with grace, and all was healed, all that long evil healed. My sons and their wives and children sat with their eyes full of hope and gladness fixed on him, and when he broke bread, he gave a piece first to James my second son, and catching the look between them, I knew it was a sign and token, and James too was delivered and become his follower. And in the midst of the meal I knew what I must do. There was after all one way of honouring him with my possessions and of sanctifying them.

"My lord," I said, "let me become one of the blessed poor. The half of all I have I give in alms; and for the rest, I will search out all whom I know I have cheated, and repay them or their children. Only I must except an inheritance for my sons——"

"No!" cried James and Levi together, "no inheritance, Father! God is our portion."

"I left all to follow the Master. Shall I take anything back?" asked Levi.

"And so we are delivered," I said, and tears sprang up again. Jesus had been listening and smiling, and now he said to me,

"Did I not tell you that peace had come to your house? For the Son of Man came to seek and save what was lost."

He came often to our home after that. I took the shutters down and kept the door wide open always for the poor to come in. Those sad women of the streets, too, of whom my daughter-in-law Sulamith had been one, they came in, not for food or alms only but because the merciful Teacher of Nazareth was often there and welcomed them. They all gathered round my table, the poor wretches of the port, the pilferers and drunkards, the beggars and the tax-collectors, they were there as often as word flew round that Jesus was on his way to my house, because he blessed them and called them God's dear ones and the heirs of his kingdom. He never shrank from them or drew back his clothes from filth and disease. The power of God's mercy was in him, stronger than all.

The elders of our synagogue rebuked me. "Do Alphaeus and his sons think they can purify themselves now? How can they know or remember all whom they have cheated?" True, we could not. But we knew we had forgiveness. We had to believe Jesus rather than the scribes: we knew we were forgiven. And he took our blame, for among the men of the Law the cruel rumour spread, "What a glutton, what a wine-bibber that man must be! See, he stops anywhere for the sake of getting a meal! There is no hospitality he is ashamed to accept!" And it was true, in a sense they did not dream; so true that Jesus used to repeat the taunt against himself sometimes. "See why I am called a glutton!" he would say as my wife served the meal. Yes, he took our shame. That is what he did not say when he called the weary and laden to lay down their burden: that he would take it up instead. But so he did. His holiness was mighty enough to bear it, to shake off every shred of pride or reputation, to enter everywhere and clasp anything. He burst through every barrier that decorum expected him to keep. He came into every house of darkness and tasted our bitterness. He lifted off our burdens and made them his own; but he laid on us instead the yoke of his own strong humility —to forgive as we had been forgiven, to love as he had loved us.

6

THE WINE AND THE LIFE

THE WOMEN WOULD follow—they couldn't be discouraged, and it can't be denied that they left their mark on the ministry.

At least Simon and I did not have a travelling mother, like James and John. She was a holy terror too. But all travelling mothers are the end! I was even annoyed with our Teacher's mother when she came running up panting, "They have no wine! It's run out!" What had our Master to do with organizing weddings? And her wide-eyed, trusting look annoyed me. Clearly, she had been used to turning to him like this in every domestic crisis, so that even now, when he was a teacher with disciples, she had only to run to him for some instant solution to be found, she seemed to assume. Women! I turned away to smell the wistaria. I heard him say in an abrupt, almost distressed voice, "Mother! What are you asking?" and added something in a low voice—I thought I caught the words "It's too soon . . ." But he had not dealt with her, for next I heard her voice, firm as ever, not one whit put off, calling to the servants, "All of you there! Come here. Do whatever he tells you."

A pause. I twisted the wistaria flower. Then I heard, "Fill up all those purifying jars, if they aren't full—right up to the brim."

I whirled round in amazement. That from our Teacher, whose views on lavish ritual washing were already notorious? He was standing commandingly. "All of them," he called again. But there was a gleam in his eye and a suspicious twitch at the corner of his mouth that made me swallow back my expostulations. However, the old Rabbi who had performed the wedding ceremony, not wanting to stay for the full feast, came past us while the water was being drawn, wiping his mouth. He checked, and his eyes widened when he saw what was going on and who was in charge of it. "Well does our honoured teacher purify himself," he said nastily. Jesus bowed, but the glint and twinkle must nearly have given themselves away. The old man snorted and went out.

Mary was standing very still, very puzzled, utterly trusting. "Draw out some water now and take it to the high table," Jesus ordered. The servants looked at Mary, frightened. She nodded: "Do it," she said. And they did it.

We waited expectantly, half fearing a cry of anger and a blow from the bridegroom or steward; but the merriment continued unabated. They had all been served up there now. Then our Master took a cup from one of the tables, dipped it into another of the great jars, and gave it to his mother, saying, "Drink, you too." She gave a little gasp as she tasted it and looked up at him with shining eyes, then drank again. After her, he passed the cup to me, knowing I had watched, saying, "And you, Andrew. For all of you must drink this if you would live."

I had never tasted such wine! It went down into me like fire, like nectar, like liquid glory itself. And there came welling up, slow at first, then stronger and stronger, such a deep, inexplicable joy, that for a moment I had to cover my face with my sleeve. When I looked up I met Simon's eyes, and saw the same in him. Everyone had been served with the new wine by now, and all the guests, the disciples, the bridal party, were looking at each other with the same hardly-believing gladness. Their very faces were changed. It was as if we were seeing each other as we never had before, as though we had a new kind of sight, or as though the wine itself were running through our veins like living sap in the vine. For a moment there was almost stillness: then the hilarity broke out. There was laughing, crying, dancing and singing—like any wedding party, but it would have had to be everyone's wedding for there to be as much overflowing happiness as there was that afternoon. We were all drunk on that wine—but was it drunkenness? We were drunk on joy, and on sheer love of one another. That was the point; yes, that was it; and it made us all young again. The women, even the most solid matrons, danced as long and as lightly as girls. How our Master's mother danced! I shall never forget it! I think she could have flown with joy that day—perhaps she did.

As for me, I found myself piping—a thing I had not done since I was a young lad, and how it happened I don't know, but I heard my own music rising in a kind of soaring ecstasy over the din. No warbler could have beaten me that day. No bird could have been as light in the air as I was on earth. For this was the Master's own festivity, and he did not give it by measure. I think he is the only man on earth who knows what rejoicing is. And that wedding day, we knew it with him.

What of Jesus himself? He was king of the feast. It was his feast, his gift to us. Yet I doubt if most people even noticed he was there, let alone knew whose wine they were drinking. He has a strange elusiveness when he wants to: a way of passing unseen. But he was king and reveller, all the same.

Whenever he speaks of his feast in his coming kingdom, where we shall all sit at table with him at the end of time, it's Cana I think of, with such a surge of both longing and remembering that I can hardly bear it.

There was so much wine—the steward could not think where it had come from, let alone why it was in the purifying jars— that great baths of it were taken out into the village, until I suppose half Galilee must have had some. I don't think anyone suggested it be given away. It just seemed right. As we sat down to the evening feast, I heard merrily skirling pipe music from over the flank of the hill from a village several miles away.

I could not look at those jars without smiling.

But I've been told too that some who missed the famous "wedding wine" now refuse to believe in it, since no more of it has ever been found and there was none left over.

I was sleepy with happiness at last. Someone else was piping, more gently. There was quiet laughing and talking all round. The stars swam like great golden olives. I went out to the back of the house to smell the sweet night garden, and jerked awake suddenly, hearing sobs a little way off. It was the Master's mother, saying brokenly, over and over again, "You shouldn't have done it—None of them understood—You should have obeyed your God, not your old mother!"

I was so thunderstruck that I stayed where I was, I did not even think of moving.

"I didn't realize what it would mean—I would never have asked—you shouldn't have done it!"

"You didn't know what you were asking, but you believed. That's why I did it. It was not because you were my mother. It was because you asked and believed."

"When I spilt the cup and saw it running red—they didn't understand, not one—they were all drinking your *life*—it was your life you gave us—I didn't understand—son, have we destroyed you?" There was a silence, and she spoke again. "If this was not the hour—not the time—when it does come, what will it be?"

"It will be life," he said, comforting her, "overflowing, eternal life." He added, "And even if they don't understand, they believe. In their own way, they do believe. And the end of it all shall be life. Don't grieve so."

But Mary only wept.

7

RUNNING

IT WAS NEARLY midnight, and still the house was full of everyone we had ever known and many we hadn't—eager listeners,
our neighbours and all their children, people who had heard that
the Rabbi was staying in Simon bar-Jonah's house. He was so
happy himself, the rest of us could not remember how to be tired.
He loved to be with people like this, and he loved our house (he
always called it home). Poor old Hannah, my mother-in-law,
who had been flat out with fever only this morning (it left her
when the Rabbi came in from synagogue and raised her up) was
still gamely handing out meal cakes and honey to everyone who
came; she said she hadn't enjoyed anything so much since her
own and her daughter's weddings. We weren't used yet to the
way all our Rabbi's gatherings tended to turn into parties if not
veritable feasts (which he did give on occasion). Eventually,
however, I saw John mouthing at me, "The boats". I remembered
then that we'd left them tied to mooring-rings at the quay. They
couldn't stay there, the fishing-smacks would need those berths
when they came in at dawn.

"Come on," I said to John, "let's go and move them now."
James looked up, but I was feeling generous and genial. "Sit
down! Forget it!" I called. "We'll just scull 'em round to the
cove." He sank back gratefully; nobody wanted to leave that
merry gathering and the Good News. Yet when we got outside,
it was such a beautiful night that all the glory and joy seemed to be
waiting for us there, like an invisible brightness falling out of the
firmament and floating over the house. There was a brilliant
moon. We could see easily as we ran down to the waterside, cast
off the boats, and each of us sculling one of them over the stern,
set off over the golden water.

John was in such an ecstasy of high spirits that I watched the
zigzag progress of the *Salome* with some alarm. "Surely we are

seeing the glory of God himself in our midst!" he called over his shoulder. "Is it not God who has visited us, and sent us such a Master?"

"It's the light of Israel who has come," I answered, and when I heard my own words trembled in sudden awe.

"And God has spoken peace to his people."

Then we were overcome and sculled on in silence, till as we were coming into the cove where we usually beached the boats, John (who had been gazing overhead and steering a very curious course indeed) exclaimed, in the words of Isaiah, "Lift up your eyes on high, and behold who has created all these! He calls them all by name in the greatness of his might, for he is strong in power; not one is let fall!"

I answered him as we beached the boats, laughing as we kept it up, "Have you not known? have you not heard? The everlasting God, the Lord, the Creator, never faints nor wearies."

"He gives power to the faint, and strengthens the feeble . . ."

"Even the youths shall faint and be weary, and the young men fall. . . ."

We had no breath to finish, because we were hauling the boats up, and because we were laughing so much (but we hardly knew why); but the next words were going on in my head: "But they that wait on the Lord shall renew their strength, shall renew their strength. . . ." It was strength he had given us, our Master, strength and new life; not only to the sick he had healed, but to us too, whom he had called as God calls the stars to uphold them; it was like being new created.

And so when we stood back panting, flexing our hands from hauling on the ropes, I understood very well when John suddenly said "Race you!" and set off running across the moonlit beach. I was beside him in a flash, and gasping with laughter and happiness we ran down the white country road towards Capernaum. And then the great still night seemed to start running with us, and we did not laugh any more, but left the road and ran inland over the rocks and through the pines and groves, and then in a sweep round to Capernaum through the moon-white wheatfields, and still we ran and did not tire. We had the strength of God in us, our Maker and Creator was upholding us with the stars and we were borne on his hand, swept along as he moved his arm to stretch the heavens out.

I think we could have run for ever, with the sweet night air flowing past us; it seemed as though in a very little we would be in flight, mounting up with wings like eagles, as Isaiah also promised. But we came in the end to the streets of Capernaum and my house, and stopped, swaying and reeling, with the sky spinning round us. And we looked at each other in fear and joy for the knowing of the strength that was in Jesus, the unwearying might of God's creating hand, that was lifting us up as lightly as feathers and calling us with the power that summons and bears the stars.

8
LEPROSY

SOME OF US have been here a long time. It is ten years since the first filth began to creep over my skin, and the priest examining me—while I crouched shivering—said heavily at last, "Unclean." For ten years, I've heard his gloomy word ringing in my ears by night, and I've cried it out by day, the word of the Lord that came to me through his priest: "Unclean thou art, unclean thou shalt be called, unclean, unclean."

After ten years, a body in a grave has stopped rotting in the early struggle and anguish. A body buried ten years has found a kind of peace; it is at rest. It is harder for the new lepers who come to join us among the tombs outside the walls, men newly stripped of their riches, their fine clothes, their families, by a stroke as inexorable as death. We old ones would watch them beating their heads on the ground and crying out to their only hope left, to God, who healed Miriam and Naaman and planted an undying seed of hope in the heart of all his afflicted. Do the dead still hope?

Travellers on the roads below see them, the outcast men, discoloured with sores and their rags of clothes all foul; they see them and hear their wailings, perhaps, but who but a leper knows how a leper prays?

"O Lord God of my salvation, I have cried day and night before thee; but thou cast me into the pit, thou hast laid me among the dead. Thou hast turned my life into weariness to me, my flesh is become loathsome; I am weary of my groaning, I have wept all night long. Why hast thou cast me away, O Lord? and hast thou no pity? Shall I cease from thy praise? or art thou praised by silence? Didst thou so loathe my songs to thee, that thou hast smitten me into the land where none rejoice? were my prayers as iniquity in thy sight, that thou hast cast me off? O restore thou me, that I may bless thee; O grant me to see thy presence once more in my life, and praise thee before I die!"

And there is one answer, ever and only one: "Unclean."

There's little comfort we can give one another. We never touch each other, any more than the undiseased do; what comfort is there in another leper's touch? There's nothing that can be said to the newly leprous, to a young man broken out in decay of his flesh, there is nothing to wish for him but that the loneliness may come upon him and ease him. For it does ease, that deep loneliness of the leper, among the hills. They let you live, the hills, they're good, they take you in however filthy you are. There's peace in being a leper among the hills. It's when you come among men, to beg or to wander, that's when it becomes lone-liness that hurts. You're rejected then. You're a dead man and you'd forgotten it. The dead would suffer the same if they could come back among the living. It's better not to go. But some never learn; they spend all the day ringing their bell along public thoroughfares, themselves calling out "Unclean", the last degradation; all so that they can stare at the people who don't belong to them any more. They would rather torment themselves into fever of the heart than accept to be dead, but they are dead all the same, carrying their own death with them wherever they go.

There's no peace for them. And there's no peace for the ones who beat their heads and cry, "Why hast thou forsaken me, O my God?" In the end, if you're there long enough, when you realize you're going to be a life-long leper, you stop asking that. You say instead, "Though thou hast done all these things to me, yet thou art my God; my time is in thy hands."

And you come to be glad that you can see your own foulness in his sight; there's no pride possible; you can bless him for his holiness out of your very filth and know that you were always filthy: the leprosy's only the sign. There was one old man who used to sleep in the tomb where I sleep, who said he had been made a leper for Israel's sake. "Israel is leprous," he would say, "but by my suffering may she be purified." We are the goats driven out with our mass of sores upon us, away from God's kindness and into his anger, but we are a living confession of his holiness; we have our own praise for him. In the end, you come to know that the dead do praise him by their very silence, and so do we; even the lepers are in his hands, the only hands that touch us now. Only he who is holiest of all can be father to the accursed. And he is our father still, though we can never be his children in a way that the sound and healthy of Israel would understand. There is no trust like the trust of a leper, even a defiant, despairing leper, hurling accusations. We pieces of rotting flesh, cursed with the curse of Cain, we know the Holy One as you strong men never will. This is what you have done for us by rejecting us: you cast us out, and God has caught and held us. But it is death all the same, this holding of his, and his hand over us is darkness.

Harvest time brings the pain back even to the oldest lepers. To see the olive groves and orchards full of laughing girls, to see all the townspeople out in gay attire to help bind the sheaves and build the stooks, to be dodging and running from them all day long, daring to go nowhere without your bell, it's more than a soul can bear without cracking; while there you are, rotten fruit that will never be harvested, and yet you remember what you were.

It was one morning in harvest when I climbed the hill above the town, groaning out as I had not for years. "O Lord, wilt thou not hear my prayer? wilt thou not turn to me? None but thou knowest my trouble; it has broken my heart to be outcast from thee. Thine anger breaketh over me, thy wrath has undone me; my lovers and my friends thou hast cut off from me, and all men are strangers to me. Spare me a little, O Lord my God, before I go down into death; for I am a passing sojourner with thee, as all my fathers were."

I sat down under a rock, praying with all the old anguish, as though my young blood were rising again in my rotted body; I was in greater pain than I had known for many months. Another man, another of us, was sitting above me on the higher peak of the rocky outcrop; I could see him silhouetted against the dawn sky, and knew that unmistakable posture of a lonely man, a leper praying alone. You know them by the set of their shoulders, by the way they lean forwards as though their whole body were crying out—the rejected and afflicted, men with their death upon them. I was comforted, strangely, not to be alone. It was good that he was there. And then at last my companion stood up, and to my amazement I saw that he was not one of us at all. He was no leper. The sun fell on his bearded face and untorn clothes. He was a stranger after all, a townsman—yet I could have sworn, when I watched him there, that he had the doom of leprosy on him. But now I saw only an upright, powerful man with authority in his bearing, and I fled down the hill so as not to defile him, crying "Unclean! Unclean!"

I could not get that stranger out of my mind. There had been something so kingly about him as he stood there on the hilltop, and yet I could not forget how I'd thought I was sitting by another leper. I remembered what my father (may he rest in Abraham's bosom) used to tell me to comfort me: that he'd heard a great rabbi teach that the King Messiah will be a leper, and sit in the gate of Rome with the afflicted of Israel round him; and this was what Isaiah meant when he wrote, "He has no comeliness that we should desire him; his face was more marred than any man." And I was full of strange thoughts.

I went to glean in the fields that had been reaped, and worked through the heat of the day; then, weary and in some pain, I returned to the other lepers at the graves. They greeted me with cries: "Look down there, in that field below us! Know who that is? It's a terrible prophet, Jesus of Nazareth! Listen, that's his voice! He has power over the devils, men say!"

I looked, and in the cornfield below, in the valley, the man who had seemed to me a leper-king was preaching to the harvesters, and a great number of them were listening in awe as they ate their dinner. I looked at him and knew that it was true: he was a mighty prophet, and more than mighty; the hand of God was with him, his holy spirit was in him, his very breath was God's life. Yet seeing him there, he seemed to me again to have our loneliness upon him; if not a leper, yet one of us. And suddenly I knew that he was sent to us, as much as to any brown-faced reaper. We had waited for him as they never had; we had known God would turn the light of his countenance to us one day. We had longed and hoped for it, while they in their happy lives had scarcely thought of it. And I cried out, "God has sent him to be king of the lepers! Come on! Let's go to him! He has the power to heal us all!"

I had already seized the skirts of the tunics of two of them, and was running down the hill, when the others pulled me roughly back, shouting, "Josias, are you mad? How can we go down there among all those people? How can we defile a Prophet? Do you think he'll want *us*?"

"He will want us," I said with certainty. "Oh, come! Daniel! Simeon! Don't you understand? This is the prophet of God's salvation!" I looked round at them and saw them hesitating. "Sanballat!" I appealed to the young Samaritan who was dear to me, who walks in God's ways, in spite of his descent. But Sanballat looked up and said "No. Because if he should refuse, I would hate him."

"Refuse? He'd curse us to our face," muttered Simeon.

"Then I'll go alone," I said, "and prove . . ." Prove what? Prove to what extremities of folly a sick man's fantasy will go? As I set off, conscious of all my companions' eyes upon me, my courage and sureness were ebbing. What if he sent me away? Would I not hate him too? Wouldn't it be better to stop, to hold off now, while I still loved him? Not put him to the test? "Of course he'll just send me away," I thought. Yet I never doubted that he was a prophet as great as Isaiah or Elisha, who had healed kings and captains of their plagues, and that undying seed of hope deep in me pushed me on, stumbling down among the stones and then through the stubble towards him. There were only a few people gathered there now; most had returned to their work. They stared at me as I came on. I had forgotten my cry of "Unclean", forgotten everything but his presence. They drew back with exclamations of disgust, but I scarcely saw them. I ran through the hard stalks and fell on my knees at his feet.

He was the only one who had not drawn back from me.

"Well, son," he said, "what are you asking?"

"Sir," I gasped out, "if only you wanted, you could make me clean."

"If I wanted!" he repeated, and I looked up, startled at the vehemence in his tone, and saw his eyes kindled. "Do you think I want you to be unclean?"

"Forgive me——" I stammered, "You're angry——"

"Not with you!" But I still shrank away. And then the world turned over, for he reached out his hand and laid it on my shoulder, the first human touch I had felt for ten years; and through that strong grasp all the fire of him came flowing, not indeed in anger towards me but in burning compassion. And it came to me that it was with the leprosy that he was angry, and with death and all evil powers, and even with the righteousness that had driven me out with my sins and Israel's on me.

"I do want to," he said. "Be clean."

And it was strange, but as I felt his power filling me with life, so at the same time all my filth and disease seemed to be being drawn off me through his hand laid on me. He's taking my leprosy into himself, I thought, and looking up in sudden fear, I saw the same deep, unmistakable loneliness again, that estrangement I knew so well, and a leper's look in his eyes; I've never seen eyes of such fire and such sadness. I could tell he was groaning within himself. I began to say, "Sir, are you——?" but he, realizing I had seen and understood, broke in, saying almost harshly, "Don't tell anyone."

I shook my head; I could not speak. I felt as though God had done what we had prayed for so long, had reached out his hand and turned my death into life, but had become himself leprous in doing so. I clutched his knee, I was suddenly frightened like a child. But he tightened his grip on me and said softly, "Don't be afraid." And I could not be. I forgot my fears of desolation and knew that he was master of it all, health and sickness alike. Not all our years of living death together could quench the strength and fire in him. The moment of anguish, his and mine, was swallowed up. I looked down with a little sigh and saw my own hand and arm, fresh and brown as a baby's; no scabs, no scars, no white, dry skin flaking off, and my eyes stung and I wept. But he was speaking again.

"You must go," he was saying gravely. "Find a priest who will declare you clean, and offer the sacrifices commanded by the Law: as under the Law you were condemned, so shall the Law itself vindicate you. But don't tell anyone, not even the priest, what I have done for you."

And I did not, for how could I? I scarcely knew myself; though I knew in my heart perhaps. But my cleansing could not be kept quiet. Ten lepers on the rocks above us had witnessed it, for a start. The whole town knew it as soon as I appeared in synagogue next Sabbath. So I was the cause of another kind of loneliness he had to suffer from then on: hysterical crowds used to mob him whenever he appeared in town or village, until he was forced to hold his meetings far outside them and sleep often on the hillsides. But he knows I didn't tell the real thing that happened, that was secret between him and me, nor how I had known him as the leper-king.

As I went back to the graves to say farewell to my brother lepers, Sanballat came running towards me with his face alight, crying, "You've proved it! You were right! It must be true!"

"Proved what?" I had forgotten my own words.

"That here's a prophet who knows how to have mercy on lepers."

He and nine others went after him when he left the town— not at once, for a kind of awe was on them and on him after my own healing—and were all cleansed later on, along the Jerusalem road. Sanballat was the only one who came to find me afterwards. I hardly recognized the shy man in new clothes who knocked at the door of the house where I was staying, but as soon as we looked at each other we knew that the same had happened to us both, we had both seen it, the suffering that lay over that man of God. And we knew we had tasted the burning mercy of God, that cleanses by the fire of his pity, for that fire was in his prophet Jesus and was running through our bodies. And Sanballat caught my hand and whispered, "It is God who has taken away our sin. It is God who has suffered for us."

And we stood and prayed to him there for his holy servant, the lover of the outcast, to bless his reign and save him from the evil one; prayed that he should not perish for having saved us, prayed that that fire should consume all death and decay at last and the king of the afflicted live in the strength of the life of God.

9

THE PEARL

I WAS SHY of him, that great prophet and teacher who had chosen my husband to be the "Bedrock" of his company of disciples; shy and frightened. I couldn't understand why Simon had been honoured so, a poor fisherman, or why the Rabbi came so often to our house, poor little house that it was. I could not understand him. He did not behave like the Jewish men I had known, like my father's friends when I was a girl. My father forbade the women even to show themselves, but Jesus kept us all with him, women, children, hens and goats, he liked to be surrounded by everything that belonged in the house. And then he let anyone come in who wanted to follow, from urchins and beggars to learned rabbis from the synagogue; they'd all sit there in our uneven little room, with the beetles running past them and the whitewash coming off on them, and listen while he preached as though he were sitting in the colonnade of the Temple at Jerusalem. We had nothing to offer them except a spoonful of honey in water—seldom much we could even give the Rabbi himself; our poverty distressed me, but though he surely could have found a better welcome anywhere in town, it was to us that he always came. Our house was his home, and he treated my mother like his own. I kept away from everyone as much as I could. I didn't know how to speak with him; I'd hardly spoken with a man in my life, except my husband. But he had a wonderful way with children, I will say that. He used to sit our little girls on his knee while he taught. But it was a long time before I heard a word he said.

There was once when I did try to be a good wife to Simon and say the proper thing to this rabbi who had become Simon's whole life. (How his great round eyes used to follow the Rabbi's every movement!) I was overcome suddenly with a sense of Jesus' honour and goodness, and saw how God was blessing the people through him, and I praised him aloud as I had been taught: "Blessed is the womb that bore you, and the breasts that you sucked! Blessed was your father when it was told him, A man child is born to you!" But the Teacher fixed me with those eyes of his and said, "Blessed rather are those who hear the word of God and keep it." He didn't want praise, he didn't like compliments for himself, the Rabbi didn't. He became notorious later for being beyond flattery. All he cared about was to get his message over. He didn't mind what people thought or said of him, so long as they listened. Our salvation and God's honour were all he was concerned for.

It shook me up, when he gently rebuked me for my compliment, but it was the beginning of understanding him for me. I started to follow him around with the other women so as to listen to him, on the waterside or up in the hills. It was funny behaviour, now I come to think of it, not really proper for any of us wives, but at the time it didn't seem wrong. What he was saying had come to fascinate me. All those stories the Rabbi told, they haunted my mind, yet always I felt that it was something else he was really saying. . . .

Then one day, quite suddenly, I heard it, and knew what he was trying to tell us. He was teaching in the house, with the Twelve and a lot of the other disciples about him, and I was listening behind him as I nursed the baby. He was telling story after story; nobody could move; yet he ended each one with his almost desperate appeal, "If you have ears to hear with, then hear!" He told us of fishermen drawing in their nets, of farmers planting, of harvesters reaping, and I don't know what else besides; then he said, "Or the kingdom of heaven is like treasure buried in a field. When a man found it, he buried it again, went and sold everything he had for sheer joy, and bought that field."

He must have heard me stir behind him, and the baby whimper as she missed the nipple, because he looked round with a smile and went on, "A merchant looking out for rare pearls found one precious beyond all reckoning; so he too went and sold all that he had and bought it."

I tell you, at that moment I sold all that I had and was and laid it at his feet, because I knew that treasure; I had been searching for it all my life; always my heart had been waiting for the joy of joys that would come when God redeemed his people. "Oh let it be now," I thought, "let it come to me, let me see it." Did I speak it aloud, did he hear it? How did he know I had recognized him, himself the pearl beyond all price? I only know that from that time on there was perfect, unspoken friendship and understanding between us. I was not afraid of him any more —though you might have thought I'd be more afraid, because I knew that God was in him bringing in the kingdom, the father come home to his children at last; that from now on, wherever he can find a heart to reign in, there his kingdom shall be. But it was only afterwards (mending nets in the dawn) that I thought of it that way. At the time, in the house, there was nothing but "Oh! Please!" and the overwhelming joy.

It's never changed or left me—how could it? Is a treasure that is God himself ever going to corrupt? It's my precious pearl, lying there deep inside me, God's own living joy, and the Teacher's.

That next morning at the nets—working with fingers *and* toes, determined to finish the rent by the time the boats came in, for it was last week's rent which I'd not had time to get down to— I had to sing as I knotted, I couldn't help it. I didn't see the Teacher coming till he was against the light. I looked up and the joy shot to and fro between us; there was no need to say anything, no place for fancy compliments now. He walked on towards the sea and I knotted a tangle and had to undo it, but I laughed. And then the boats were coming in, splashing and hailing, and in a minute I was in Simon's arms. I hadn't realized till then that we had grown a little estranged because I was so nervous of the Teacher whom he worshipped. I remember him looking into my face with amazement, and then a great radiant grin broke slowly over his own. Oh, that blessed time long ago and his dear grin in the dawn!

Not that he ever wholly understood, the way the Teacher had right off.

Long afterwards, in Jerusalem, when we had Gentile women

to cope with, Peter—as I've at long last learnt to call him—said to me once, "How I wish all wives were like you—with their jewellery inside!" I dropped my distaff with a gasp, remembering suddenly the Lord's parable long ago, and how it had seemed to me he was speaking to me, offering me that pearl beyond price, and I had given all and taken it. I began to laugh for happiness, but then it changed and I was crying, though still for happiness: and Peter, thinking he had upset me, came and put his arm round me and said clumsily to comfort me, "That's not to say you aren't beautiful outwardly as well, you know! I've never seen a woman more beautiful! But with you I always feel——' and here he could hardly find words at all—"there's a secret inner you inside your heart, who never shows herself, with one precious jewel, a more precious jewel than anyone's ever seen—only God sees it. That's how I feel about you."

A pearl, I thought, a shining pearl of pearls, the one, and I smiled at his sweet humble ignorance of his own heart full of treasure.

But if it's been so for us, if there's been joy like that for me, what will it be when Jerusalem finds her pearl and sells all for it? When she looks up at last to see the joy and salvation coming to her, as I knew it long ago, the desire of all desire and the hope of all hope: God's redemption? Then, I think, my pearl will be taken up and set in heaven, and become the morning star.

10

THE RAISING OF THE TRIBES

AFTER JOHN THE BAPTIST, my dear master, was put in prison, I began watching Jesus of Nazareth in earnest. It was John himself who had told me to. But it was strangely hard to watch him. In a way he baffles watching. For one of the most characteristic things about him is the way the pattern keeps changing: the sudden recognition of him in a wholly different picture, the shift of pattern. It's like seeing him and knowing him for who he is for the first time; but why should there ever be an end of these moments, for who is he?

The shifts come to everyone at some time or other. Then you see a sudden dazed halting, the fixed, prophetic stare, sudden terror in the face, a raised hand, the invariable stammered phrase: "It's the fulfilment of Scripture! He's fulfilling the Scripture which said . . ."

There was such a seeing for me, soon after John's arrest. I began by accounting him as simply a successor to John, a teacher with his disciples, until it came home to me that he had *twelve* disciples—precisely twelve—and I saw with a shiver of fear, as though I had indeed seen them raised from their graves, Israel himself and his twelve sons, the fathers of the twelve tribes. I fell on my face on the stony mountainside with all the reverence and awe for my veritable ancestors welling up inside me, those long-ago patriarchs walking through the land again, yes and there was fear too. Then there were once again just twelve men and their teacher, but though the moment of vision passed, the picture —and the reverence—won't leave me. And so I've come to know him as the new Jacob, God's favourite and beloved, the bearer of his promises, the father of a new people.

John the Baptist had a flash of seeing while I was with him once, and neither will the memory leave me of how he stopped dead as though paralysed, up to his thighs in water, and murmured to us and to himself, "See the firstling, the chosen one, God's consecrated lamb." So when I joined Jesus, as he travelled the countryside preaching, I could see him too as the first of the new flock, the ram without blemish, going before the flock to lead it; sometimes as the young ram of God, consecrated to him, and sometimes again as the shepherd, for I'd seen him working amongst shepherds once, and neither I nor Andrew and Simon, who were my companions then, have ever been able to forget it. So I found myself murmuring, as I watched and listened to him, "O thou shepherd of Israel, thou that leadest Joseph like a sheep" —and then checking myself, afraid, for that is a direct prayer to God. Yet the Lord has many shepherds: not least our forefather Jacob.

After the seeing of the pattern, there is the almost greater joy and terror of seeing it work out, beyond possibility of fantasy or coincidence. So it was too on those early journeys. By the time I joined him, after John's death, he already had a considerable following of folk whom he had healed, or freed from devils, or declared forgiven, and all their friends and family; it was really like a tribal march. Yet I could hardly believe what I was seeing, and kept a little distant from him still, asking (as many people did and still do) why he did not advance on Jerusalem, why he was content just to travel round the Sea of Gennesareth, why he kept himself exiled in half-pagan Galilee, that lost province beyond the even more lost and wholly pagan Samaria? Others (I was not one, for I was used to John, who also was friend to the poor and despised) asked similarly why he spent so much of his time and strength on the unclean, the sinful, those sunk below the Law, those whose ignorance of it was beyond remedy, all the outcast from the pure community. And he would answer again and again, "But I was sent to seek and save the lost", "I was sent to the lost sheep of the house of Israel", and often his joyous cry to a newly-healed or penitent man or woman was "For this too is a son of Abraham, this woman whom Satan had bound is a daughter of Abraham!" And slowly, hardly daring, I understood. He was journeying through the territory of the lost and scattered tribes, calling them home, rousing them up to follow him, the

Shepherd of Israel indeed. And they came, those forgotten and downtrodden remnants, those few semi-Gentiles still calling themselves by the name of Asher and Zebulun and Naphthali, the tribes we had counted dead and extinct: they remembered who they were, God's people, and came after him. It was truly like raising them from the dead. He was journeying through lands as forsaken as Sheol, lands that had known the fulfilment of Isaiah's prophecy to Galilee: "They shall fret themselves, and curse their king and their God, and look upwards and earthwards, and all they shall see is darkness and dimness of anguish, and they shall be driven to darkness." And now Jesus came among them preaching the good news of the Kingdom to them first, to the fallen and forsaken tribes, and I found myself saying in my turn, under my breath, "It is the fulfilment of Scripture! He is fulfilling the word of Isaiah: 'Land of Zebulun and Naphthali, Galilee of the Gentiles! The people that walked in darkness have seen a great light; and on them that sat in the shadow of death light has shone.'"

So I saw him raising up the people of God, and they followed him more trustingly than ever Israel of old followed those God sent to her. We were the new People on the march, and since everyone there had been set free from something—poverty, sickness, the hold of evil, the threat of death, the tyranny of our own sins, the burden of guilt, perhaps simply ourselves—we sang and danced (or some of us did) as joyously as once Miriam and Aaron: "I will sing unto the Lord, for he has triumphed gloriously; the horse and his rider he has thrown into the sea."

Yes, I've been watching prophecy fulfilled, promises coming true. And if that would send a thrill down the back of any Israelite, how much more for me, who had lived with all the Scriptures as prophecy, copied them endlessly, and copied the interpretations of the Essene teachers, seeing in every word dark mystery and hints of the irruption of the Kingdom of God? Was it not part of our teaching, for instance, that the Twelve Tribes would be reunited in the Kingdom of the Messiah? And what am I seeing now?

Today there has been another shift, a new pattern. The Master (as I do acknowledge him now, loath as I was to take any master but John) was already rumoured to have power to raise the dead. I was half ready to believe it. But this morning when we came to the little town called Nain I saw it. As we entered we met a funeral procession for a young man, with his widowed mother so shaken and consumed with sobs that she could not even wail. Jesus strode into the procession and took her in his arms as though he had known her all his life, halted the bier and cried out to the dead man, "Stand up and live!" In that passionate moment there was no room for doubt in any of our minds. Jesus' burning compassion caught us all and we thought of nothing but the woman and her grief. It was impossible that the dead boy should not be caught up in it too, and so he was. Slowly, a little stiffly, he began pulling himself up and saying "Mother . . . Mother . . ." There was no marvel in it, only the urgency and the release that were in Jesus himself. But afterwards we marvelled, for we realized that we had seen the Scriptures fulfilled again. "Thy dead shall live, they shall arise; awake and sing, all you that dwell in the dust!"

But I was possessed by the memory of that young dead body slowly sitting up, and it was another prophet who was ringing in my ears, Ezekiel who foretold the resurrection of all Israel from dry bones when God breathed on them. I saw the bones lying all over Galilee, and Jesus in his burning pity calling them, "Stand up and live!" I saw the breath of that cry going into them and gathering them together; the flush of life running through them, the flesh glowing on them, transparent at first and then the strong flesh of a man, and then the movement. In my mind I did not see the army of risen warriors described by Ezekiel, but a single gigantic figure slowly pulling itself up and rising to its feet by the lake-side, straddling the lake, the mighty figure of renewed, risen Israel itself. Nor is it any marvel. When God calls with the power and urgency of all his pity and love, how can anything that has died help but rise?

11

THE EASY THING

As we left the synagogue the screams of the possessed man were still sounding in my head, and they were to echo on there and in my dreams for a long time. We disciples reeled out after our Teacher, dazed, stumbling, seeing him still the figure of command towering over the wretched lunatic, seeing in our mind's eye still how the devil-driven body had fought and convulsed, screaming terribly, against the one who was setting it free. Yet no one watching had doubted that the passion of evil had met its master; that our Rabbi from Nazareth had power over the devils. . . . I was beginning to understand now what Simon Peter had felt when he first called us. He had borrowed Simon's boat as a platform to preach to the crowds from on the waterside (we felt very honoured). Afterwards he came fishing with us, and with him there, we made such a haul of fish as we had never seen; the boats were sunk low in the water by the weight. But while my brother John and I were exclaiming and struggling with the nets, we saw Simon in the other boat sinking on his knees and seeming to push the Rabbi away with his hands, crying out, "Go, my lord, leave me, I'm such an old sinner! Please leave me!" Not likely. It was the beginning of the closest of bonds—sometimes one might say, of friendships, but not always, not then for instance, and not after such episodes as the healing of the madman in Capernaum synagogue. But it was Jesus who chose, one might almost say put himself upon, Simon; poor old Simon was scared to death. John and I couldn't help laughing at him a little. Jesus said to him, "Don't be so alarmed —they're only fish! But from now on you'll be catching men." And, Simon says, that frightened him twenty times more.

Poor Simon! He's so easy to tease. But he saw more than we did, all the same. In every healing he does, the Rabbi seems more full of power. So far, we had been delighted, had marvelled and respected him, in common with all the people and scribes. But that exorcism was the beginning of something different. There began to be fear now: fear among the people, fear among the scribes and Pharisees, fear among us. And fear sorely also among the demons.

It took different forms. The common people worshipped him, we shrank from him, the scribes and Pharisees began to harden themselves and watch him closely, and well they might. Such power at loose in Israel, after all, was their charge, for them to call to account. They could not merely watch. They should have —Oh they should have come after him, as we had; there should never have been such bitter enmity; it was not to destroy *them* that he had come. But they took him for threat, because they could not exercise authority over him. Had they forgotten the great and holy power whose servants they were? If the Lord himself had intervened, even on their behalf, could they have exercised authority over him? No more they could over Jesus. But they did not say, "This is the Lord's doing." They grew only more hard and more afraid.

It is precisely authority that is in question. The people do not make his lot easier for him by their constant unfavourable comparisons of their own teachers with Jesus and the comment, heard so often: "He speaks with authority—not like the other rabbis, who never do anything but mumble out reverent interpretations of the Law—or even of the rabbis of earlier times. This man speaks as if he had *written* the Law—as if he were Moses!"

But the scribes said they neither claimed nor exercised authority: that was God's alone; they were the faithful custodians of his word; and what authority did Jesus have? They've challenged him, as they must, as he knows they must, again and again. And he never answers. He never gives them a sign. If only he would give just one sign to prove that his authority is from God! Why will he not? Doesn't he know what they say of him? That his power is diabolic and his authority from the devil? How can we go on defending him when he will not defend himself?

I have to admit that there are some people who show no fear or unease with him at all. There are all these women who follow him around for instance. Any woman will come up to him and start tugging at him, yelling, "My baby!" or "My husband!" with a familiarity that makes my heart come into my mouth.

They treat him as they would no other man, surely not even their own husbands. It's not as though they could understand his teaching, or were even interested. But he always takes an interest in their troubles, and in fact I've known him side with them when we were trying to shoo the most tiresome of them away. The children too. They are utterly unafraid of him. They seem to think he was sent from heaven to be their playmate. Wherever we go we are surrounded by swarms of women and children, who take besides not the slightest notice of us. But all who are not infants, idiots, or women trying to get their own way— anyone, that is to say, capable of thinking—stands in fear and trembling of our Master.

Well, it's happened. He's given a sign. But of what?

We were in the house at Capernaum; the place was packed— it was like Solomon's judgment-hall. He was preaching the kingdom. No one stirred, no one could stir. Then there came a pattering of dirt from the ceiling, then a shower of bits and debris from broken mud bricks, and then we heard a board being ripped up. The Master stopped speaking. I leapt indignantly to my feet and was about to shout a furious curse when I saw the Rabbi was laughing. We just had to stand and watch while these four profane fools ripped half the roof off (covering us with dust) and lowered a fellow on a stretcher through the hole (Simon Peter and Andrew held their peace better than I did, considering it was their parents' home). Jesus looked at the man and looked up at the four craning hopefully over. He was so full of laughter that one by one we all began to laugh. Even the scribes sitting by the door were laughing. But presently Jesus had pity on the mortified faces looking down through the clouds of dust and on the paralytic. He leant down, put out his hand and touched him—the gesture made us fall instantly silent. But then he did not heal him. He was still laughing. He said, "Your sins are forgiven, son."

And the man began to laugh. Lying as rigid as before, his eyes began to narrow and dance, his face twisted into a grimace and a convulsion shook him. Jesus and he were sharing a joke. The hand resting on him was less like a healer's than a man's laid on the shoulder of a friend who has done something to delight him. They were absorbed in mutual merriment. He had forgotten us— forgotten the crowds. Almost we were swallowing the astonishing situation, his astonishing words; then suddenly he straightened and looked round and there was no laughter in his face any more, but a deep anger and sorrow. He was looking straight at the doorway where the teachers of the Law were sitting in a huddle. "Why must you always have such thoughts? Why?" he cried out.

The elders looked at each other, then Rabbi Hananiah stood up, flushing, and said, "Honoured Teacher, you force us to say what we would willingly have left unsaid." Then in a tone of sternness to match Jesus' own, he thundered, "You have spoken blasphemy. God alone can forgive sins."

So it was said—what we had all been on the point of thinking, if it had not been for the sight of Jesus and that man in such perfect mutual understanding and mirth. But now it was different. I felt horror go up my spine as I realized what Jesus had really said. I saw dismay on the faces round me. Someone wailed out, "Oh, Master, why did you say it? Why didn't you just heal him?" It was the question in all our minds. "He's done himself now," muttered Simon beside me. "He'll never be able to justify that."

"When has he ever justified himself?" I whispered back bitterly.

But Jesus said simply, "Is it blasphemy to forgive, but not to heal? Why?"

In the silence which followed he went on, "Which do you think is easier: to say 'Your sins are forgiven', or to say 'Stand up, take your mat and walk'?"

Silence again. The hectoring flush faded from Hananiah's face. He looked in perplexity at his colleagues. They avoided his look, bewilderment spreading.

"Why, healing surely is easier, since that's permitted to men," I said to myself, "at least—unless—but no——" And everyone was muttering the same.

"What does he mean? God could do one as easily as the other, but only God——"

"Perhaps he means that healing is not easy——"

"Well," Jesus said, "since you can only believe in the one and not the other—" he went on to the paralytic— "you'd better stand up and take your mat and walk, and let them see."

And he did. Grinning hugely, he stretched, swung himself off the stretcher, stood up and slung it over his shoulder.

"And yet my other words were blasphemy?" asked our Teacher. The elders were scowling in annoyance and embarrassment. A new murmur was going joyfully through the crowd, a murmur of relief.

"God would not have let that man rise at his word if he had really blasphemed."

"God has given him the right to forgive sins on earth!"

In the swelling jubilation I saw the scribes making their exit arguing amongst themselves, and knew what they were debating. "Which is easier . . .?"

The same question dins round and round inside my own head. "Does he treat forgiveness so lightly? Was it true forgiveness? Or did God overlook his pride for once? We know he can heal. But can he forgive? What are we supposed to have seen?"

He had given a sign. But I can't read it. And I wish with all my heart I had the simplicity of some people, of my brother John, who consider that he has proved that he has the right to forgive sins in God's name. "And therefore his authority is from God."

Those easy words . . . And how easily he had spoken them. But forgiveness is not easy. To turn away God's wrath is not easy, not a matter for laughter and merriment and buffoonery like breaking in through a ceiling. Forgiveness means repentance and grief, the affliction of the soul; it means, for God, dimming the burning of his holiness. Can even he forgive easily, like that, at the sight of the absurd antics of those friends, at that comedy of impatience? Can he forgive out of delight, for fun?

Or is healing easy?

I only gradually came to realize that the trap was to try to answer the question at all. The scribes were trying, and were reduced to sullen argument. John and the others had leapt straight over it. But I had fallen in, and there I am, stuck fast. I don't know who he is. I don't know how he heals, or how he forgives, or whose is the power. I'm afraid . . .

12

THE HARDEST THING

... I'M AFRAID.

We were still not used to his ways. We had, indeed, learnt by now not to set out in search of him if he was missing when we got up (the first time it happened we scoured the neighbourhood, thinking—I don't know what—that the spirit might possess him and drive him wild in the desert again, that the Pharisees might have kidnapped him, that he might have left us like Elijah to go to Horeb or Sinai). We knew by now that he liked to pray by himself for hours before dawn, but it still came as a shock when he sent us home from the hillside where he had been teaching, and said he would not follow us yet. "Master," gasped John, "you're not staying here to pray all night?" Jesus laughed at that and told us not to be anxious on his account: he had been forty days and nights alone in the wilderness once: "The angels looked after me," he said. "But how hard was the struggle!"

"Master, then let us stay with you!" cried Simon.

"Simon, could you face Satan beside me? Can you fight the fight I must? Which of you knows what I must undergo?"

Always that loneliness. It was true, none of us knew either what he had been through or what he must still face. I dared not speak. Ever since he had made the open claim to forgive sins, or rather, since he had forgiven in God's name that ludicrous man let down through the roof, I had been so full of trouble and doubt that perhaps I only stayed with him because of my brother John. I had seen his power; I could not tell if it was holy or unholy; and more and more the rumours flew that it was diabolic. Now as we made our slow way back to the village where we were staying, leaving him on the hillside, I was wondering in gnawing anxiety: He confesses that he faced the devil in the wilderness; but who won? Who came away leading whom captive? I remembered with a thud of fear his own remark,

"No-one can rob a strong man's house, unless a still stronger enters and binds him." He was the strongest man on earth, but what was Satan? I was terrified at the picture of the two of them locked in combat, the strong and the stronger, the robber and the robbed, in the bleak hills with nothing but the stones to eat. And this was the man to whom I had given my life, at his bare words, "Follow me". Where was I following him? I shivered in the dusk. It was a cold night. I missed the lush lowlands and the water. I had never before left the lake to wander up into the hill country.

Early the next morning we went back. John was there ahead of me. I don't know if he had been speaking with Jesus before I came; now, as all the company of disciples slowly assembled, trudging up from the villages, a great silence fell. The Rabbi sat on a rock near the top of the hill and watched. He looked more refreshed than many of us. I think there was not a word spoken till the sun was high in the sky and a hundred or more disciples were present. They were still the men, mostly. By midday the number would be five or six hundred as the women and sick arrived. Then Jesus stood up, in that expectant gathering, and called, "Simon, son of Jonas."

Simon started, leapt to his feet, and bolted up the hill, then seemed to lose his nerve and fall . . . fell back, recovered himself and slowly made his way to Jesus' side with his head tipped back and his mouth open.

"Andrew, son of Jonas."

We began to guess how solemnly he was naming us.

"James and John, sons of Zebedee. Levi, called Matthew."

Twelve of us he called, and we went up to him out of the gathering like the elders going up to Moses from the camp of Israel. We were like those elders and the people were our people. They watched with deepest attention. The solemnity never lessened. They knew the Master was ordaining us as their leaders, his officers.

"You twelve I have called," he said, "to preach the Kingdom of God with me. In my name you shall do all that you see me doing. The power that is in me shall be in you to heal the sick, raise the dead, cleanse lepers, cast out devils. And you must announce the Kingdom wherever you go."

And a slow and creeping terror, like paralysis, began to come on me, as I realized that his power, that strange and fearful power, was going to come into me, that I must know it in myself.

He was speaking to the whole assembly now: "And all of you are God's flock. Never be afraid: God has chosen to give you the kingdom. . . ." Another day of teaching was beginning. And before the end of it John had healed a crippled child, and Philip driven out a devil. But I did nothing, did not try; I was afraid of what I might do.

The twelve of us did not go our separate ways that nightfall; we knew that where Jesus went, we must go. We all accompanied him down to the village, but I ran up to him and pulled at his arm, drawing him a little ahead. "Master," I said in a low voice, "why did you choose me? Why in God's name did you not choose John and leave me?"

"I know whom I have chosen," he said smiling.

"Master, in God's name, tell me, what spirit is it in you?"

"Ah, how I wish you knew! For it is your spirit too." Then he stopped still, put his hands on my shoulders and said, "Don't reject the spirit. Above all things take care that you don't reject the spirit. For that can never be forgiven, because you'll have rejected forgiveness itself."

The sternness in his tone was very different from the almost lighthearted way he had spoken of forgiveness in the house at Capernaum. We went the rest of the way in silence. I did not dare to ask, "Can you forgive me now, or is it already too late?" I was not thinking now that forgiveness for him was easy. It seemed terrible, the hardest thing, easy in nothing but in rejecting it. And yet still there was that gnawing fear, "His power is evil, and if you don't let it possess you it will destroy you."

In the house he told us that he was sending us out, two by two, the next day, to preach all over the countryside while he himself went on to the next towns. "Don't be afraid of anything," he said "Don't take anything to protect yourselves but go poor and defenceless. Don't take any money, any spare clothes, any food, but let your heavenly Father look after you. Anyone who takes you in will be blessed as though he had taken me in, and not only me but the one who sent me. And give as freely as I have given to you, give all I have given you." His spirit, his power. . . .

John was so blithe and full of faith, it was easy for me, at first, to remain silent and unnoticed. For two days we went together through the hill territory in the direction of Mount Carmel, and I watched the fire and power in John and grew bitterly ashamed. How could I doubt him, my brother, who had always been so dear to God? How could I doubt my lord and master Jesus? Yet I did doubt.

Then on the third day we came to a town where a girl ran out to meet us screaming, her head lolling. "What have you come here for, you messengers of the living God? We don't want you! Get out!"

"It is not us only," said John, "it is the Kingdom of Heaven that is upon you."

"Get out! Get out! Take the Kingdom away! You'll destroy us!" But I saw the frenzied pleading in her eyes, pleading against her own words.

As clearly as I could hear the devil's voice, I could hear Jesus' within me. "Cast it out," he was saying. "Cast it out by my power and in my name. Set her free from Satan's bondage."

"Hold her for me, John," I said, stepping forwards. He was so surprised that he complied without question. Other townsfolk were running out by now, shouting. I scarcely heard them. There was nothing but the closeness and violence of evil, as close as the girl lashing and biting my hand. I let her bite it and held the other on her head. Her froth and my blood dripped on the ground. But in a way I was even glad of the pain. I could easily forgive it her. And suddenly, in that age-long instant, I found myself thinking: "Satan binds in sin. If Jesus looses from sin it can never be Satan's work." And I cried out in exultation as much as command, "In the name of God and of his holy servant Jesus, I command you to leave this woman!" She gave a shuddering scream and fell at my feet, inert. "Pick her up," I said to the bystanders, panting and gripping my hand. "She's alive."

But they shrank back. "She's a sinner," they were saying. "She's the devil's own. She's unclean."

Then power really came and I felt myself towering over them. "She is no longer a sinner, and she is set free from the devil. She came running to us for healing in spite of the evil spirit that possessed her. It is God himself who has cleansed her. Take her and cherish her!"

For I knew the power now, the spirit that was forgiveness itself, and I knew that God does not dim the burning of his holiness to forgive; no, he burns so fiercely that he burns the sin all away and his blessedness can reach through and touch the poor human creature within. Now I understood how great our Master's joy must have been when he could touch it in a flash, immediately, in that poor, comical paralytic and his friends, who had desired nothing so much as the burning-away of their sin. All the power of Jesus is the power of forgiveness; in all that he does it is God's mercy at work. As for healing, it is harder than holding down a madwoman, it's the very struggle with the devil. But forgiveness is the piercing-through of mercy, the supreme touching above the conflict, the simple burning, the easiest thing that yet costs God of his very nature. It was not that paralysed man alone whom Jesus has forgiven, but in all whom he has touched, all whom he has healed, that pure burning of forgiveness was at work; he has been glad, yes glad, to bear the pain of humanity's crazed biting. Only a blind Pharisee would set himself up to judge between his healing and his forgiving. Only a blind disciple could fail to see who was the strongest man of all, binding the devil and loosing his creature in one single work, as easy as laughing, as hard as willingly suffering; yes, in love and joy easily doing the hardest, hardest thing.

13

POWER AND JOY

So THROUGH ALL the towns of Galilee we went, twelve poor men, with the power of God in us and the joy of the Kingdom in our hearts, working our Teacher's own works for him; and God himself fought for us. For now wherever John and I came, evil things shrieked and besought us not to use the name of Jesus against them, for it had power nothing could withstand. And I no longer shrank from wielding that power, but it was joy and glory to me deeper than I had ever dreamt of, to be the bearer of that power and have it in me, and to speak that name. All darkness fled away before us, not the devils only, but wherever men were nursing evil, their thoughts were laid bare by our mere greeting and announcement of the coming of the Kingdom of God, and they broke down and confessed their sins. Divided families were reconciled, tax-gatherers gave away their gains, those who had slipped away into the superstition of the Greeks cried out that the Lord was God and Jesus his holy one. So everywhere we brought the sword of judgment and the oil of mercy, even as the Rabbi Jesus himself did; we felt the kingdom flaming about us, and we left its peace with all who accepted us, and we knew that Jesus' words were true when he said, "Whoever receives you, receives me, and whoever receives me, receives the One who sent me."

We had nothing, we rejoiced to have nothing, not so much as a change of clothing. The Master had wanted us to let people give us things, because, he said, "If anyone gives you so much as a cup of cold water for my sake, he will assuredly not go unrewarded." We received many such "cups of water" and many were blessed. But woe to many others, who would not hear, who refused our word of peace, who shut their door in our faces! Woe to the hardened hearts and blind eyes! For rejecting us, they rejected him who had sent both Jesus and us. And we spoke stern prophecies against them.

As we came back to Capernaum just before Passover-time, all the hosts of heaven seemed to be marching behind us, in the cloud of white dust hanging over every road; and we were at their head, in the place of Jesus. As we came in sight of the familiar lakeside villages where we had first followed him we broke into singing as we walked, for very exultation. Somewhere here we were joined by Philip and Bartholomew, as all the pairs of apostles converged on Capernaum, who heard our singing before they recognized us, and when they saw who we were shouted with laughter: "James and John! You sons of thunder!" (so Jesus had nicknamed us). And the four of us went together along the high road through Magdala singing psalms of jubilation: "Let God arise, and let his enemies be scattered; let all who hate him flee before him!" we sang. And so it was. Still before our face the powers of darkness scattered and the light behind us grew, for God himself was our rearguard and all his redeemed were with us. So rejoicing in his glory and majesty we came to the village farm a little to the west of Capernaum where Jesus had promised to await us.

We saw a figure on the hill behind the farmhouse, which we guessed might be he, and left the road to make our way up through the orchards towards him, and he came down the flank of the hill towards us: I shall never forget that meeting among the quiet trees, how the four of us stumbled uphill breathlessly but triumphantly singing the last verses of the psalm: "Sing to him who is seated in the heavens over all . . . fearful and glorious is he in his holy places, the God of Israel gives strength and power to his people; blessed be God!" And Jesus' voice answered us, "Blessed be he for ever", and looking up I saw such blazing joy in his face that for a moment I felt suddenly ashamed. Our singing and jubilation, it was children playing, we had had no idea of the true glory and victory of it all. But then I was crying out, forgetting even to greet him, "Master, in your name, even the devils are subject to us!"

"Yes," he answered, "I watched how Satan fell like lightning out of the sky. And now you see that I have given you the power to tread underfoot snakes and scorpions and all the forces of the enemy, and nothing will ever harm you."

"It's true, it's true!" I shouted. "The only power that could have harmed us is bound for ever—you have bound the Evil One, Master, in the abyss!"

"Have I?" he said with a smile. "He has lost his lordship, true, but he doesn't know it yet. While you are in this world you will have to fight him. But you will be armed with power from above."

"Master," I declared, "we have been fighting with that power; we know it."

He smiled again, a little sadly, and said, "Yet what you should rejoice over is not that you have power over the devils, but that your names are written in heaven, yes, and your seats are set at God's own heavenly table."

Then the great and blazing joy came back into his face so that we fell back from him in awe, for the Spirit was mighty on him, and he raised his hands and cried out, "I bless you Abba, Father, Lord of heaven and earth, because you have hidden these things from the learned and wise and revealed them to the little ones. Yes, Father, that was your choice!" And though I understood then that the rift with the scribes and lawyers was bitter to him, and their rejection more serious than I had realized, yet what I saw was a man consumed by joy, his life nothing but a great thanksgiving in that fearful power of the Spirit I had shrunk from so long, uttering his shout of "Yes, Father!" with every pulse of his blood; and if he saw the sky rent by the lightning of Satan's falling, truly I saw heaven and earth filled with the exultation of the one who had cried among the pines, "I bless you, Abba, Father!"

And it was for us that he blessed him, for us and our playing at joy, for our rejoicing compared with his was the games of "little ones" indeed; but it was for us that he thanked his Father then.

He was silent then for awhile, but the intensity of his cry of prayer seemed to ring on and on in the spring air, while we stared out over the blossoming hillside and the lake. At last he turned to us, and I saw suddenly that there was grief as well as joy in his face, grief for the incomprehension and rejection of those who should have been most his friends; and he said to us now, "Amen, I tell you, only a father knows his son, and only a son his father." There was bitterness, yes and loneliness, in his tone, but then his eyes lit up again and he went on, "Yet the son can share what he knows of his father . . . for he belongs to the house and he it is who has the right to make others free of it." Then he cried out to us, "Blessed are your eyes, to see what they see! For I tell you, many prophets and kings desired to see what you are seeing, and never saw it; and to hear what you are hearing, and never heard it."

We were seeing, we knew the father, because we knew his son; he had made us free within his family; comic, scruffy children, he had made us God's little ones, he had shown us what he could not show the proud and learned. And a deeper gladness kindled in us than all the exultation of our return, and as we went slowly down towards the house, where our hosts were calling to us, John said to me in a low voice, "This is his real spirit, this. . . . All that power—I don't know; but this is what it is to him." I nodded, I could not speak. We both knew it. All of us there had been caught up for a moment beyond ourselves in the sweep of our Teacher's love and joy, for his Father and for us, and for that little space of time we were still spinning in that fiery circling, we were in his spirit, and we knew father and son almost as they knew each other. This was the source of his power and authority, that the scribes and Pharisees had challenged him to declare, this was the force in him that I had felt and feared. For that moment, we tasted it and had it in us, and knew the love and joy that drove Jesus on; I understood then (though later the understanding failed me) that even if he had to go right to death for his Father's sake, he would do it in a passion of love and joy.

14

THE BRIGHT SPLENDOUR

I'VE LIVED BY the lake all my life, and always loved it. I remember how when I was a little girl the shimmer used to flicker on the courtyard walls under the vine-trellis where I was playing alone (for we were right on the water's edge), and I used to cry out with joy and dance with it. Later when I was a girl ready to be married the lake threw a veil of light round me as I sat in the same courtyard painting my father's and brothers' pottery. Always the light, the water, the air, the smell of wet wood, the smell of fish, the swaying palm trees, the cries as they hauled the boats in. Always the shimmering splendour was there, the hidden splendour, God's own glory wandering unrecognized among us. I loved to dream that I was glimpsing the Shekinah whenever I saw a sudden flash of lake-light. A girl's dreams. I lived with eyes only for the hidden splendour, and never guessed that someone was living with eyes only for me.

Ar-shebna came often up the lake from Herod's city of Tiberias to buy jars, cups and vases from my father, for his brother Chuza was Herod's steward, and sat in the house drinking our honeyed lemon and watching me through the door. But I was hardly aware of what went on inside. I was immersed in the patterns of light and shadow under the vine leaves, and in trying to transfer them to the vases I painted. I loved to cover them with vines and wavelets. Ar-shebna bought everything I made at a high price, but I was not doing it for him.

I loved the lake in its wild moments too, when sudden storms came spinning across it from the Decapolis territory, and squalls of tremendous wind beat against the house. Then I could hear the power in the water outside, and it seemed to me like the voice of the Lord thundering again as it had at Sinai. When the water beat like that against the houses on the lake—rain and spray—no-one could use the rooms fronting on the lake.

We could not endure the lake in its fury, nor even look at it. But I used to open my shutter and smell deeply the wild smell of a storm on a freshwater lake: the smell of untamed water. And always the beauty of the light, by night or by storm: the glinting, fierce or gentle, the shimmering, the splendour hidden in the depths of the water giving itself away.

Dreams, a girl's dreams, far more fragile than the truth; no-one can master light and water, but anyone can smash a dream. Ar-shebna said he would give me a palace of dreams, but he only smashed or smothered my own. He said he was taking me away to be a bride—not yet: his son's, when he came to manhood, according to Jewish custom. He must have paid my father a heavy bride-price, or slave-price rather. So I left the vine-covered courtyard and my father's house and lived in a room over the tanner's shop with silk hangings over the windows. They gave on to the lake too, but I never looked out now. As for my wedding, either Ar-shebna had no son, or he is many years from manhood. I began to understand I should never be a bride. And there was no light in that room but the light of tapers, and I seemed myself to be smothering in scents and embraces. I saw no-one but Ar-shebna and the tanner's family. And I knew I should never see the bright splendour now, for I was no bride, I was a whore.

How long was I imprisoned there? Two years, five years? Then there came the morning when I descended from my chamber to speak with Hannah the tanner's wife and buy some fine oil. I stood in the doorway of the shop talking with her and looking idly out at the sunlit sand in the roadway. Then a little boy came running down the street yelling "He's coming! The Prophet's coming!" He gave me a smack with his hand as he passed and called "Get inside, dirty woman! The Prophet's coming by!"

I did not answer his insult, I did not get inside, for there was such light in the street, all the brilliance of the early morning, and he—the Prophet—was striding so lightly and joyously down towards the waterside that it was as though the very dayspring itself were moving there. The houses were bathed in it, that sweet fresh light, the water glinted with it. And as the figure came level with me I whispered under by breath, "Oh, Master."

I only whispered; yet he stopped and turned, looking straight at me.

"Oh, don't come near me!" I said aloud. "Keep away from me, prophet, I'm an impure woman!"

But he crossed to my side nevertheless and said, "Who shall call unclean what God has called clean?"

I stared at him in amazement while his words sank in, and all the radiance of the young morning sky behind him seemed to be in his face. "Does God call me clean?" I asked, and already looking at him I knew it was true. "Can even God restore innocence?"

"All things are possible for God."

And I knew that he had; through the Prophet's words, he had; I was a girl again with my heart beating with hope at the sight of the lake-light on the walls, dreaming in a rapture of the coming of the bright splendour. But again it was not the same, I was not dreaming now; it was not a mere flicker of light that was making my heart leap with joy within me; no, it was not for the sake of the sweet brilliance of that morning that I was looking up at him with the beginning of hope and wonder so great that it could find no words.

"Blessed are you who have had eyes to see," he said quietly; "I tell you truly, the Kingdom of God stands open to you. And further I tell you that your eyes shall see heaven open and God's angels ascending and descending upon the Son of Man. Be ready for that day and never stop watching!"

"I will watch, oh I will watch!" I cried in a transport of joy, and then my heart fell as I remembered: "Ar-shebna will come back. I belong to him."

"You have never belonged to anyone but your Father who is in heaven," he told me. "And if he lost you for a while, do you think he'll let you go again now he's found you?"

I clung to his robe, and some of his own gladness and certainty must have come through to me because I stood up suddenly and laughed. The morning was beautiful, the lake was shining.

"Let him come!" I said. I knew that nothing had power now to separate me from the vision given back, from the glory returned, that the innocence of forgiveness could not be robbed from me.

"Have you anywhere to go?" he was asking me.

"I'll stay here," I declared. "I'm not afraid. I'll give Ar-shebna back his silks and live like a widow. I'll serve the tanner's family— Hannah, you'll let me, won't you?" I turned to her and found her in tears, but she hugged me silently. The Prophet watched us and said to one of his followers, "Judas, have we anything in the purse? Give it to them." And aloud he added, "if you could only hear the rejoicing there is in heaven now!"

We begged him and his disciples to stop and break their fast with us, but they wanted to make the crossing as early as they could. But I went to the quay and watched them setting out, sniffing the wet wood, the lake smell, the fish smell, the tar smell. It was so long since I had watched the boats. Passers-by stared at me, but when they saw I was under the Prophet's protection some of them smiled. I followed the boats (the disciples waving to me) with my eyes until I lost them in the dazzle; then I came back singing to the house and threw everything Ar-shebna had ever given me out of the window. And the less there was of all that stuff the more the Kingdom of God seemed to be pouring through. I was free of the stifling bondage, free of the heavy caresses that had choked my life and my joy away. My life and my joy, they were God himself now, who had touched me with his brightness in the person of his prophet. Long afterwards, in Jerusalem, one of those apostles (as they came to be called) told me with awe and sternness how once with their Master they had seen him transfigured with the Shekinah of God overshadowing him. And I'm afraid I laughed. "You saw it just once?" I said. "And he didn't want it known, bless him?" But he walked through the lakeside streets and quays with it all over him, as the morning radiance was over the town; you'd have had to be blind not to see it if you met him as I did that morning. He could no more help showing it than the lake could help reflecting the light.

Ar-shebna came back a few times. I met him in the shop and talked to him there where I had talked with the Prophet. He was unable to understand. He thought the Prophet of Nazareth must have bribed me away from him. He said, "But I gave you everything! What can he give you? He is a wandering poor man. His family is of no significance. He'll never give you any present. Why, why have you preferred him to me?" Then thrusting his face close, he asked, "Is it because he is younger than me?" Another time he asked, "Is it because I never brought you to court? I will, I swear it! I will take you to Tiberias now!"

But I stood by the door and looked out on that waterside where the Prophet had stood clothed in light, and laughed softly for joy, because he had clothed me in it too; he had given me no silks, no, but he had cast his own glory round me. And the freshness of the shimmering lake, yes and the power of the wild stormy lake, were promises of what was to come.

15

LETTING GO

I *Jairus the Synagogue Ruler*

BLESSED BE HE, who createth new life continually! Amen.

When my brother sent to tell me that he was returning from Egypt, I wrote joyfully and replied, "Come and see how the Lord has blessed our estate and my wife's womb, and you will never again want to leave the land of promise!" I received him with the best of all I had, and the dearest of all, my little daughter, brought him wine and pomegranates. She served him so prettily, that I was amazed when he asked when she was gone, "Now, brother, I am waiting to see how the Lord has blessed your wife's womb!" His eyes were searching the fields as though expecting someone.

"But my little Miriam was before you just now."

"Why, has the Lord given you no son?" he exclaimed, his face falling, and we spoke of other things and never again of Miriam. It is true, the Lord has given me no son, but is she not enough for me? She is the delight of my eyes and the joy of my heart, and my brother spoke as a fool.

When we used to go in the spring to visit my wife's parents in the hill country of Upper Galilee it was my happiness of the year to cross a certain watercourse, dry later in the year, but at that time requiring to be forded. The women and Miriam and the baggage used to go over on muleback, while the men waded. But when she was still very small, as we reached the ford one year, a shepherd and his flock were going over before us. He had led the first sheep over and was waiting while the others followed. But one last lamb, the weakest, stood on the far side bleating piteously, too afraid to enter the water, and at last the shepherd had to come back for it and carry it across. Miriam was so excited: "Abba, abba!" she cried. "You go across and come back and get me! I'll be a lamb!" And every year she remembered, and we played that game at the ford. I would cross and watch while the mules got over, until only Miriam alone was left on the bank; then I would cross again and carry her over in my arms, or on my back when she grew too big. And I would tell her as I put her down. "Even so does the Lord, the Shepherd of Israel, carry his own people tenderly in his arms."

Until she was eight years old, we played shepherd and lamb at the ford, but not after that. For the last time, as I lifted her up, I felt her trembling suddenly, and she began to shriek, "Put me down, abba, put me down! You're going to drop me! I'll fall in!"

"No, you won't, my little one."

"You'll drop me! You'll drop me into the water! I want to go over on a mule!" And we had to send a mule back to fetch her. She was crying with terror, her face scarlet. I said to her, "I would not have dropped you, sweetheart."

"Yes, you would! You would!"

And a little later on, she asked, "When the Lord God is being our shepherd, does he ever drop the lambs?"

"Of course not! The Lord never lets go of his own, never!'

And yet it was true that I had been thinking with sorrow that the Lord never visited his people any more, but left us crushed in captivity to Rome, and turns his ear away from our prayers.

"It is not true!" I said fervently. "The Lord loves his lambs and carries them safe for ever! Not for them the fear of any water to cross!"

But Miriam would never play the game of the shepherd again.

II   *Esther the wife of Mabi*

I had been bleeding so long, and defiling myself so long, that it seemed as though to be pure again were as hopeless and pathetic a wish as to be young again. I was so tired, my own body had wearied me to the very bone and bled itself out. My husband had divorced me—he could hardly do otherwise. I was nothing but a great ache that could never be rested, for as long as I lived I was a daughter of Israel still and it was my duty to the holy God to seek purification. "You shall be holy, for I am holy." But every time I stretch out for holiness, for purification, he takes it away and sets it out of my reach, leaving me dragging myself from doctor, to priest, to doctor, to priest. I hadn't any more money, I hadn't any more strength, but still I bled and must struggle on. And no-one could help me.

Until I saw the healing prophet of Nazareth passing with his crowd of followers on the waterside where I was trying covertly to buy fish, without touching and thus defiling anyone, a harassing, humiliating business. I saw him at the same moment as the fishwife whispered to me as she gathered up my coins (avoiding my sleeve), "There goes the Prophet Jesus! He's a healer, did you know?" I left her kindly hint unanswered. I couldn't take my eyes off him or think of what she was saying. "There's help," I thought. I saw the strength in him and all my body seemed to sigh and ease itself. "There's help. He could help."

I forgot my fish, I forgot my coins and was creeping after him on the edge of the crowd already. It was out of the question to ask him to lay his hands on me. Yet perhaps—perhaps? I might be able just to reach out and touch his hem. "Lord God of my fathers," I prayed in my heart, "if you ever mean to have mercy on me, have mercy now. Let me come close enough to touch him. Don't take your holiness away any more. Don't punish me any more. Forgive me now. Let me touch him."

I had no right to be in that crowd at all. I know I must have rubbed against some of them. I could feel myself bleeding, all my joints were aching, my hot clothes clung to me, the flies swarmed on me—they alone fearing no defilement. I should never get near him! How could I have thought it? Did God mean to give me purity at a touch, suddenly, easily, now, like that? Had he not ordained me to the long seeking of his face?

And one thing I never thought was that by touching him I should in fact defile him. He would burn up all my filthiness in a flash and it would be no more. All I wanted was to touch him without his knowing. More, I did not even think of hoping for. "But I shall not be allowed to touch him," I thought with increasing certitude.

Yet I kept on. Every time I looked up and saw him I hoped again, and made a fresh attempt to wriggle near. And at last he stopped, talking to a man who was bowing low before him, long enough for me to come right up close behind. Everyone around him was so engrossed that I went unnoticed. I was almost there—when Jesus' voice came warm and loud over the others: "I remember your little Miriam! Not for nothing did I bless her when you brought her to me in the synagogue! I will come at once."

And he started forward on his great man's stride, out of my reach.

Now I was only a little way behind though. I ran, hardly caring for dissimulation any more. All my seeking for God, all my striving after purification, all those weary years of reaching and longing, went into that last urgent push and tumble of reaching, and his robe was under my hand, was in my hand. For a second I held it lightly to my cheek and then let go, expecting to see it swing away as he strode on. I had lost my balance, I was on my knees in the hot dust; but there was strength coming into my body, it was true; God had given holiness to the one who had sought so long; strength was welling up where the blood had ebbed . . . but the robe was not swinging away, it was swinging round, and Jesus was saying, "Who touched me?"

I scarcely had time to get behind someone's cloak. My head was pounding, my eyes swimming. I knew he must see me. Indeed I knew I must let him see me. But for a moment I truly could not move. One of the men with him called out, rudely enough, "Master, there's half Capernaum treading on your heels, and do you say, 'Who touched me?'"

"Someone did touch me," he insisted, and looked straight at me where I cowered. And I fell on my face before him because he looked at me so, and now I was bitterly ashamed of having tried to hide, and steal his holiness, and yet even now I could not face his look.

"Oh, Rabbi!" I gasped. "I dared not come to you—I was unclean! Forgive me that I touched you!"

But he bent down and raised me up, and turned my face

with his hand to look into his. And I knew I had to pay the final price for holiness, the price of confrontation. Not to seek God for ever but to let him find me; and it was the hardest thing of all.

"Daughter," he said gently, "it's all right. Your faith has saved you. Go in peace, free for ever from your trouble."

And so I was brought face to face with God at last, he stood before me and I before him, and there was silence, in those moments when I stood with the Prophet's hand turning my face to his. And this was the meaning of all those years of my running and his withdrawing: just so that at the end I should stand, and know, and be healed.

I don't know how long that utter stillness held us. Then there was dashing in the crowd, and a man's voice hoarsely, urgently whispering, "It's too late. The child's dead. Tell the Rabbi not to come any further."

III Jairus

It was the Rabbi Simon, more than myself, who had become friends with Jesus of Nazareth and used to invite him to preach in our synagogue. But I too revered him as a man of God, sent to us to prepare us to receive the Kingdom. And though he was not a father himself, he loved the children, and loved Miriam. When the fever began to burn her out, and we saw that she was beyond the help of medicine, my wife and I looked at each other and knew we were thinking the same. I rose, saying, "I will go and ask the Rabbi Jesus to come and lay his hands on her. He can save her from death." I was surprised to find the strength of my own certainty. "He can save her from death!" I repeated as I went out.

It was easy to find him in town in those days. The crowd collected wherever he was. The people parted to let me through, and I ran and flung myself to my knees at his feet; and as I tried to tell him, I could scarcely speak for weeping. "She is dying, Rabbi," I said: "my daughter Miriam's dying. She can't last the hour."

"Little Miriam!" said the Rabbi: "I remember her! I did not

bless her for nothing. I will come at once." And he added, "Don't be afraid. She shall not die."

I could not doubt the warmth of feeling and compassion in his voice. That he meant to come and heal her before she died, I am certain. And yet he stopped, he delayed. Why did he stop? A woman came up behind him seeking his help. He turned, he asked after her, he stood and called her. I waited with my heart sinking and sinking. He seemed utterly absorbed in this new demand for help, it was as though he had forgotten Miriam. As we all stood halted about him the tears began to flood my eyes again and I wept silently there, wept because I knew in my heart that now it was too late. And yet I could not feel anger but only the sorrow of it, the sorrow of what might have been if he had not delayed. I scarcely needed the arrival of the messenger to tell me she was dead. "Why trouble the Rabbi to come any further?" said my servant, with a hostile look at him. But Jesus' attention was back with us.

"Don't start doubting now," he said to me urgently. "You have trusted me. Don't start doubting now." And I shook my head, too choked to speak.

The professional flute-players and mourners had been waiting, like vultures, outside the house, ever since they heard there was sickness there, jostling me even as I went out when she was still alive. Now as we approached, we could hear them already, having seized their opportunity and pushed in at the very moment of death. Jesus spoke to them sternly: "What's all this for?" he said. "Get out! The child is not dead, but only asleep." They laughed at that, loudly, unpleasantly, but it was in a great hush all the same that my wife and I led Jesus and his three closest disciples into the room where Miriam lay. "Shut the door," he said to me. He did not want to be watched by the household. He strode in and went down on his knee beside her, all the urgency of grief and love in that movement, and when I saw it, I could not ask any more why he had delayed. He could not have loved our daughter so if he had not loved the other who crossed his path. He knelt over her, looking at her, for a moment and then took her hand.

IV *Miriam*

The water was deep, fast-flowing, dark green. She had been standing on the shore so long, waiting for the shepherd to come. She knew he would come. He always came. But this time was the real time. She knew she had been dreaming, the other times. She wasn't dreaming now. She stood all wet and cold and waited for him, calling out for him with little bleats of fear.

And at last she saw him come, the Lord God, dressed as a shepherd, coming to find his little ones. Of course he had not forgotten, he would never leave them behind. He came across the water, swinging himself on his staff, calling to her, with his hand held out to her, and she leapt and danced for joy. "Come, my little one, come on, my pet," he said to her, and bent to lift her up. She was safe, she was on his shoulder, the Lord God was carrying her safe across the water. How wide it was. She was glad it was so wide. She wanted him to go on carrying her for ever. She sang to him and he sang back. The dark water rushed past below. She wasn't afraid any more.

But suddenly, in mid-stream, she felt him stop. "Oh, my little one," he said. "Listen."

She listened and heard the distant, terrified bleating of a sheep through the water.

"Oh, my little one," said the Lord again, "I must let you go."

"Yes," she said. She knew now she had always known it. All the times he had carried her across, all those dreams, they had only been preparations for the one real time when he must let her go.

"You won't be afraid, will you?"

She whispered, "No." She knew that the other sheep, crying through the torrent, was far more afraid than she.

"I'll come back," said the shepherd. "I won't forget you." And he began to lower her from his shoulder, to let her down into the water. She cried out and clung to his sleeve; then she remembered and managed to let go, and sank with a little gasp into the darkness. The noise went rushing over her head, through her head. It was cold. He was not there to cling to any more, she knew he was gone. Then she sank down further and there was nothing any more but the cold.

V *Esther*

I stood reeling in the empty street, overjoyed, appalled. He had turned, he had turned and looked at me with kindness and pity in his face, at the outcast who had presumed to touch him: "Daughter, it's all right. Your faith has saved you." God had lifted up the light of his countenance on me, and the little girl had died. Because I had touched him, stopped him, for my salvation, a little girl had died. I hardly knew how I stumbled home. The light followed me and shone on me all the way, the light of the Lord's living holiness, like a touch laid on me. And it was comfort: when I remembered suddenly, and cried out because of the child I had brought to her death, the answer seemed to come: "She was not dead, but sleeping."

I could not do anything till the time of purification was past. It was a deep, deep purifying. He who had turned seemed still to be standing before me, cleansing and healing my whole life with his presence. And the light of God shone steadily on me, shone right on me. All for me was life, sight, meeting. And for her was it only darkness, silence, aloneness? Was she bound in that empty sleep for my sake?

In the end I went to the house of Rabbi Jairus. I will ask, I thought. I will only ask of the servant at the door whether the child is alive or dead. So I fell on my knees in the gateway crying out to the first slave I saw, "Tell me, I implore you in the name of the Lord, tell me how goes it with your little mistress? Is she alive?"

And I heard a glad voice calling from a window above me, "You've come, you've come! I knew you would!" I looked up in time to see an excited shape turn in from the lattice, and heard her shouting through the house, "Mother, Mother, she's come at last, can she come up here?"

Before I knew where I was she was grasping my hands,

pulling me in and up to her chamber, whispering joyfully, "He saved you in time, didn't he? He got to you in time. I was asleep, you know, I was dreaming about you."

I looked round, amazed and bewildered, but the girl's mother caught my eye and shook her head. "Not asleep" she mouthed, "she was dead."

"Who—who awoke you, my little mistress?" I asked the child.

"I'll have to tell you my dream," she said. "I've been waiting such a long time to tell you. Come here and sit down."

And I looked at her and knew that whatever had happened, even her death if I had helped to cause it, had been for her good too, because there is no division in love, nor does it ever let anything go.

VI *Miriam*

The darkness was no longer the cold gloom of the ford, it had become so deep and great, it must be the very waters under the earth that she was lying in. She had fallen so far, had she sunk right through the centre of the earth? How would the shepherd ever find her now? But at once she knew that the night which was wrapping her round was the Lord God's cloak, his shepherd's cloak, and that he had caught her, he had only let go of her so as to catch her and hold her with all his might and power. He was holding her so closely she could not have fallen out of his arms if she had tried.

"Come on, little one," he said, "we must go up again now."

"Did you find the other sheep?"

"Yes, of course."

"Shall we be together?"

"If you like."

He was carrying her, though she could not see the flood below her this time. At last he was kneeling on the bank looking down on her in the water, her hands in his. "One more step! Be brave. Stand up, my little lamb."

She felt herself being pulled slowly to her knees in the familiar room. The rush mat felt ridgy under her. Her parents were standing by her. The air was sticky and close. But he was still there, more real for the moment than her parents or her room, her own shepherd on his knee beside her in the smoking light of an oil lamp.

I've been asleep in the middle of the day, she thought. I must have been ill. For an instant panic seized her, the panic of having slept at the wrong time, of not knowing what was going on, not knowing where she had been, and she felt her throat seize up with a sob. But then the hand grasping hers gave a squeeze; and she looked up at him and remembered, and all fear fled.

"It was a long way, wasn't it?" he said.

"It was true," she mumbled. "It wasn't a dream this time. It was true."

She seemed still to be able to hear words sounding on in the shuttered room, as though it would never let them die away. "Talitha cumi. Stand up, little lamb." And she was standing. She began to move, shakily at first, and then running, to fling herself into her father's arms and then her mother's. But then she was by her shepherd again, to touch him, hardly believing, and yet knowing so well.

"Lambs need feeding," he said, "especially lambs that have swum so bravely through such rivers as that." He was smiling down at her so that she hardly heard her father exclaim, "Of course! I should have thought of that!" and open the door and clap; and even when the shepherd looked quickly up and said, "Tell no-one about this. Let them think the child was only sleeping," she did not think what the words might mean. She could only gaze at him and know that she had dreamt true, that she had fallen so far into his arms that she could not ever again fall out, that he was carrying her safe through fathomless waters, his little lamb.

16

THE SINGLE ONE

THE MAN I had been struggling with all yesterday was waiting for me when I went down to the road to get my alms of bread and herbs. I knew he would be. He was standing between me and the road laughing. Since the moon changed he had been laughing like that, standing there by the road and laughing at all who came till they fled with their eyes half out of their head. Yesterday I fought him and got away at last, leaving him bleeding and stunned. I shouldn't have come back. . . . But I wanted my food. He was weaker, though, today. I was afraid of him at first when I saw his bare, emaciated body and heard the terrible laughter again, but when I threw myself on him I felt how much weaker he was. I knocked him down, grabbed the bread and ran back up the hot, stony hill. I could hardly believe I had really left him behind. But wait a minute! Whose shadow was that flying over the yellow earth beyond mine? Then I could scarcely see the sunny earth-colour for shadows, all fleeing in despair, triumph or panic from the road, a shadow of each single time I had run like this. And now I was running alongside a man slavering as he ran, clutching a loaf he could not eat for fear until he was alone, and he would never be alone. I hated him. He was more disgusting than any beast. His bare ribs stuck through his burnt skin and his face was covered in flies and froth. I ran faster, but he was already running at my fastest speed. With a yell of loathing I threw myself at his feet and pulled him down. He was stronger than the laughing man because today I was not laughing but running. We wrestled desperately. Both our bread was lost. In the end I struggled free, and left him there, his legs still kicking as he ran for ever and never found anywhere to sit down and eat alone. He had cheated me of my meal. And already I was locked with a vengeful, starving man, who hated me because I had cheated him of his meal. I was all but powerless against that passion of desperate hunger, of howling remorse for bread lost. At last I panted, "I'll go back and find it! I'll find your accursed bread!" He let me go then and I ran back towards the place. . . . But a weak, crying skeleton of a man came and caught me gently by my knees, oh, so pitifully, and tipped me down the precipice.

I fell a thousand times and then I saw the chained man. He was the worst of all because he had been there so long and I had met him so often. I forgot my bruises and my fall and ran from that fearful place, back towards the tombs, my only home. A howling man leapt out at me from the first tomb. I knew him well, in fact, I might as well stay and howl here now. So I did. But then I saw the crawling man coming at me from the depths of the tomb. He had lain there for many days once in a drought. The crawling man's face was too terrible to meet. I was afraid of his thirst. I ran from the tomb and from every tomb mouth a man leapt and ran with me.

Screaming, I ran to the hilltop, and such was my fear, I forgot where I was and looked towards the sun over the lake. It was madness! If there was one thing I knew it was that the eye of God looks across the lake when the sun's up, the Living One, the Single One, He beside whom there is none other, sending a straight, single path of light over the water. I had rather meet any treacherous, ferocious naked man than the eye of the Holy One. But today I looked and met it. Had it called me there? It was coming towards me over the lake along the straight path of its own light: not It—He: the High and Lofty One, the Blessed One, whose name shall be One in all the earth on the last day (but I no longer prayed for the revelation of that Name. It would be the end of me and who can pray for his own destruction?) The Everlasting One who was the first and shall be the last, the Unchanging One. And now I was running, running down the stony hillside as though all the men of the tombs were after me (but they were not; I was running alone)— running into the eye of his power as though I longed for that final dissolution, and all the screams I had ever screamed were flying through the air like thunderbolts with me.

There were a number of men on the shore, beaching a boat, but I saw One, standing up against the sun; I saw him burning in the fire of the divine simplicity and then I was on my face before him feeling the burning already, the last disintegration beginning. And with the audacity of terror and despair, I did the bravest and most foolish thing I could have done. In a last attempt to gain the mastery, I took hold of him by his own holiness and hailed him. I called him by his name. Had I overheard travellers on the road talking about him, had I learnt it straight from the abyss of hell? How should I know? I tell you I saw the Undivided One blazing in the fire of unity, and a thousand bare-skinned men fell in their ripped chains shrieking, "What have you to do with us, Jesus of Nazareth? Have you come to destroy us before the time? I know you—the Holy One of God! In God's name do not torment us."

I had called on God's name and his own name. But he looked at me and threw my own weapon back at me; he asked, "What is *your* name?"

I thought, "That I'll never tell him"; and then I knew I could not—I had lost my name long ago. Then I let out a great howl and cried, "There is a multitude of me! There is a legion! Legion, that's my name! Caesar would be proud to command me!"

He had forced the confession from me, forced me to know what I was. And I fell prostrate not in defiance now, but utterly conquered before the True and Faithful One, the Mighty and Holy One, and knew that all I had ever been, every self and shadow of me, was delivered into his hands. I waited for the annihilation to strike and shatter me at last into a million ghosts, but I whimpered as I lay there: "Mercy, mercy. Not the abyss. Not nothingness to wander in for ever. Not the abyss. It's not time for that yet. The world still endures."

And he did not smite, but paused, and said, "What then?"

I looked up eagerly, hungrily, and said, "Give us a place. Give us earth. Give us a body. Let us die. Don't send us wandering!" I remembered something I seemed to have seen, was it today or long ago?—pigs feeding on the mountainside. I looked round and it was true: there they were, a great herd of several thousand. "Give us those pigs!" I screamed. "Give us them for our place! Let us go into those!"

"Go," he said. And then I could bear his presence no more, the searing burning of his truth. For all those minutes I had endured it, but now flesh and spirit collapsed, shattered, fled screaming in innumerable fragments, crying for a place, for earth, for hiding, for death. The quiet lake received me with a mother's welcome. I sank gratefully into it, come home at last, unchased, unvexed any more, swallowed up in that blessed deep. I drowned a thousand times, sank down in thankfulness from a thousand tormented selves, and his pure light could not hurt me any more.

Then a strong hand was grasping mine, pulling me out, and arms caught me as I fell forwards, weak as a new baby, but they didn't burn me now. They were holding me like a child, dressing me, wrapping me in his own cloak. The sun was sweet as water on me, the air was kind. I sat on the ground at his feet, and he sat on a stone beside me, and all my old bruises and chafes were healing even as I sat there. And I could remember nothing of all that time in the tombs. It was drowned, every moment and memory of it. I was remembering other things now; the village well and my mother coming swaying and singing with her waterpot, the shady corner by the house where the tamarisk grew, mending nets with my toes in the early morning after long fishing, heaving the boat in with my father and brothers. And singing the praise of the Blessed One, whose name is Everlasting. . . .

I don't know how long we sat there. There was no time, no hurry. There was nothing and no-one to flee from, no escapes to plan, no sudden springs to watch for, and he beside me was no sickening burden of my own company but all my salvation. Yet eventually people did come, running over the hill, waving and shouting. The one beside me stood up, seeming to sigh deeply, and laid his hand on my shoulder as they came crowding, pointing, exclaiming. I could not understand their fear and excitement, the repeated words, "You should have seen those pigs go mad! They just rushed over the cliff"—and again and again, "devils . . . prince of devils. . . ." I did not know what could be the matter. There was only the great one peace. But it was fear in them all the same. In the end one man in robes and turban stepped forward and said distinctly, "Go away, please go away from us. We don't know who you are, but please leave us. We are simple folk and we can't take this."

So he beside me sighed again and turned towards the boat with his companions (whom I had scarcely noticed hitherto). I cried out, "Wait! Let me come too! Let me stay with you!"

"No," he said, "not yet. It's home that you need. Go and find your own people. Tell them of the mercy of the Lord your God—your God and my God. There'll be plenty of leaving and following later, but not now, you must find them first."

So he sailed away again across the lake, in the haze of distance, the Only-beloved, the Chosen One, rejected by all the good people of that countryside, welcomed only by the madman who feared and hated him. I had a sort of wisdom from my own loathsomeness; I knew that the divine simplicity burnt, that his truth shatters, but these people had to learn it. They were the ones, not I after all, who could not bear the shattering. And I was the only one to find that in the end he had not destroyed me, but had made me whole.

17
THINGS

I FIRST HEARD him preaching on a public waterside. I was on my way, I remember, to see over a new farm my father wanted to buy, but in the end it was past noon before I got out of town. I simply could not stop listening. I had never seen a man so full of strength and faith. He made me want to do everything for God's sake alone and be his true child. At midday, however, I tore myself away to recite the noon prayers. He seemed to have forgotten them, along with his own meal. The urgency of the coming kingdom was on him.

It came off on to me, you might say. Now at last I found myself able to perform tasks that had previously been beyond me. For instance, I came in that night from my journey and straight away knelt down to wash my father's feet as he sat at table. I had always known of course that this is one of the highest ways of honouring one's father, but had never been able to force myself to it. But I did it now just by thinking of the joy on that man's face.

And how eagerly I recited all the prayers! How my heart burnt! I increased all my tithes by a third and gave to every beggar I saw. When I prayed to God the Father of Israel the tears ran down my cheeks. I resolved to take Nazirite vows and began to purify myself. Never again would I avoid making pilgrimage to Jerusalem thrice yearly, and I would take at my own charges any poor pilgrim who had never been able to afford to go.

The other pupils of Rabbi Eliezer laughed at my new zeal, kindly, warning me not to vow too many things before it wore off. Of course, I was indignant, and yet I had to own that I began to flag. How I reproached myself! The trouble was, in fact, not so much loss of zeal, as that I thought of too many things I could do to the glory of God, and once having thought of them, how could I now leave them undone? The crisis came when one day as we were sitting down to meat in my father's house, I thought of holy Tobit. At once I remembered how my Rabbi Eliezer had taught that the perfect Jew would not eat before he had seen that every dead body in his town was buried, and that no circumcised flesh was lying as carrion because his family could not afford to bury him, or because he had none.

I rose from the table in distress. It was too much to ask! The lakeside was thickly populated and the poor died like flies in the heat. Must I work as sexton every day for several hours before I might even eat? Yet the voice of Jesus seemed to ring in my ears—with a new tone of accusation—"You must therefore be perfect as your Father in heaven is perfect."

And in the end I went to him. Did he recognize the handsome young ruler of a few weeks before in the weary, anxious, sweating boy who came dinnerless to him as the sun began to dip? I had resolved to ask him. Whatever he told me to do, I knew I could do, if it meant feeding all the poor with my own hand. I fell on my face at his feet, almost too overcome to speak; and already I was comforted just to be kneeling at his hem.

"Good Master," I cried at last, "tell me, for God's sake! What are the things I must do to inherit eternal life?"

But he answered sternly, "Stand up! Stand up, and don't flatter me. There is none good but God."

It pulled me together. I realized with a start that I had not been thinking about God—had forgotten him, in fact, since early that day. But Jesus went on, "And why do you ask me about things to do? I think you know quite enough about good deeds, don't you? You have the commandments. Consult them."

He still sounded almost angry. I was deeply puzzled at his attitude today. Gone was the transfiguring light in his face. I could tell I was annoying him, yet I was too desperate to give up. I plunged on, making bad worse.

"But *which* commandments, Master, which are the ones God most desires us to fulfil?"

His relentless voice came back at me. "Honour your father

and mother. Do not steal. Do not commit adultery. . . ." I felt myself blushing with humiliation. The commandments which the veriest infant in Israel learns.

And suddenly my misery burst its banks and I cried out, forgetting ceremony: "I've kept them! God help me, I've kept them all! And I know it's not enough!"

He looked at me differently then. Or perhaps it was not differently. Perhaps it had not been anger so much in his tone as—what? pain? disappointment?

"Yes," he said almost to himself, "you do want to enter the Kingdom, don't you? You do want to be free of all that, don't you?" Then his abruptness returned and he suddenly threw out words: "Then make the break! If you want to go the whole way, go it! Sell everything! Forget all the things you ought to do! Give it all up, give up all you have, and come after me!" He leant forward as I stood reeling and dumb; it was he now who was pleading with me. "There is no other treasure. That *is* the only treasure. Come on, let yourself go! Don't you want to?" And he knew how much I wanted to; yet I still could not answer. "Let there be a bit of joy in it! What is the good of hoarding things—good deeds, riches, your own self? What are you keeping them for? If a man finds buried treasure in a field won't he sell all he has for sheer joy to buy it? Could he be happy doing anything else?"

Looking at him then, I knew that this was his own joy he was speaking of, that he was himself one who had paid the price of everything. And behind that, behind him, did I seem to guess a greater giving still, a principle of all for all that was the life of God himself?

I had stepped forward, my eyes were on his, my hands seemed to be raising themselves, palm upward. Sell all I had? And what was that? The house, the orange-groves, my father's signet ring which would one day be mine floated into my mind. Well, obviously it wasn't all mine to *sell* exactly, though I could *abandon* it, and there were some things I could sell. . . . At that point I suddenly remembered that I had not left the steward with enough coins to give the daily afternoon alms. And I remembered that I must wash and change today before the evening Shema', for it is not fitting for a son to come with dirt and dust all over him, as I was; I must put fresh oil on my head, out of respect for my father. And with these two sudden recollections sanity reasserted itself. Abandon the patrimony? What had I been thinking? In fact, I had to complete the purchase of the new farm that very evening. My sense of responsibility had returned. I must go at once. I should be late. I bowed deeply to Jesus and turned to hurry off, hardly remembering the words that had passed between us, wondering a little what crushing load was weighing down my spirits, until I had time to think as I hastened along the quiet road under the olives, and knew then how bitter and bitter the disappointment was that Jesus' discipleship was not for me.

18
TRUSTING

No-one can say that I consented lightly to becoming an old, diseased woman.

It overcame me slowly, that shivering disintegration of my body, the rebellion of my limbs. I fought it at every step, from the first trembling of my hands, when I refused to give up the measuring of the household grain and oil, to the last stand when I still thought I could hold off bed-riddenness. Mastering my weakness, I continued to run the household as usual, overseeing my daughters-in-law at their spinning and the men at their dyeing, teasing out the fleeces for spinning as only I knew how, until the very end. I could not bear that they should see my straight back bent, my knees giving way. For months, I went on measuring the grain and oil, doing it alone, fierce, I know, in my secrecy, so that no-one should see the slow agony of it and how much I spilt. I fought as hard as mortal can fight against the gradual advance of death. When I was defeated at last I lay on my pallet, in mid-morning with all the tasks to be done, the beasts to be watered and the next day's merchandise to be prepared. I lay there while the children did it, with tears running down the side of my face and into my pillow (but I did not sob), and prayed for death to come and complete his work. But he did not come. I was left there to lie, and lie, and lie.

Sometimes I woke feeling so well I tried to rise, and then the weakness would throw me down and death would stand behind me and laugh.

Then there came the day when my son Jonathan took a mule-load of fine dyed stuffs into Gadara to sell, and came back full of an amazing story of how a wandering healing preacher had total hold on the neighbourhood. Jonathan had seen with his own eyes the main market-place all laid out with sick folk on their mattresses, to the great hindrance of business, so that they might catch hold of the fringe of his garments as he passed. "I've never seen such a sight!" said Jonathan. They had been lying there since early morning, all because he had been glimpsed at dawn coming down a mountainside nearby.

"It's a pity you didn't stay and watch whether he could really heal them," I said tartly. I spoke angrily, because the sweat of apprehension had begun to prick all over me. "You could have asked him to come here."

"Would you really have wanted that, Mother?" asked Jonathan anxiously and in surprise. "A wandering preacher with no credentials? We don't know anything about him. He could be anyone. Would you really have wanted me to bring him?"

"No, of course not," I snapped. "He's doubtless a charlatan. Indeed I don't know why you had to fill my ears with such a story."

I was ashamed to think that my strength and health might lie in the hands of such a man, a roving marvel-monger. It would be impious to call him in, I thought. In any case, I could not bear that a stranger, a strange vagabond, should see me in my weakness and set eyes on my wasted limbs. I wanted to die and let the world remember the woman I was, truly am. For I know well that I am of one blood and one spirit with Deborah, Jael, Judith. If I must suffer and die I will do it as they would have. No-one shall witness my defeat except my own children.

And yet I knew in my heart from that day on that I must encounter the wandering Galilean healer who had such power over the crowds; I knew surely that he would come to our village; I felt him coming, inescapably, drawing nearer and nearer. Reports of his activity reached us. I did not follow them. I knew he would come here and I dreaded it. "If he can heal, a man young enough to be my son, come from nowhere, just a labourer from across the lake, why cannot I?" I thought, and strove every day to raise myself up from sickness; but my body did not know me any more, nor could I stir hand or foot when I tried. But it used suddenly to dance, wildly and uncontrollably, kicking and springing against my will as I lay there on my back; and I who had never feared pain or sorrow became afraid now of my body. For its dancing was the dancing of death and the devil, triumphant in me.

The healer came. News reached us at last that he was in the next village, and all the sick had been laid out there in the street and healed as he passed by laying his hands on each. I went cold with revulsion and dread, but I knew what I must do. I said to Jonathan and Ephraim my sons, "Tomorrow you must bind me on the mule's back and carry me into the village, and lay me there in the market-place with the other sick. The man of God is coming. Maybe he will lay his hands on me."

"Mother, he shall come here and heal you in your bed, whether he wants to or not!" cried Ephraim. "You shall not make that journey and lie in the market-place!"

"Perhaps he is only a charlatan after all," added Jonathan.

"You will do as I say," I replied. "He is a man of God."

And they did it. They bound me on muleback and so transported me into the village. And as I had expected, the jolting set my body dancing. Almost my will to do this thing failed, when I felt that mad kicking and jerking begin again, but my own spirit obeyed even when the spirit that had taken my body would not, and my sons laid me, dancing crazily and fearfully under my blanket, among the other sick in the little market square.

The whole population seemed to be there, ill or well. The children ran up and down staring at the sufferers, but only the very boldest stood and gazed at me. Their elders stared at me from a distance, unable to take their eyes from me. "She has a devil in her; look at it!" they murmured. I lay with my teeth clenched while the sun crawled up the sky. I could not pray.

And then the young man, the healer, was among us, and I was forgotten. Another burning focus had replaced me in the thoughts of everyone there. He strode from bed to bed crying out, "Arise, old father!" or "Stand up, little one! Shall any remain in bonds when the Kingdom of Heaven is at hand?"

"And Jonathan believes him to be a charlatan!" I thought contemptuously. "Can he not recognize a man possessed by God?" I knew what he was when I first heard of him.

The living power of him, of God in him, moved towards me

through the square. I closed my eyes. My legs danced. I was drenched with sweat, not only from the sun. Then I realized he was standing over me, while I jerked at his feet with spasms of grim mirth. "Quiet now," he said. "Be still."

And Death ceased his cavorting and stood howling over me. But he was not gone, the devil, he had not given up my body. I could feel the quivering in my limbs still, ready to break out again. Then the words came that I had waited for and dreaded.

"Stand up, mother. Give me your hand."

And now I could not. Whether my body would have obeyed or not, my spirit would obey no longer. I could not bear what I feared, that the weakness would take me again and throw me down in front of them all, even after his word. I could not even bear to stretch out my hand to him, seeing it in my mind shaking like a branch. I begged him with my eyes to move on and leave me, but with a half smile he shook his head and bent down to take my hand.

"No, mother, but you must stand up."

I felt no strength or life flowing into me, as I used to imagine I would. I felt nothing but the old, familiar trembling. There was only the weakness, the sweat stinging my eyes, the gaze of the man bent over me fixed on me. There was no strength with which to stand up: nothing but the weakness, the deadly weariness, the heat.

"Then let me fall," I thought, "I don't care; let them all see me fall, for if you cannot heal me there is nothing left. I will suffer whatever I must suffer for your sake." And I began to haul on his arm to pull myself upright, and felt, now, suddenly, his own strong pulling. I was sitting up in his hold; my body was gathering itself together, I was half up; I was standing. "But I shall fall when he lets go of me!" I thought, feeling my knees caving.

"Shall I let go?" he asked softly.

"Yes," I said. "I'm up now."

His eyes shone and he moved his hand, but only to my head, blessing me. I did not fall. I stood there on my own poor legs under his hand.

"Go in peace," he said. "The healing you have found is your own trusting."

I could have fallen down and kicked in front of them all and it would not have mattered, now. A deeper healing had begun that could never be reversed. But I knew I should not fall. I called my sons, and we went away. But I left my trust, and my strength, and my weakness, for him to keep in his strong hands.

19

WIND

I THOUGHT IT was a beggar plucking at my sleeve, but it was the boy slave of some wealthy household, and he was beckoning me into one of the richest houses in Jerusalem; I had marvelled every time I passed it, though I was so preoccupied at the moment that I'd forgotten where I was. Mystified, I followed him in, and into a beautiful watered courtyard, where a white-bearded Jew of rank stood nervously fingering a goblet, with a youth lounging by a pillar behind him. I greeted them in the Lord, and the old man replied as though hardly hearing me; then he said, "Aren't you Matthias, the apostate initiate from the holy community at Qumran? My son Joses pointed you out to me in the street a few days ago." I looked at the curly-headed youth and recognized with some difficulty one of our former novices at Qumran.

"I am Matthias," I said, "though as for being an apostate——"

The man silenced me: "Forgive me—I said what I did not mean. I am distracted in my mind." There was a pause while he twisted his cup; then he looked up and said, "Do you understand your master's teaching?"

"My masters at Qumran?" I asked in surprise.

"No." He looked away again, and I understood that he wanted to question me about Jesus of Nazareth, but did not dare to name him. I said, "The Rabbi I follow now teaches us of the kingdom of God in many parables. You would understand them better than I. Why don't you speak with him? He is up for the feast now."

"I have spoken to him already," he said. Then after another pause he shook himself: "Forgive me. Take a seat, I beg you. Please do not be modest. I know of the learning of your community. I am asking your help."

So we sat down on carved seats. I was given a cup of spiced

sherbet, and then my host asked abruptly, "Do you know what it is to be born again—of water and the spirit?"

I smiled involuntarily into my cup. "I think I know nothing else," I said. He seemed taken aback, and asked carefully, "Does it mean the purifying of the spirit, as the body is purified by water?"

"Did you never hear the preaching of John the Baptist?" I asked. "He taught that he washed both body and soul for repentance, but he warned that another should come after him with a far greater and more terrible baptism—the baptism of fire and the holy Spirit." I felt the fire kindling in me as I remembered; and I cried out, "So John prophesied, and this is he! His baptism is not for cleansing, but for making a man altogether new. I tell you, the Spirit of God is stirring over our land as it moved over the waters at the beginning, and bringing forth new life. God's power is at work among us!"

"Your Teacher said to me," said my host, with difficulty concealing alarm, "that the wind blew where it would, no-one knowing whence or whither, and so it was with all who are born of the Spirit. But how can this be? We know too well who we are and where we have come from. Can you explain to me the parable of the wind?"

"What! Do you, a rabbi of Israel, ask me about the blowing of the breath of God?" He flinched as though I had struck him, but I could not stop to wonder why. I put down my goblet and stood up, to feel that free blowing (though no breeze stirred in that courtyard), with all the power of the desert wind that had swept through Qumran and carried me away from it, the wind in which I had lived and breathed when I was a disciple of John the Baptist.

"Of that breath the world was created, and Israel was born. You know this, yet you do not know where the world came from, nor how it shall end, nor yet do you know of Israel. God called us, and we came; he breathed on us, and we were. You know that wind. It is the life that gave you life. Do you refuse to breathe it? Can you live without the wind?"

"I am afraid," said the old man. "Your Teacher—I do not

know where he comes from, or what he will become. I am afraid. I am afraid of lawlessness."

"But the Spirit is the spirit of holiness!" I exclaimed. I was seeing John the Baptist as I spoke, so filled with the untamed holiness of the Spirit, with God who is never possessed, even by Israel, but gives himself always. I could see John so clearly, with the hot wilderness behind him and the sun in his eyes, that it took me a moment of blinking to see the courtyard of palms and greenery again. My host was staring at me, his hands clutching the carved arms of his seat. "What is it in you and in him?" he cried. "It's the same. I am afraid. What is it? Can you not even say that the spirit blows from God? Is your Teacher—is he truly sent from God? Have mercy on an old man and tell me plainly!"

But my mind was with John, and when I tried to think of Jesus it was through John's eyes I saw him, as he had once described him to me. "The spirit came mightily on him, and I fell as one dead, for heaven was opened. And then the spirit drove him away into the wilderness." I knew that if Jesus had talked of the spirit blowing as freely as the wind to my host, he was speaking of that which he knew well. I looked at the troubled old face, so earnestly searching for words of law to rest in, and saw in my mind the arid desert of Judaea, the all-powerful wind, and Jesus driven, driven on by the strength of the living holiness of God to face danger and temptation among those burning rocks. I said at last, "You are afraid, because God is with him. Well may the earth tremble, for great is the Holy One of Israel in our midst! I tell you this is the wind and fire of God!"

The poor old man covered his face with his hands, but when he looked up, it was with a smile. "You are all wild young prophets of the desert," he said. "But there was another thing your Teacher spoke to me of. He said that Moses had lifted up the brazen serpent in the wilderness for the salvation of Israel, and so should he be—set up not for judgment or condemnation, but for salvation. There was mercy in the desert. What have you and your other master John to say of mercy to an old rabbi who can't get his breath in the wind?"

It was my turn now to hide my face in my sleeve, leaning against a palm trunk for giddiness in the wind that had so suddenly turned, had changed in my face, and was blowing against me. In the end I found words.

"If you have learnt that from my Rabbi—that he is sent for the salvation of the world—then you have no need to hear from me of his teaching: you know it."

I looked up then and saw the old eyes widen and come alight with joy, and the palm leaves stirred and rustled as a breeze rose at last.

20

THE MAT

WELL, HE USED to come along to the pool and stand there. Just walk around, looking, and sometimes he came and stood over me and I thought he was going to say somt, but he never did. And once, the angel came down into t'pool right when he was there, and I thought, surely he'll give me a leg up and hoik me in. But he never.

And it's funny, I've always had this feeling as like someone was standing behind me, see, all these years, I keeps getting that feeling, but it wasn't him, was it, not thirty-eight years ago! I don't think! Eh, he wasn't born when I first came here.

And you know, it warn't so bad after awhile. I mean, these bubblings of the water give you something to live for. To look forward to, y'know. I mean you never know, it might be your lucky number next time. Keep hoping, that's what I say! So it warn't too bad, lying there, in the end. There was always going to be another bubbling, warn't there. In fact I thought I saw one just beginning that last time he came along and there he was slap in the way, so I said "Mind out, mister! I want to get in the water!" But he didn't move, did he, so I missed it. And who knows, that one may have had my lucky number.

Then he says "Do you really want to get well?"

I ask you! So I says, "Well, if someone—on their, feet, like you, f'r instance, gave me a push-in instead of getting in my WAY . . . I can't wriggle, you see, like some can, so they always beats me to it. . . ."

"But do you *want* to be well?"

I saw he was after somt, so I went crafty-silent, like.

"Get up, mac!" he suddenly shouts, "get up then!"

And I was so astonished that I sort of shifted, and d'you know, I was half up before I knew.

"C'mon!" he yells, "up!" He was laughing. So was I, mate.

I was on me feet, wobbled a bit, so I throws me arms round him! "There you are," he says, "now pick up your mat. We're breaking camp. You're never going to lie down here again."

Well, I stopped laughing. I don't know. There was somt in that I didn't like. I mean, I was tired already. Still, I bends down and does up the poor old mat in a roll. I felt quite fond of it after all these years.

"C'mon!" he says, so I set off beside him. "One thing I'd like to ask," I says, "why didn't you do this first time, if you'd a mind?"

"I would have if you'd let me," he says. And I sort of remembered that ghosty feeling of someone hovering around, and I had a mind to ask him about that, also who he was when he was at home, but I was that out of breath, I couldn't speak. I just wanted to lie down right there in the street. He wouldn't let me though. So I was crafty again. I just fell behind a moment, then got away in the crowd to some gent's fancy porch. I was only going to sit down a moment, mate! But just as I was heaving-to me mat roll what do I hear but the voice of the law? "What do you think you're doing?" says one of the nobs, appearing in the doorway. "Carrying your mattress on the Sabbath?"

Well, blow me, I didn't know t'was Sabbath. I had plaguey all idea what day it was. So I felt a bit narked, but I just said politely, "I'm just following instructions, sir!"

"Whose?"

"*Doctor*'s instructions!" And I told him why I was lugging that flipping mat around when all I wanted was to lie on it. And that I didn't know if it was Saturday or doomsday.

"Who was this who told you to carry it?"

But I didn't know. "He wanted to get me out of there, see. Perhaps he didn't know it was Sabbath either."

Ooh, you should have heard that toff hiss when I said that! Had I put my foot in it! But he just says, "Tell me if you see him again," and tells me where to find him on duty in the Temple.

Well, I had to go to the Temple anyway, didn't I? Offer cure sacrifices and all. I won't give you the story of how me sister took it when I showed up. True, I warn't in the best of moods by then. I felt, y'know, as though this healer man had told me to walk till I dropped dead, and as if I couldn't stop till he gave me leave, just had to keep on walking after him. Well, I could have wished meself back at Bethesda, that's all. Thirty-eight years, I hadn't that much longer to run, had I? It would have passed there all right. Now all this jumping up was fine enough, but how many years of foot-slogging am I going to have to notch up? And me past retiring age!

So I was feeling a bit ironical when I took me sacrifices in. And blow me, there he was. Up he comes so I couldn't dodge him.

"Come off it now, mac," he says, no preamble. "Or you'll get yourself into a state where even I can't help you."

"What do you mean?" I asks.

"You know what I mean. You're crippling yourself twice over. Can't you just be happy about something for a change?"

Well, to be quite frank, no, I couldn't. I mean, all this jumping up cured is okay, but the thought of ten-fifteen years of riding Shanks' pony ain't so much fun. That's something you don't think of, somehow, lying there. But then if you got cured the regular way I suppose you could take things the way they suited you—in my case, easy. And this guy still wouldn't let me. We just stood there looking at each other and was it a battle of wills!

"Oh, snap out of it, mac!" he exclaimed at last.

And it was a dead near thing. I could have burst out laughing for joy or bashed his face in, and it was a toss-up almost. You know?

But I was aching all over and it was hot and, well, all this novelty, it was too much for me. At least, I didn't actually bash his face in. I just said "Beat it, mister." And he did. But soon as his back was turned I scooted off to the Court of the Gentiles, where my Pharisee toff was holding audience, like he'd said.

"Bloke you want's just going out the gate there," I yelled. Well, I was fed up. Was it that bad a thing to do? I'm sorry if I got him into trouble. But he didn't ought to have got in the way of my lucky number.

There's too many strings attached, the way he does it.

21

GLORY

FROM THE FIRST, we of Capernaum honoured the Rabbi of Nazareth. Indeed, it was I, Rabbi Simon, who insisted he should be so called, for of course he was not trained at all, but I could not help regarding him as my colleague, as I had myself for most of my life been specializing in the use of parables. Naturally I was exceedingly interested in such natural talent and his uncanny skill in hitting the nail, and used regularly to come to listen to him; and he, very properly, returned the compliment, and was often there standing thoughtfully when I spoke. Between us, there grew up a great liking. If he was to some extent my protégé, I felt always refreshed and even inspired by his company. After the good turn he did my Terentius the centurion, whom I had myself led to become a fearer of the true God, we even addressed each other as friends, without the title of "Rabbi". I repeat, at that time there was no animosity at all. This is not to deny he was rash and outspoken. But I, having been trained in Jerusalem, had perhaps the finesse—at any rate the sophistication—not to be too easily shocked. At Nazareth, a far more conservative place, he was thrown out of the synagogue, but there was nothing like that here.

What bound us together, at a deeper level than techniques in parables, was of course hunger for the Kingdom and the revelation in the sight of the Gentiles of the Glory of God. He was as filled as I was with the holy thirst. I have often thought that all my blessings and joys, which are many, are as dung and ashes to me while Israel is thus humiliated; I have begged the Lord to take them all from me and grant me but one, to see the restoration of Israel, and his Glory vindicated; but enough of that! We prayed together sometimes on my rooftop, and I shall never forget how passionately he would stand and pray:

"Heavenly Father, may the holiness of your Name be known

and glorified! May your kingdom come and your will be done on earth, as it is and for ever shall be in heaven!"

Those were days when a deep and wonderful joy seemed to be taking possession of me and of all of us, like a growing and abiding warmth within. If my first request—to see God's salvation —is not to be answered in this age, then I would have another: let me have those days back, let me live them again, and all that followed be undone. And both my prayers are more than a man may ask, and I know it.

He is known, not as Jesus the Rabbi now, but as Jesus the Sorcerer. That is a crude and fearful way of trying to name the essential alienation from us we began to feel in him. It is easy to dub a man demon-possessed and I do not do so. But I know what makes them do so; I felt the change too. In Jerusalem, he was sometimes called a Samaritan, which expresses the same unease, the same doubt if his God was ours. I know he was not a Samaritan, but again I know the feeling that lies behind the charge. What happened? What divided us? What made him change? Was it when he first saw the might of Rome in Jerusalem, no longer with the dazzled eyes of a pilgrim but with the bitterly clear sight of a teacher and leader; when he first truly understood the captivity of the holy city, did his faith in God's deliverance begin to waver? Did he begin to think that the Lord's arm was shortened or his power lessened because he does not choose to exert it? But who shall keep faith if the leaders of the people doubt? And so he joined the ranks of the false shepherds denounced by the prophet Ezekiel: he who had told the parable of the true one.

The first I knew of his rejection of us, or rather his defiance of us, was in his increasing recklessness in consorting with the unclean and sinful. He seemed almost to want to pollute himself. He threw concern for purity to the winds. He would eat quite flagrantly with tax-collectors, those vermin of Israel, and heal the uncleanly sick by touch. Doubtless, there was compassion in this—which of us does not feel compassion for these people, and long to bring them back within the Law to serve their God in holiness? But there are things a Rabbi has no right to do.

He may not demean himself so, for by so doing, he is sullying the purity and holiness of God. He must not compromise himself with lawlessness, with the unblessed. Above all, and above all, he must not neglect the commandments himself, and this is what Jesus did: the Sabbath law in particular, and the rites of washing. A true Rabbi, a true shepherd, should observe all these with double stringency to atone for the breaches of the people, and as an example. But Jesus became quite deliberately lax. There may, I repeat, have been compassion in it, but there was also certainly insolence. It was, in particular, an insult flung in my teeth, his friend and mentor.

I restrained my anger and dread. For he drew the line nowhere, not at Samaritans, not even at Gentiles—for he said to Terentius, that the nations from every corner of the world should come in and feast with Abraham, Isaac and Jacob, and the sons of the kingdom be cast out. Terentius told me this and I pondered it in great anxiety, but I held my peace at that time. Yet his rebellion (as I must call it) was harming us, for the multitudes who fell under his spell no longer paid the same regard as before to us; our influence, in face of his, was waning—and so was observance of the commandments.

I saw too well what he was trying to do. He was trying to make an *easy* law, an *easy* worship, one that would appeal to the Gentiles, so as to vanquish them by concessions, as it were. But this is utter unfaith, unless he were a second lawgiver, divinely commissioned. If the ancient holiness of Israel does not stand, the Glory of God on the earth does not stand. But they shall stand. It is vain too for him to protest that he does not break the commandments, only rejects our tradition, for what is our tradition but the centuries of our glorifying God?

God's majesty cannot be served by bare humanity in its frailty. "Behold, his Holy Ones are not pure in his sight," said Job the wise. So I came to know that I must denounce the man of Nazareth as I had once acclaimed him. Many other doctors of the Law had reached the same conclusion, but it was harder for me, because I still loved him and was in many ways still his friend. So I held my peace, against my conscience. Indeed, I continued to invite him to my table, avoiding controversy. I was criticized, I may say, by other Pharisees for this, for it was known what sort of table-company he otherwise kept.

What's more, it presumed its right to every table he might sit at. For then there came the disgraceful incident with the prostitute who followed him into my house and her scented oils. I said nothing, I repeat, nothing, while I watched her caressing his feet with her hair, but my silence did not spare me his lashing rebuke, which has become such a famous tale up and down the countryside. Everywhere it's repeated how the Prophet of Nazareth told Rabbi Simon that the prostitute who kissed his feet loved him more than Rabbi Simon because she had been forgiven more than he had. But this was no mere casual judgment. Only I perhaps felt the bitter reproach underlying his words: "She has loved me as you never have, she has given me what you have refused me."

I did answer this time: not directly, but I sent him a parable by one of my pupils, not only about the woman, though she and the humiliation he had inflicted on me were included, but warning him about his whole activity. I took one of his own favourite themes, the king who gave a banquet, to drive home my point. In my version, the king's steward allowed so many of his poor relatives and so many beggars to come to the kitchen where he was in charge, that not only was the best of the banquet eaten beforehand, but the house itself was left trampled and despoiled and the king's name held in mockery far and wide. "When the king comes to see his banquet, will he praise his steward for his generosity? For he has dishonoured him." But Jesus sent back the message, "The king will praise the steward for his wisdom. For he has made for himself many friends. It is the king himself who will summon the poor, because they will come in gladly when the invited guests have disdained to come. Tell Simon to learn what this means: 'I desired mercy and not sacrifice'." So then I knew my fears confirmed. He wanted to throw open the doors of the Kingdom and he cared nothing any more for the sanctifying of God's Name.

So then I went to see him, in case by any means he would

listen to authority and, yes, to wisdom. But when I went into that smelly little fisherman's house and greeted him, "Blessed be thou in the Lord, and may the Kingdom come in thy time," instead of repeating it back to me, he said, "It is here, at the very door, but will you enter into it?"

"It is the kingdom of God's children," I answered stiffly.

"It is indeed the kingdom of children. But what child can carry the burden that you are carrying? Why will you not lay it down and turn and become a real child?"

"It is no burden to uphold God's Glory," I replied.

"You do not know what God's glory is. You are only speaking of your own. If you knew what his glory truly is you would believe in me. But you cannot, because you are only seeking your own."

"It is my honour to honour and glorify God," I said, "but you dishonour both him and yourself. Oh, Rabbi in Israel, why do you want to debase God? Why will you make him a footstool for the Gentiles? Why would you have his people and his kingdom disgraced and defiled?"

"Unless a seed falls into the earth it can bear no fruit. All who love their life shall lose it, and all who lose it for my sake and the kingdom's shall find it. I have told you this often, Simon; do you still not understand?"

"You would not maintain that God's seed must die in the earth, that the people in whom he has set his Name must lose their life?"

"If I lay down my life," he replied, "I am truly glorifying my Father, and he will glorify me who have not sought any glory but shame."

"Has Israel not suffered enough?" I cried. "Does God desire more desecration? Has the time not come once again for the Temple to be filled with his glory?"

"You say so," he said, "and yet I tell you that you yourselves will destroy his Temple."

I was too aghast to speak.

"And I tell you further that when you do, he will raise it again in three days, a new and glorious temple, not made with hands. Oh, there will be glory! The glory of the Father will rest then on the Son of Man and on all who have served him. For is it not written, 'My righteous servant shall justify many'? But many who are first shall be last, and the last first."

I said very gravely, "Beware what spirit is in you, Prophet of Nazareth." And I left him, greatly afraid, for him most certainly, and for the nation too, for I suddenly wondered what truth there was in his dark words.

It came to me later that when he spoke of the true glorifying as the laying down of his life, he was not as I had first thought speaking hypothetically. It had been no abstract or symbolic conversation for him. And I was the more afraid.

I thought that was the end of our relationship. But in fact he seemed to exert more power over me when he was absent than when he was present. (I had noticed this before, and with others, too.) It was a few days later, meditating under my walnut trees in the evening, that I realized that I did know what it was to glorify God in the loss of all, when I prayed that I might exchange all my blessings for the sole one of seeing his salvation. And as I sat still, struck by my thought, I felt myself, as it were, feeling with his feelings—sure, for that instant, that I did know what the glory of God was to him: life itself, his life and his death. But this glory was unseen. It was a pressure, a weight, a shout, a darkness, it was the fullness of the evening and it was utter nothingness. Almost I said, "Yes, this is his true glory, and the forgiveness of my manhood and my frailty." For this was hidden glory, that could fill a poor hovel as easily as the Temple—more easily, for that arrogant and brazen place could not bend itself to such humble glory. But then I remembered the rams' horns blowing at sunset on the Day of Atonement over Jerusalem, and the sunrise seeming to set the golden Temple on fire, and the chanting of the pilgrims making their slow procession up from Jericho at Passover, and the rhythmic Shema' coming from every mouth and every heart all over Israel, like a great cry of faith ringing out in trust and longing in our long night; and once again I knew that this must never, could never, perish; here is God's true glory, who has made Jerusalem his hearth, as Isaiah said.

And then, a day or so later, I would find myself thinking, "No. Let us go into the dark, into the pit, of his *unknown* glory, let us learn to know it as Jesus of Nazareth knows it." And that alternation filled my life like a battle, while Jesus was fighting his own battles up and down the country, and Sabbath after Sabbath went by and still Capernaum was the only synagogue where he had not been denounced. For I could not and Rabbi Jairus, of course, would not.

And to this day it goes on, the sudden uncertainty. Who was he? Holy or accursed? Shall we ever know? Usually it seems clear to me, as to most of us, that here a great soul had gone wrong and become a renegade. But then the sudden hunger bites again to know the Glory as he believed he did, with that immediacy, almost that familiarity. But again the doubt returns: was his God our God, and whom did he call Father?

I heard from him once more. I knew he was in Galilee, though he was keeping hidden. In the early spring he sent one of his disciples to tell me: "The Master says, My hour is at hand. I am going to Jerusalem to glorify my Father and receive glory from him." I understood that he meant his death and sent the reply, "Tell your Master that I honour him for it." For going in his bare humanity, in his frailty.

So he was crucified, the death of the accursed. Did he indeed glorify God in it? Perhaps. And perhaps he glorified him in the lanes and slums of our towns. May his blood avail for the salvation of Israel, which if he had lived, he would have destroyed.

22

BREAD AND STONES

YES, YOU SCORED your point very neatly, didn't you, Master? "Don't you untie your beasts on the Sabbath and lead them to water? Then why shouldn't I untie this woman from Satan's bondage?" Yes, very neat. Hinting that their concern was perhaps not altogether with proper keeping of the Sabbath. But, all the same, do you think they like being made fools of in public? You'll do it once too often, Master, you really will. There's no need to be a very bad man not to like being made a fool of. We all have our natural pride. Are you so eaten up with the glory of God that you can't understand that? That some people are not going to repent and keel under when you make them smart, but are going to turn on you? I'm not saying that you have to kiss the Pharisees' feet. But don't you know how you make us all smart sometimes? Well, I hope I can take it; but some aren't going to take it for ever. And I wouldn't altogether blame them.

Even for me it's hard. Hard knowing how much you know about me. True, it was the red-letter day of my life when you came into the tavern so unexpectedly—you must have seen me jump up from the table and slink into the shadows, horrified. For I knew who you were. And you looked piercingly after me and said, "Who's that? Tell him to sit down and finish his meal." The innkeeper it was who gave me away, roaring out, "That's old Judas Iscariot! The old rogue! He daren't sit down in your company, Master! Know how come he's being fed free here for as long as he likes?" (with an affectionate slap on my shoulder; how I shrank!) "Or in most places in town? He's got half Capernaum in his pocket, so he has, by cooking the books in our favour so long while he was steward to Jason of Nicomedia. Used to halve our debts, didn't you? Well, Jason booted him out at the end, but he never knew the half of it, eh, Judas? Jason thinks he's a man of influence in the town—oh, no! Not compared with our Judas! Eh? We know he's a man to keep in with, see? Never know but what he'll be Pontius Pilate's chamberlain next. But don't ask him to sit at table with you! Eh, Master?" And another ear-splitting roar of laughter. I scowled and tried to back towards the door. I tell you, that innkeeper had forfeited for ever the favour he prized so much. But you, Master! You weren't shocked, you neither stormed nor sniggered. You just smiled and said, "You've got a lot more sense than most of the so-called children of light! To prefer to have friends all over town to making a pile for yourself, that's real wisdom, that's what hardly anyone chooses. To halve debts! What rare understanding!" Then you added, "Follow your choice to the end. Come and learn the real wisdom of light, come and learn about the whole remission of debts." And suddenly I was on my knees, weeping into your cloak, crying, "Oh, Master, teach me!"

I never wanted anything as I wanted that. As I still want it. But oh, you're a hard teacher. You're a hard man, a hard teacher, and the hardest thing you've done is to trust me. Yes, putting me in charge of the common purse, that was the hardest thing, not for my light fingers, but because every jingle of it told me again that you loved me. Do you think it's easy, being loved? Is it easy to be known for what one is and to have to endure being redeemed from it? To sit at table with you in the tavern of my own degradation—to sit at table with you anywhere? I know the bitterness of your sorrow over the Pharisees' conceit and stupidity. You've said you can't save them until they have seen what they are, and that's why you speak to them as you do. Do you think it's easy for them either to have you loving them, you fierce burning prophet? You don't need to tell me you love your enemies. I know you do. That's why you have so many of them. And all of us—Peter, James, John and Judas; Mary, Martha and Salome—every single one of us is a little bit your enemy. You know that too. And you know we love you all the same, and there are many who would if they could. But you are too hard.

I've heard you speak so sadly of the Pharisees, and sadly to them as well—as though your sadness were not even harder to bear than your anger. That parable of yours of the two bad sons, for instance, the runaway and the churl, and how they grieved their father—who but you would have dared to end the story with gentleness from the father? "Son, you are ever with me, and all that I have is yours." You put your own heart into those words (and God's heart too, I have no doubt); all your grief over those proud men who should have been the first to receive the good news. Although I'm more like the runaway than the stay-at-home, you're silently saying the same to me all the time: "Judas, you are ever with me, and all that I have is yours." How could that elder son have borne it?

I haven't been able to bear it always. When I stole those silver pieces from the bag for my youngest sister's wedding, do you think I cared about her or her wedding, or that I was really trying to curry favour in the old way with my brother-in-law? You knew what I had done, and I wanted you to know. I wanted to hurt you by betraying your trust. There were the other times too. You're the only one who understands. Matthew said kindly to me when Bartholomew caught me out the other day that he knows the itch, he wouldn't be surprised if he did the same himself one day. I nearly killed him for his stupidity and because he might persuade you, too, that it was only itch. But we understand each other too well, you and I. Oh-oh yes, I understand you, Jesus son of Joseph; not that you have the darkness in you that you can see in me, but you could have, oh yes, you could have, or could *have had*, perhaps. And I think I'm the only one of all the Twelve who knows that.

If you were not what you are, holiness that has never walked on this earth since the Lord God walked in Eden, you would be the greatest and most monstrous evil. For even you have known temptation. How I had to smile at the innocence of the others, when long after you had told us how to fight the devil, some of them beckoned me aside one day and asked me whether I thought it was perhaps your own story you had told us. For you had said, "When you know that your heavenly Father will give you all you need, then beware; for the devil will say to you, 'If that is true, then command these stones to turn into bread for you, and they will obey you.' But how then should Scripture be fulfilled, which says, 'Man shall not live by bread alone, but by every word that comes out of the mouth of God'? And when you know that your angels stand always before the face of my Father, then beware; for the devil will say to you, tempting you, 'Then cast yourself off the parapet of the Temple, and the angels will bear you in their hands.' Never hearken to him; for Scripture commands, 'You shall not put the Lord your God to the test.' And when you know how glorious is the inheritance your heavenly Father has prepared for his children, then beware; for the devil will come to you and show you the kingdoms of the earth in their glory, tempting you, and he will say to you, 'If you desire glory, worship me, and I will give you all these.' Never listen to him, but turn your back; for Scripture says, 'You shall do homage to the Lord your God and worship him alone.'"

Master, as I listened to that, I saw it all; I saw you carried in vision, like Ezekiel or Habakkuk, to the Temple parapet, or to a mountain-top with a view over many kingdoms; I saw you, faint with hunger, picking up the stones; I saw you commanding Satan to get behind you. Old Simon the Zealot refused to believe it. He said you could never have desired the glory of the earthly kingdoms, because of the far greater glory of your own kingdom. But I know you did desire it—yes, and I know you rejected it too; but you desired it first. I know, oh yes, I know, the way Satan would have led you, and you might have trodden it— the way of rebellion against God, the way of pride and madness. Yes, Master, you could have gone into madness and thrown yourself off the Temple, or into sorcery and made unholy bread, that you could never have stopped eating until it came out at your nose. And you could have taken the power and glory to yourself, and become rejected, an abomination to God.

Master, you who tasted pride so nearly, you should understand, you should have pity on us whose mouths are full of its foul taste. For no-one ever wholly refused the devil's offers but you. All of us are a little mad with dreams, restless with lust, crazed with pride. You know, Master, you know how I've sucked stones. All the time I was steward to Jason, deceiving him, I was heaping stones over myself, hoping they would turn into bread, but you took them all away and fed me on God's word instead, that is your own whole strength; the devil was not able to turn you away from your obedience to God. You've chosen the bread of God's will and he could not make you eat any other. But we've all eaten stones.

John it was—the hot-headed innocent—who asked you once, when you were warning us of times of testing to come, why we should be liable to them. "Why should we be given over to the prince of darkness to be tempted by him? He has no rights over us! You've set us free, and we belong to God." You answered, "But still you are in the world, and he is lord of this world yet for a while. He has no rights over me, either, yet I must be given into his power, so that the world may see that I love the Father and never swerve from his commands." You love the Father; there it is, that's what you brought away from your time of temptation in the wilderness, your spoils of victory—utterly faithful, triumphant love. Can you no longer remember what the temptation was like: the veering of love into hatred, the swinging, the staggering? No, you are steady now. You could never turn against your Father now. In a way, it's that very faithfulness of yours that makes you so hard to bear, for you're a living judgment on us, the veerers and staggerers, the unfaithful in love. It's not that we are without faith and love. I do have both—sometimes. But with you it is not sometimes, it is always. Master, I have wished that you had been unfaithful. You are hard, hard to bear; you are relentless in what you are and what you ask. Have you never hated God for his very holiness? No. But I have.

So I used to talk to him all night in my mind. I reproached him, I pleaded with him, I poured out love to him, but I never dared speak it to him. He knew too well. I could not really speak to one who knew and saw so much—he would always have seen more than I wanted to tell.

Then there came that quiet day of sun and haze, soon after our first mission without him—in fact the last pairs of apostles were still straggling in—when news came of the murder of John the Baptist, and Jesus, shaken and sad, called us away to a quiet place to be alone. But it was impossible. The people saw us set sail, and followed us round the lake on foot. Also, Jesus seemed to gather strength during the voyage. When we landed, and the people came panting and stumbling up to meet us, we saw the compassion come into his face; "They're like lost sheep," he said, "looking for a shepherd. No, don't send them away. I'll teach them here." And he did, all the rest of that day and all the next, and they hung on his words; thousands of them, they could not have enough of him. He had to stride up and down among them the whole time, speaking to all of them, healing their stammers and sores. It was always the way; but there was something about the isolation, the lonely peace of the place, the brooding hills, the sense of being a people called apart in the wilderness (though he had not called them); and there was something different in him too, the grief and foreboding John's death had caused him, making him appeal to them more urgently than ever. Whatever the reason, a strange intensity grew. There were, as ever, the whispers, "Surely the Kingdom will come now," but here, this time, we could all believe it. It was among us already, we had found the field with treasure in it, and surely, surely, it was time to dig now.

And I saw something on our Teacher's face like a great hope. He was sharing the slow, hushed, mounting excitement. It was as though, for once, he were one with the people, they were hearing and understanding what he said, and a great hopefulness was growing in him that they were ready to accept it; so it seemed to me. "You are salt to the earth," he told them, "you are light to the world," and he taught them how to live as children of the Kingdom, giving all and asking for nothing back, blessing their persecutors and leaping for joy at insult for the sake of the good news of the Kingdom. And they still hung on every word.

Late in the afternoon of the third day, he came to us reeling with weariness and with a strange light in his eyes. I looked at him and suddenly I was afraid of him. The intensity and solemnity of that impromptu gathering had increased, not lessened; the heat-haze shimmered on the hills; the very earth and lake seemed to be listening. "It's enough," he said, "it's enough. We must end it now. We must feed them and send them away."

"Master! Feed them? What on? There are thousands of them—let them go away and buy for themselves."

"No," said Jesus. "They would faint on the way. We will feed them."

"It would cost hundreds of denarii! And where could we buy food for them all, anyway?"

"Haven't you anything? What, are you withholding your own food? Five loaves? Five whole loaves? And two fish besides? You've got all that and you'd have let them go away hungry? Shame on you!"

I saw that he was teasing us. It annoyed me.

"Give those loaves to me," he said, "and tell them to sit down."

They were willing enough to obey; they saw that something of deep wonder was going to happen, when Jesus stood up with one of the loaves in his hands. In the perfect silence we all heard him clearly as he broke it:

"Blessed art thou, O Father, Lord and God of the universe, who bringest forth thy bread from the earth to feed thy children; amen." It was the blessing I had used too all my life; why then did my heart start to thump so strangely and a mist come behind my eyes? But I had no time to think. Andrew pushed one of the fish-baskets from the boat into my arms. "You do the people over by the rocks," he shouted, and seemed to be buried in more baskets, passed over his head by the other disciples, before he had finished speaking. I took my basket across to the rocks as he had bidden me. It was full of fish—and of bread.

There was bread. There was more bread than anyone could eat. There was no seeing where it all came from. But I know that we had had at the outset five loaves and two small fish, and that for nearly an hour we were toiling under the weight of the food

we distributed, serving at the feast which Jesus gave those folk
of Tiberias among the lakeside hills that day. There was never
an end of it. Even when they could eat no more, and most of
them were filling their water-skins at the lake, our baskets were
still full. I looked up then and saw Jesus standing there, that light
still in his eyes, watching the feast he had made, listening to
the murmur of awe and gratitude—but none of those guests of
his can have known the real wonder, except the Twelve, who
were present when the loaves were counted, and it's just as well
they did not. I looked at him there and a great crawling horror
came in me. I thought, "It was stones. All that bread was stones.
You've done it after all. You've made bread out of stones." And
I saw that he had fallen; that for the sake of pleasing the multitude,
he had betrayed his Father; he had taken the devil's power and
bewitched the stones.

He was not eating, but the rest of the Twelve were hungrily
setting-to. Philip, his face glowing, turned and said "Why,
Judas, haven't you got any? Here—take." I shook my head
and turned away, my mouth too dry to speak. I suddenly felt
John's dark eyes on me; they seem to have caught some of the
Teacher's own quality of piercing. "Eat, Judas," he said, "you
must eat." I shook my head again. He rose and came over to me,
and laid his hand on my shoulder. "Please. Just a little. Just
to say you did share. Don't you see that the Master has kept
Passover today?" (It was shortly before the days of Unleavened
Bread.) I shook his hand off and went away. That bread would
have killed me.

As I wandered alone through the well-fed gathering I heard
new murmurs. "He is the man God has sent us! He is our new
Moses, our new David! He will feed us and lead us!"

One man cried out, "Here is a king who will not make us
his bakers, as Samuel warned the Israelites of Saul—no, he'll
be *our* baker!" There were laughter and cheers, and the cheers
seemed to catch like fire in brushwood and spread through the
camp: cheers, and the words "Here is our king! . . . our king! . . ."
And the sick shock came again; I thought, "Bread from the
stones and the kingship of this world. Bread and the kingship."

Then Jesus was calling us, standing very erect, his eyes flaming, the tranquil gladness all gone now. There was a passionate imperiousness in him. The other eleven jerked their heads up, dismayed, but I understood well enough. He was taking control now of that seething, adoring mob. Even so is Satan adored in the abyss.

"Peter! James! Andrew! All of you! Be off, leave this to me. Don't stay here any longer. Take the boat—I shan't need one. Go quickly, now—quick!"

I didn't need to be bidden. I was racing with the others down to the shore, throwing myself into the boat off that accursed beach. I couldn't get away fast enough. Yet part of me was straining back, in a deadly curiosity, to see and hear what he did now, how he took the power and glory from the rabble of Tiberias, to see him let them make him king.

I am not a strong man, and certainly no seaman, yet I rowed so hard on that crossing that Peter called jokingly, "Whoa, there! Don't let that bread go to your head! Remember we've all got to keep the stroke." It seemed we would never get away from that shore. The wind was against us, and rising fast. It was dusk when we left, and we settled into our rhythm and rowed through the gathering dark and I chewed my cud of bitterness.

He had been the Lord's Anointed. I knew that as I had always known it. But the Lord has rejected his Anointed before now: Saul, the first, disobeyed, and the spirit of evil madness came upon him in place of the holy spirit of prophecy. The first king and the last. Between two poles of evil the windy night seemed to stretch over me. The spirit of madness and destruction was blowing again, that had driven Saul to attempt to murder his beloved protégé David, and in the end to despair, necromancy and suicide, accursed as he had once been anointed. And had our hope and the hope of Israel now disobeyed? Every beat of the oars, every gust of the wind, every crash of the water, answered yes, yes, yes. The hours passed, we groaned as we rowed, the shore came no nearer. "If only he were here," muttered someone. I thought, if he were here, the lake would yawn in horror and the abyss be laid bare for the terror of the evil it was seeing, and the bottomless pit would engulf us all; and indeed I felt as though I were falling into it already.

Then the moon came out suddenly, and I saw a figure: spectral, rising out of the sea, but I knew it as I knew myself. My scream tore through the wind, echoed by the cries of the others as they too saw him, borne up on the water by the hands not of angels but of the devil himself. Oar after oar flailed up, lashed, lost hold; the boat juddered and swung to the swell, as they piled into the bottom, bowing or hiding; some of them prayed aloud. But I sat still. Then I stood up. Already, you are damned already, and so am I. I'm coming to you.

Before I could jump or move the voice came, as warm and human as ever, hailing us and calling, "Don't be afraid! It is I."

Then as Peter leapt to the side, taking my place, volunteering to jump out and come to him, I sank down with my face in my hands in a terror and joy and shame so great that all sensation failed. I felt nothing, I thought nothing; there was only the cold wind blowing, and my knuckles pressed into my eyes, as I began to understand that all my fantasies were false. It was he— the same he, still himself, faithful in love to his Father, the son not of Saul but of David. It was not on him but on me that the terrible spirit of suspicion and murderous jealousy had blown. It was I who had played the part of Saul.

I don't remember any more wind or rowing. We were bumping on Capernaum quay almost at once.

And at Capernaum the disappointed kingmakers of Tiberias found him, a couple of days later. We were coming out of synagogue on the Sabbath, when a shout of menacing triumph went up from across the street: "There he is!" And at once we were surrounded by a grinning knot of zealot scoundrels calling, "Why did you try to give us the slip, king? Did you think we'd give you up? Oh, no! We ain't fickle! Now you stick by us!"

"It's only bread you're after," he said, and suddenly raising his voice cried, "You don't know what bread is!"

And standing with his back against the white sunlit wall of

the synagogue he told them, and still more he told us, what bread is, what that bread was he had fed them—fed us—on, among the shore hills that day. It was not bread from stones, but bread from heaven, not the bread of sorcery but the bread of truth, the sign not of his disobedience but of his very life with God. "If you had known what you were eating!" he cried. "Then you would be asking me now for bread indeed, the bread that God really gives. It is God who fed you that day. I can give you nothing, it is God who gives everything; it is he who had given me to you—to be your bread."

A burst of nervous laughter went through the crowd, and a stab through me. The laughter died away into uneasy murmuring, yet still every face was turned to his, and more people were collecting every moment. He stood there above them all, unmoved; tall, brown, full of an authority they could not help knowing; yet a man with his back against a wall.

"I tell you this," he said. "I fed you that day with bread and fish, but next time it will be with my own flesh and blood, which I must give for the life of the world."

And they stared, and backed away, not in derision (though some of them laughed to cover up), but in terror, and I backed with them. For I hadn't needed his words now. I knew. I had known all along. I had known that that superabundance of bread was his own generosity, that the constant increase was not from stones but from his very self, that it was his own life he was giving us and I was helping to hand round. I had known it, and that was why I could not eat it. I knew now how desperately I had lied to myself, persuading myself that he had fallen, was evil, a thing abhorred. I hadn't feared it, oh no. I had hoped for it, how I had hoped for it; I had longed for him to be evil, if only I might wriggle free by any means from the grip of his holiness, the goodness I could not bear.

And now I was back in his hold, and still I could not bear it. I could not even follow the retreating crowd out of his sight, but on the far side of the market square I turned and shambled back to him, kicking the stones. He still stood under the synagogue wall. The Twelve stood or sat round him, hunched and silent. At last he shook himself and looked at them a little wonderingly.

"Are you still here?" he said. "Don't you want to go away too?"

At that Simon Peter jumped up and exclaimed, "Master, where should we go? You have the words of eternal life."

But the sadness only deepened in Jesus' face, though he smiled, for he was looking at me. I looked away.

"Didn't I choose you, all twelve?" he said. "Yet one of you is a devil."

Yes, Master, yes, I am a devil. But who blew the spirit of the devil on me? Who sent me mad as David sent Saul mad? Who sang the sweet song of the Lord in my ear, as David sang it to Saul, until for its very sweetness the spirit of devouring jealousy and bitter hatred came on me? Did Saul indeed slay himself, or was it not David who really slew him? Was it not to save himself that Saul tried to kill David first? And who are you but the son of David? Who called me, and loved me, and trusted me, with a love and trust that I could not bear? Who shone on me with such brightness that I was blinded, and my light turned into darkness?

There's always a black and red mist behind my eyes now. But sometimes it lifts, or it's rent—as you rent it that day teaching on the mountainside, a little while after the feeding of the multitude, when you seemed to look across at me through my own darkness, saying, "Would the worst man among you give his son a stone if he asked for bread, or a snake if he asked for fish? And shall your heavenly Father cheat you if you ask for the Holy Spirit?" The mist cleared then, and I knew I was doing again what I had done at the feeding: I was trying to believe you evil, trying to believe God evil, and sender of the terrible spirit upon me; and I saw you there in your truth and remembered God, who he is, the faithful and holy one, and I collapsed there on the rocky hillside as I had broken down in the boat when you spoke in your own voice. I fell in such racking grief and shame that I could not breathe, I could not sob. I was choking; a little more and it would have strangled me. For I can't do it. I can't believe you evil. I can't commit that sin, though I long to, the sin you warned us against, of calling your Holy Spirit evil. Every time I nearly succeed, you force a crumb of the bread of truth down me. I can't swallow it, I tell you! I can't take your forgiveness!

I stole five silver pieces from the bag again yesterday. I spent it on wine with one of my old clients. I did not want it, but it's all you have left me to do—the only futile little way I have of hurting you. When you've nothing more I can steal, I shall sell you yourself—anything, if only I can repudiate your trust. And all the time knowing that I can never do it. I'm conscious always of your compassion and friendship, burning me. If I were really to sell you, you'd say, "Go on." There is nothing I can do to stop you bearing with me. And you've learnt that from your Father; for it was said of old that Israel should fear God for his very mercy.

Yes, it's your mercy and God's that I fear. Am I Isaiah, who could eat burning coals from the Temple altar to purge his sin? I can't eat the burning coal of your bread. It is that which will kill me, one day—the strangling remorse as the last blackness lifts. Master, don't ask me to eat your bread. The foolish old innkeeper was right after all: I can't sit at table with you. On the day you make me eat your bread I think I shall kill you. Why must you give us bread? Why must you give us yourself? Why could you not give us stones? I want stones! I would rather have stones! I don't want you to trust me, to trust yourself to me! For I know you've given yourself into my hands like a piece of bread. Master, don't ask me to eat it. . . . Give me stones, O God my God, give me stones, don't give me bread, don't give me thyself; O Lord of heaven, thou blessed one, who knowest not evil, wilt thou trust us so? Wilt thou kill us by trusting us? O God of Israel, give us stones.

23

SON OF MAN

WE WERE TIRED out from the journey back from Jerusalem after Passover and already we were off preaching the Kingdom of God again. This was what Jesus had meant by choosing us Twelve to be with him and share his life.

We tumbled late and weary into strange beds. I had scarcely greeted my host and hostess, though I half-heard Jesus greeting them with his usual courtesy and blessing the children. Peter, John and I were lodging with him here and the rest in other houses in the town: this was becoming his usual practice, when we slept under roofs at all. He had started singling us three out some time back, and I tremble at what it may mean.

I awoke when a sunbeam struck me and sat up. The room was empty, I was suddenly filled with hunger and excitement. A new day to glorify God in, a new day with such a Rabbi as ours! The joy of the Kingdom was in my heart and I ran down to the waterside. The first morning light shone on the lake, the fishsellers were busy on the quay, as eager to come out and meet the new haul as the weary fishermen were eager to turn in. I saw boats riding at anchor outlined against the dawn, those that had not been out that night, with here and there a fisherman peacefully sitting and chipping floats for his nets, or only watching the bustle. I strained my eyes into the bright distance but couldn't recognize the *Rose of Sharon* in the glare, until a hearty voice called me, "James!" Then I saw Peter crouched in one of the nearer boats, caulking a crack. "Here," I said, "I'll help you. I'll start this end. Poor old *Rose*, she's falling apart! She's never had it so tough."

"Like us," said Peter. "Judas has gone to buy some more pitch." He was black with it; I couldn't help laughing. He kept passing his arm unconsciously over his face, a habit of his when he was worried. "What's wrong?" I asked him, but he only shook his head, perplexed at himself. I asked "Where is everyone? Where's John? Is there anything to eat?"

"There's you-know-what," he said. "Bread from Tiberias. That locker's full of it. It's all right if you dip it in the lake; I've had some. John's brought up the *Salome*—" he nodded across the harbour towards it, and I saw with a shock that the fisherman quietly carving out net floats and watching the bustle on the wharf was our Teacher himself, and that was John sitting by him, sewing at a sail. I was involuntarily rising to call out, chiefly from sudden, strange alarm, when Peter tugged at me: "No, don't call him, James, he doesn't want to be recognized." And certainly if those sellers and buyers on the quay had known who was there, there would have been bustle of a very different kind: a crowd would have started collecting at once. But John saw me and came across and swung himself lightly into our boat. He took a piece of the bread I was eating, murmuring: "Real bread, not manna, which vanished overnight; it's real bread, true bread. . . ."

"What's the Rabbi doing?" I asked, and heard my voice hoarse with a kind of fright.

"Just watching and listening. He doesn't want to teach today. We're going travelling by ourselves. He says there is something we don't understand yet."

"I don't understand *anything*," groaned Peter. I no longer wanted to ask why he was worried. The same nameless disquiet was growing in me too, yet it was linked with the strange joy and excitement I had woken with. I said, wondering aloud, "For there is the fear of the Kingdom, as well as the joy of it."

"Fear?" said John, raising his head incredulously.

"Yes, fear," said Judas' voice behind us. He had come up unheard and was squatting on the quay. "Salmaeus the ropemaker is sending his son with a barrel of pitch," he added to Peter.

"Fear of what?" persisted John.

"Fear of him," Judas and I said together.

John stood up, eyeing us as though hardly able to believe his ears. "What? Still? Now? I know, at first we were all afraid . . ."

"Much more now," Judas said.

"But fear is to do with being hurt!" cried John. "When you come to love someone you stop caring about being hurt. You can't be really afraid of someone you love."

Judas shrugged, Peter groaned, but my own temper rose in answer to John's flashing eyes, as it always does. I stood up too—the boat rocked uncomfortably—and shouted, "How dare you *not* be afraid of him? Of a man whom the wind and sea obey? Who do you think he is?"

Perhaps they were words that should never have been spoken. Silence fell. It was the first time any of us had mentioned the terrifying night, that we would willingly have believed was common nightmare, when we were caught in a storm so that the boat was swamped, and then Jesus stilled the storm by a word. That stilling was more fearful than any storm. I glanced round; Judas had gone white and his eyes were staring, Peter and John were looking at each other with stricken faces, but beyond them the quiet fisherman still whittled away at his net floats. And suddenly I was more afraid of him then, so much one with humanity, so ordinary, unnoticed even by the sharp-eyed fishmongers, than I had been on that strange night when he rose up in the boat with the power in him. And even then, we had not guessed what he was going to do; it was not ever power that showed, fire from heaven; he had been asleep on a cushion in the stern, drenched with spray, until we woke him because we thought we were going to have to swim for it. The mystery of him was worse to bear when he so often seemed just like one of us—and then you would realize from something he said or did that his feet stood in hell and his head in heaven, that he lived all the time in heights and depths we never dreamed of, that God spoke with him face to face as a man with his friend, not only on a holy mountaintop but all the time.

Then John said, "Yet he did not say 'Have more fear', but 'Have more faith'. He had the faith to sleep in an open boat in a storm because he knew his Father would not let him die in vain, before his hour had come. That's how he'd like us to be!"

"And when his hour has come, and you see him as he truly

is, do you think you won't be afraid then? Do you think you'll be able to love him then?" flung back Judas, and I looked at him and saw his eyes on the figure across the harbour with a fear close to cringing loathing in them. I was terrified by his look. There was none of the awe and holy dread which you'll see on faces in Temple or synagogue, the marks of the fear of God. It was closer to the blank, mad fear that we saw on the faces of the demoniacs in the presence of our Teacher. For a second I saw it staring out of his face, that look of hell, and then he had turned on his heels and was running away from us into the town. We looked at each other in dismay. It was a relief when young Bar-Salmaeus arrived trundling the barrel of tar.

Hell and heaven kept yawning open at our feet and behind our heads in those days. Well might we cherish memories of tranquil days on the water. We needed them all, for suddenly our nets would break with all the fish of the ocean and the love of God; or eyes would stare and gibbering words would scream out the evil of Satan; we began to guess what lay under the fathoms of that lake we had known all our lives. And all the more we silently cried out, "Who can this be, whom the winds and waves obey?"

When the *Rose of Sharon* was patched up and *Salome*'s sail repaired we sailed to Bethsaida and beached the boats there. It was late in the summer before we saw them again. Then we made our way on foot farther northwards still into really pagan regions, right into Phoenicia, with Mount Hermon rising up closer and closer every time we looked. The Rabbi seemed preoccupied and was trying to avoid crowds. He wanted to be alone with us, yet even to us he did not speak much. He had John the Baptist in his thoughts a good deal, and those other suffering leaders of our people, Moses, Elijah, Jeremiah. He skirted Tyre and led us east, into Ituraea. We could not guess where we were going or why, until Andrew pulled me aside and said, "We are close to Caesarea Philippi. James, do you know what the Essenes teach about it? About all this part? Matthias told me when we were with John the Baptist. They say the mouth of the abyss of Gehenna opens close by and it is only a yard under the earth. Do you think the Rabbi will take us to preach in Gehenna?"

"I should not be surprised!" I said grimly. But indeed the abyss of hell seemed only a yard underfoot below the whole land of Israel in those days, and our little country rocked and tossed like a pancake floating on a boiling saucepan, ever since the Spirit returned, since John arose to prophesy and Jesus to lead us into the Kingdom. There was no place for mortal flesh to shelter before the terror of the majesty of the Lord and the desperate struggle of Satan. I could well believe that the Master had led us here to the mouth of hell because he must challenge it in the name of God. And truly it may have been so, for we hardly ever knew what battles he fought in the spirit. And so we walked day after day in the silent northern hills; until one hot, oppressive day, close to Caesarea Philippi, Jesus called us to him.

The sky and solemnity of it alike weighed on us. The sky darkened even as we stood there gathered in a semi-circle in the dip between two stony ridges. A wild goat ran along the top as we assembled. I saw Judas shiver and hunch himself. Simon rubbed his arm over his face again and again.

Jesus said, "Tell me, what are people saying of the Son of Man? Who do they think he is?"

We looked at one another.

That name. It was an indication of the gravity of his question. Although it was an ordinary enough phrase, such as anyone might use, yet he tended to call himself son of man when a certain mood was on him, the prophetic mood perhaps, a bitter mood it seemed sometimes. When the longing for the kingdom was fiercest in him, and he was in pain for the hiding and delaying of it, then he would speak strangely of the days of the Son of Man; or when the authority God had set in him was derided, when it became too harshly clear that he was indeed after all "just anyone", then he would fall into speaking of himself as son of man. "The Son of Man came eating and drinking, and men say 'What a glutton, what a wine-bibber!'" "Foxes have holes, birds have nests, but the Son of Man has nowhere to lay his head." It was as though the indirectness and ambiguity of the phrase answered to a perplexity in himself, a question in his own mind, as though he like the rest of us had to face as he could the humbling of God's power. Because of course it is a name of power too; we all know that Israel will be saved by "one like unto a son of man" in the last days; but for Jesus it was always power humbled, and he was just anyone, a son of man; he spoke it often in wistfulness and irony.

We were all becoming nervous of the words. I flinched to hear them, however harmless in their context. At the last farm we stayed at, for instance, our host tried to lift an iron pot off the fire without a cloth, and snatching his burnt hands away exclaimed, "What a silly old son of man I be!" And John and I jumped, and flushed in confusion when we caught each other's eye. Those words, son of man, had come to hold in themselves all the fear and wonder we had in our minds for Jesus, they were the great question we never dared ask; and I've thought it was so for him too.

And now there he stood asking it, asking us. "What are people saying of the Son of Man? Who do they think he is?" A shiver of unease ran round the circle of it. I braced myself and answered boldly.

"A lot of folks think you're John the Baptist. Herod for one," I replied.

"Or Jeremiah, or Elijah, or one of the old prophets."

Yes, I thought, it is true. Prophecy never burnt with more fire than it does in you, Rabbi, son of man and son of the spirit.

"And you?" he asked. "What do you say?"

I, as senior of the three he had called most closely to him, thought, "I must answer. Go on, son of thunder. Tell him he is the greatest prophet of all. It's the truth." But I could not speak.

Then Simon Peter blurted out the answer none of us had dared to make; and sky and earth seemed to fall apart at his words.

"You are the Messiah, the son of the living God."

The swirl of the Teacher's robe startled me in that immobile gathering as he threw out his arms to grasp Simon by the shoulders, and cried, "Blessed are you, Simon bar-Jonah! For flesh and blood did not reveal that to you, but my Father in heaven."

They stood there, the two of them, the grey clouds tearing behind them, the lightning coming and going. Simon was shrinking and quailing under the Rabbi's look and those powerful hands. I heard thunder, and then—not heard—but felt it again, answering thunder, underfoot, underground. A yard! Hell was not a yard down, it was barely six inches, it was rising, erupting; would the abyss split open in front of us, mounting its last desperate attack?

The Master must have felt it better than I; and still gripping Simon, he cried out, "Have I not called you Peter, the Rock? And now I tell you I am building my church on that rock, and the gates of hell shall never prevail against it. You shall hold the keys of the kingdom of heaven, and all that you open shall stand opened, and all that you close shall stand closed."

The lightning split the sky, the mountainside shook under me, yet neither hell nor heaven opened. They heaved and pressed at their gates, but the power of unsealing was laid in Peter; all that pressure, all the authority of our Rabbi, rested in us, and the point in Peter.

Why us? I wanted to cry out. Why us? What is man, that you remember him, and the son of man, that you visit him? Why have you set him between the angels and the nether-world, to be crushed or torn between the two? Who can stand in his flesh between hell and heaven and not be split, strained, tortured, destroyed?

The Rabbi dropped his arms and turned to the rest of us, but it was towards me he looked. "This is true too," he said: "the Son of Man must suffer. The delivering up, the binding, the crucifying—yes, it must all come."

"But not to you!" exclaimed Peter, taking him by the arm: "not to you! We're all sons of men. It doesn't matter if we suffer, but not you! False Messiahs are crucified, not the true!"

And the Jesus turned with such blaze of anger as I had never seen. "Get out of my way, Satan!" he cried in a terrible voice,

and through poor Peter—the doorkeeper—the words rang down
to the bottom of hell. Then he added more gently to Peter,
"You're thinking as men think, not as God thinks. But don't
try to tempt me to an easier way. It cannot be."

So I knew that he was thinking all I had thought, and doubtless
more; he knew all about the stretching, the sundering, the
destroying; but he had taken the name of Son of Man for his
own. He would not leave us to bear the pain in his place, it was
the other way round: he it was who was taking the weight of
hell and heaven in the place of all the sons of men.

"You'll have your share of it too," he said. "No-one can be
my follower who does not say goodbye to all that is dearest
to him—even to his own life—and take the cross of his own
execution on his back, and come after me."

We gaped at him; he had spoken sombrely and sternly
before, but never with such words as these. And I saw suddenly
the weariness in him and knew how deeply he himself shrank
from whatever fate it was that he foresaw so clearly and I felt
obscurely: the rending of him that was the price of his lordship
over the kingdoms of God and of Satan. He was a son of man
and could not avoid thinking as men think, he too, even though
he chose as God had chosen. I could not see him any longer as a
towering figure filling the heights and depths. I saw only a
weary man forcing himself on, pleading with us not to make
it harder for him, on the grey, empty hillside with the thunder-
clouds behind him.

24

SON OF GOD

THE TWELVE OF us and Jesus journeyed on through the thundery, half-pagan mountains, and though there was no mistaking the deadly fatigue in our Rabbi now, all that had been said was relief and release, and there came—muted at first, then swelling in all our minds—a sense of something close to jubilation. We were catching it from our Rabbi, as we tended to catch all his moods. It was not our own jubilation, indeed, we scarcely understood it; at first I thought it was because Peter had said at last what we had not dared to think; then it seemed to me it was rather to do with the words that had followed and the parable of the cross. He spoke to us freely now of "the exodus that I must accomplish at Jerusalem", with a kind of triumph in his voice. My heart began to lift. I thought of Elisha following Elijah on their last journey together through Israel; how Elisha had sworn three times over, "As the Lord lives, and as you yourself live, I will not leave you before the end." I remembered how for his faithfulness he had been allowed to see his master taken up to heaven in a whirlwind and a chariot of fire, and been found worthy to inherit a double portion of his spirit. Surely we were following no less faithfully, in spite of poor Simon Peter's blundering, and we had a greater master than Elijah! If for him there had been heavenly chariots and horsemen, what would there be for Jesus, the promised Messiah? And would he not grant us to see the glory of his ascension?

So I would think; and then I would remember how he had spoken of suffering much before that glory could be his; of being delivered up to his enemies, of binding and of crucifixion. "Surely he was speaking in parables." I thought uneasily. I understood well enough that he must suffer, for he was the son of man; so Israel must ever suffer before God vindicates her; but death? How could Messiah die, how can Israel die, truly die? "It was a parable of his victory," I thought again. Or perhaps indeed Messiah must fall in battle, and be raised from the battlefield in glory. That could be; but crucifixion, that accursed death, that heathen obscenity, this could never come to him; Peter surely had not been wrong there.

I was all the more certain, because of the quiet, growing exultation in our Teacher as he led us round the northernmost shore of the Sea of Galilee, telling us that soon he must be "received up to heaven", and that "the Son of Man shall come in the glory of his Father and of the holy angels, to judge and reward each man; and some of you shall not taste of death before you see the kingdom of the Son of Man". Another time he told us that we would not have time to preach to all the towns in Israel before he returned in power. But we understood nothing, though we thought we did, for we knew neither what his triumph was, nor his exodus, nor his glory, nor his kingdom, nor his power.

But we could not help sensing that hidden rejoicing in him as we travelled on through Ituraea; until at last, a week or so after the scene at Caesarea Philippi, he could contain it no longer. We had reached a little town of goatherds and poor mountain farmers. Here he told the nine to wait, and took Peter, John and myself with him, half a day's journey up the mountain behind the village. He wanted to be alone, and this time he succeeded in contriving it. At last he halted, out of sight of the valley. It was very still, the sky heavy; the thunder had never really cleared away. There was an intense hush in that secret dell so high and unvisited. The thyme smelt sweet underfoot, and one eagle rose and fell, rose and fell.

"Stay here," he said. "Wait for me." He withdrew a stone's throw to pray, as he often did. We watched him for a while standing with his hands raised; then the heavy air must have sent us to sleep. It was not the first time, nor was it to be the last; we could never pray as he did.

I don't know how long we slept and he prayed; we were awoken at last by thunder and rain. Cold drops were falling on us, the sky was dark; then, rolling over, I started up in terror,

for a ball of lightning had fallen on to the hill not ten yards
from us, just where our Master had been praying. I half rose
and called out hoarsely. But this lightning did not flash and
vanish. It hovered and stood, and the whole wet hillside shimmered to it. And at last my half-blinded eyes saw that there was
no lightning, but our Master himself, still standing there in
prayer, and he was the ball of white fire. I could see the move-
ments of his garments now, and that he was flanked by two
other figures, shadows of light against his blazing light, and
they were speaking, or singing, the three of them exulting together; and they sang, one answering the other,

"When Israel came out of Egypt, and the house of Jacob from
foreign captivity,

Judah was his sanctuary, and Israel his dominion.

The sea saw it and fled; Jordan was driven back.

The mountains skipped like rams, and the little hills like
young sheep.

What is troubling you, sea, that you have fled? Jordan, that
you should be driven back?

You mountains, that you skip like rams? or you hills, that
you skip like young rams?

Tremble, O earth, at the presence of the Lord, at the presence
of the God of Jacob,

Who turned the rock into a pool of water, and the flintstone
into a springing well!"

And I knew that I was seeing Moses, who led the first exodus,
and Elijah, who ascended to heaven, rejoicing with him who
should soon depart on a greater journey than either.

It was raining heavily, and the brilliance of our Master was
shining from drop to drop till the very air seemed alight with a
hidden, rose-gold radiance, and the glistening rocks seemed to
have become translucent, his splendour welling up through the
very stones.

The Splendour! The Shining of God's presence! It was no
light of earth we were seeing. The Shekinah of the Lord was
filling that thundery hillside. Even the dark clouds above us
were illuminated by the shining of God on his last and greatest

messenger to Israel. We all three realized it together and fell on our faces. I who had wanted to watch Jesus' ascension in glory, as Elisha had watched Elijah's, had no courage now to look, but buried my face in the earth; but I heard Peter behind me—the ever-courageous, ever-blundering Peter—calling out in a cracking voice, "Master, what a wonderful thing you are letting us see! Shall we make a tabernacle for the Glory?—or three tabernacles, one for you, one for Moses and one for Elijah?"

"Oh be quiet, you prating clot," I thought, but the Three who stood there cannot even have heard him. As Moses had spoken with God in thick darkness on Mount Sinai, and as Elijah had hidden his face in his mantle when he was called to speak with God on Mount Horeb, so now, the three of them were wrapped in the cloud of brightness where God had descended. Sideways through my sleeve I saw the whole mountain glowing as though—yes, as though a pillar of fire stood against it.

Yet God remembered us, three prostrate, terrified fishermen, for through the thunder and the rain and the song, his word came into my ears and into my heart, as it had come to the generations of my fathers: the word to all that comes to each.

"This is my beloved son. Listen to him."

I thought death would take me soon, for that joy and terror were too great for flesh to bear. But it was a firm human touch that I felt: a hand was gripping my shoulder. "Peter! John! James!" came the Master's voice, with laughter in it. "Stand up; don't be so frightened!"

I hardly dared to look up; but when I did, I saw no ball of lightning held on the hill, no pillar of fire, no Moses nor Elijah. There was only Jesus, with gladness in his face and his clothes dark with rain, the same Jesus we had always known. We stood up slowly, staggering, and looked at each other. Heaven had overflowed today as hell had all but overflowed last week. When I had said to myself that he stood with his feet in hell and his head in heaven, I had not guessed half the truth of my own fancy. We were afraid now, not only because we had been in the presence of God, all sinful and ordinary as we were, but because we had begun to understand in what deep places Jesus, our Master, had loved us; we had glimpsed the heights and depths of his love, though we might never know it fully. For we had seen his joy and glory with his Father, that had refused to remain hidden any longer, so great was it now in the time of his acceptance of his suffering; and with the fathers of Israel, who had refused to keep silence any longer, but their exultation had had to burst out. And we were witnesses.

"Come," he said, "it's time we rejoined the others."

We went dog-tired and stumbling down the drenched hillside in the dusk. As we went, he charged us, "Don't tell the others what you have seen. Don't tell anyone, not till the Son of Man has risen from the dead."

And now, I said to myself, I know that it is a parable. But Peter said in my ear, "Will Elijah come back, do you think, to carry him away when he suffers? Is that what he means?" And John said, "No, no. He means that next time his glory is revealed, all the earth shall see it, not us only." For we still did not understand.

"No," Jesus said, answering only part of our questioning, "Elijah will not come again. He has come, and his work is done. Yet you saw what men did to him; for no-one recognized him. How then can it be any different for the Son of Man?"

And perhaps, if we had understood, we would have known he was answering the second part of our questioning as well. But we did not. We said wisely to one another, "Aha, he means John the Baptist. I always said John was Elijah." And Jesus heard us and smiled, a little sadly.

It was cool at last for the first time in many days. The birds were singing after the storm as we came down into the valley. A great peace had filled us as we walked. The earth was still wet and soft, almost rose-coloured; the rocks glistened. It was as though creation could hardly keep its creator's secret, but the radiance was showing through. And it was showing in Jesus' face. Looking up suddenly and catching him unawares, I gasped and fell back; then he turned and I saw only sunset light. Yet it was not my fantasy, for when we came at last into the village square, where the nine others seemed to be involved in something approaching a brawl, and Jesus called out sternly, "What's this?" every face turned to him and I saw amazement and terror on them all, for the brightness of the splendour and the majesty on his, the glory of his Father.

For whether he stood in lightning on a mountain, or in a stormy sunset in a crowd, he was always the same.

"What's this?" he asked again.

"Rabbi," a man answered hoarsely, "I brought my son to your disciples, because he has a terrible spirit in him that keeps trying to kill him—making him go rigid and throwing him into fire and water. We couldn't find you, Rabbi, they said they didn't know where you'd gone, but they tried to cast it out in your name and couldn't."

I saw Andrew and Philip flushed and angry, Thaddaeus arguing volubly with the two old rabbis from the village school, who were, unfortunately, dressed as Pharisees. I saw that the crowd was siding with the teachers. The shrill-voiced elder of the two called out, "Yes, we know you, Jesus of Nazareth! We may be an outpost but we aren't ignorant of you, Jesus of Nazareth, you impostor and seducer of Israel!"

Our Master did not look at him, but he said wearily, "What an unbelieving and perverse generation! How long shall I be with you? How long must I endure you? Bring the boy to me."

The father and another man came dragging the rigid boy. The crowd parted sullenly.

I was distressed and angered by the upset, the insults, the stirring violence, the ugliness and hatred of the scene, following so immediately upon the blessed revelation on the mountain. But the Master, though he must have been more tired than any of us, was concerned with nothing but the boy and his father. "How long has he been like this?" he asked, and when the man answered, "From childhood; it's nearly killed him hundreds of times," Jesus sighed and shook his head.

"Rabbi! Can't you do anything?" cried the man. "If you can do anything, have pity on us and help us!"

The crowd catcalled and pressed up, grinning.

"If I can?" retorted Jesus to the man, and suddenly smiled. "There's nothing that can't be done for someone who has faith."

"I do have faith!" cried out the poor father, "I do! Help me to have faith!"

Jesus glanced up at the crowd for the first time. They were watching like beasts ready to pounce. If he failed as the nine had failed they would stone him. I saw one or two covertly picking up stones already. Yet at his look they fell back now.

"Deaf and dumb spirit, I command you to come out and never trouble the child again."

The boy screamed and fell foaming and rigid. Then suddenly the scream died away and he collapsed, limp.

"He's dead," said a voice in the crowd. "He's killed him."

But the Master took him by the hand and raised him up, and gave him to his father. There came a low, evil mutter from the crowd, and it melted away, slinking home. The darkness grew in the market square. Still Jesus stood there alone. We dared not speak to him. The people of that little town had not known, had not wanted to know, what light stood among them; only a poor father crazed by grief had known; the rest, they had seen in him only darkness, and now darkness had fallen on them indeed.

Then at last I heard him say, almost to himself,

"Yet the third day he will raise us up, and we shall live in his sight."

He was speaking the strange old words of the prophet that haunt the ears of all Israelites with the stir of an unnameable hope. And though still not understanding what he meant, I realized that he was seeing beyond the shadows closing in, beyond the darkness, beyond the rejection and suffering. His shining was greater than the darkness of men. We only had power to bind ourselves and him in the kingdom of darkness, but he had the far greater power to deliver us from it and bring us away into his glorious light, into the kingdom that belonged to him, God's beloved son.

25

HEARING

"The Doubter", they nickname me jokingly among the Twelve. "Gloomy Thomas." But haven't I reason to be? I know too much about hardness of heart; about the hardness of the world itself.

Ours is a hard country. Hard soil, hard stones, hard weather. And we've been hardened. Man was created in the image of God to be tender and compassionate as he is; but that was long ago, and we are hard now. We of the northern hills are like outcrops of the hills themselves. Judaeans tell us that their land is far harder still, burnt into mountainous deserts, but we don't listen to them. We don't listen to any outsider. We know God has given us the worst share and we mutter in his face. That's how it is with my father, and I'm my father's son. For one blessing he speaks to God over his fields at harvest time, he has grumbled a thousand curses during the year. So have I: not for the soil but for the people; I have cursed God for this people of mine, the hard nation of Israel, who love neither their God nor their neighbour. And do I?

There's my mother. She doesn't curse God, she doesn't bless him. When I rebuke her for cheating over her tithes, or neglecting her purification, or serving us unhallowed food, she laughs and says, "Oh he's far away, in Jerusalem! I'm sure he doesn't watch us!" And if I scream at her, "Do you not care, do you not care for the holiness of the Lord your God?" she only smiles, because she does not care, and I see her eyes wandering to where she has been baking cakes to offer to Demeter with the other women of the town. When I go past the shrine and see the cakes lying there I take them and throw them to the swine. But it's too late. The offence to God is in the offering. I have railed at her, I have pleaded with her, I have wept before her, but she doesn't listen. Neither to God nor to man does any Israelite listen, and we go on bullying our tenants, cheating our landlords, diddling our patrons, pushing widows and poor litigants out of our way—and then we curse God because our fields are barren!

We are all deaf and dumb, I used to cry in my heart, shivering at the sight of my brother sitting upright and alone, unseeing of anything about him, closed in in his own world. Well may the spirit of deafness and muteness make its home in him, for we are all possessed by it!

I can hardly remember what Joset my twin was like when he was a child. We were contented enough playmates for a while. But childhood doesn't last long among us. On the threshold of manhood, when we were eleven, he was struck with a sickness that left him stone deaf and seemingly made of stone. He was a man suddenly, a dour, unsmiling, lightless man living in utter isolation amongst his own family. He ceased to try to speak when he found he could no longer hear our answers. The very devil of silence was in him, he seemed like the devil of silence himself, sitting in our midst, brooding over us like the rocky hills above us. We were afraid of him. We all shouted at him, though we knew he could not hear. I have seen my mother take him by the shoulders and shake him, screaming at him, as though she would force him to hear by her very panic, but his face never quickened or changed, he scarcely saw her, let alone heard her, and soon she lapsed back into her usual indifference.

Yes, we are all bound fast with chains and locks in our own deafness and dumbness, stapled into our own rock-hard hearts! God's wrath will come upon us and we will not even hear it coming! I have tried to warn them, God knows how I tried to warn them. "He will not tarry," I cried in our village, "and he will not overlook our evil!" But they saw no worse terror coming than a storm at harvest time, or a traveller they were robbing while he slept starting up on them armed. Yes, a storm will come on them at harvest time, the storm of God's fury on the day of his judgment, and he will indeed start up on them in the night with his sword of truth in his hand!

Then I heard how John the Baptist was crying for repentance in God's name in Judaea, and after vainly trying to persuade my kinsfolk to come with me, I started south to him. But I never reached him. Before I came to Samaria he was arrested and shut up in prison by a king who could not bear to hear him. And as I halted, hesitant, cursing all evildoers and wondering what to do next, the news of another man swept through the towns and villages of Galilee, because Jesus came proclaiming the imminent kingdom of God. And I went straight to him and joined him.

There was all the power and passion in him that any prophet could have asked for, all the urgency after God's holiness. Indeed, he was a prophet. And that should have warned me from the outset that Israel would not hear him, no, nor the Gentiles either, for what prophet has ever been listened to? But I was swept off my feet by the first touch of joy and hope I had ever known.

He was the trumpets before Jericho! He was the thunder of the voice of God! We went through the countryside crying and shouting like the messengers of God's salvation which we truly were, "Turn again! Turn again, O Israel! For the reign of our God is upon us!"

And this was the proof of his truth, that a few did hear. Some, some everywhere, heard and believed God's word and turned to him with all their heart. Truly, even before the time, God was reigning already wherever we went. All those who heard and received us, we left behind us as the children of the kingdom and its heirs. All who were God's own recognized his word on the lips of Jesus. Because Jesus was himself the one great hearer of God's word, the true listener. That was how it was that he could enter men's hearts and lives where others could not—where I, for instance, had failed.

"The Lord God has opened my ear, and I did not disobey, nor turned away back; he wakes my ear to hear, morning by morning, that I should know how to speak a word in season to him that is weary." So prophesied Isaiah, and he spoke of Jesus.

But the next words of that prophecy, again, should have warned me:

"I gave my back to the smiters, and my cheeks to those who were plucking out my beard; I did not shield my face from shame and spitting. . . ."

I forgot them, I did not read them. But Jesus remembered them. It was hard for him to cry to our deaf hearts, harder than it had been for me to weep and plead with my old village. It was only rarely that we understood how hard; sometimes it broke out of him—

"I have come to set fire to the earth," he cried once, "and how I wish it were already kindled! I have a baptism to undergo, and how hampered I am until the ordeal is over!"

For he knew the cost to the prophet to speak a prophet's word, he knew better than my father knew how hard it is to plough a thankless field, he knew in the end more than I ever could how bitter is rejection. But he went on ploughing and he did not curse. I cursed for him, sometimes, until he forbade me.

And I was half-aware that even I was not hearing him. My deaf-mute twin seemed to be beside me wherever we went. I remember how long it was, above all, before I in the least understood the other side of Jesus, his silence. If he was the messenger of God, it seemed to me, he was a strange messenger. After he had cried the good news anywhere he let his voice die away, he let silence follow, silence overtake his word. Though he sounded like the trumpets of his namesake Joshua, when the walls did not fall down the first time he did not blow until they did, but suffered them to stand. I could understand his urgency, this I knew too; or I thought I understood it. But I could not understand his patience. I could hardly bear it when he let the people reject his word and God's and did not shout it at them until they did surrender. I am not a gentle man and it was long before I understood the gentleness in him, or could tolerate it. Long before I could accept the next words of the prophecy, that he should turn his cheek towards those who struck it, although he told us plainly, quoting those very words, that he must and we must. It was my brother who taught me.

We went in the second summer on a long journey through the coasts of Tyre and Sidon, eastwards to Caesarea Philippi, and southwards towards Decapolis, through my home country, the steep hinterland of Bethsaida. It was a terrible journey. He was teaching us all the way, under one image after another, that he must soon die. None of us was willing to understand what he meant, all of us sought one loophole after another, refusing to accept his words, while patiently and inexorably he led us through the lonely mountains and drove it home. We were filled with sadness and fear. I was thinking, "Why do you not fight to win, like the other Joshua? Why do you silence God's thunder before his fire has fallen? Why do you not blast the unbelievers? Why do you 'whisper in the dark' and tell us to 'shout it from the housetops'—why don't you shout it yourself, from the housetops, from the Temple top? Why do you not crack open our deafness with your word of power?"

So it was with a strange hesitation that I said to him one evening, "Master, we are nearing my home village. I have a brother who is deaf and has forgotten how to speak. Will you lay your hands upon him and speak to him? For there is no man else who can open his ears." I was secretly adding, "Oh Master, can you, can even you?"

Jesus looked hard at me and said sternly, "Bring him to me when we come there."

I rose early next day and went on ahead to the village. I was received, not indeed with welcome, but with a flicker of curiosity; children ran out and shrieked at my travel-dusty face, my mother asked where I'd been jaunting off to (though she didn't wait to hear), my father asked if I'd brought them anything. Seizing the moment, I said, "I have brought you the word of God." As their eyes dulled and they turned away, I caught my brother's sleeve and cried, "And there is one here who will hear it!" And brief amazement showed in their faces and made them look again at me; made them appear in all their doorways when Jesus and the other eleven came striding into the village.

"Master," I cried, running out and kneeling, "here is my brother, deaf since childhood." I beckoned to Joset to follow me, but he stood still as a pillar of salt by the house, and Jesus stood looking at him over my head. I shivered at the tense silence, the hostility, the watching eyes, the two still figures, the air charged with thunder. Then Jesus went to him, took his arm, and led him away from those eyes, between two houses and into a grain field. The Twelve moved uneasily after him, but the faces at doors and on rooftops fell and turned away. Jesus could not break that monstrous indifference. He was concentrating all his power on breaking one man's deafness. As we watched, hovering in the alley, he was gripping my brother's head, so that their eyes must meet, pressing his hands into his ears; then he seemed to kiss him on the mouth; through every sense, through every organ, that power and that urgency were dinning into my brother, and still I saw from Joset's dangling hands that he was refusing it.

Shout! I was crying in my mind, oh, shout with the word of God and break him open!

But Jesus did not shout. Not since babyhood can my brother have been dealt with so gently, caressed like a child and faced without anger. And what was the good? None, we were all thinking as we watched. We saw Jesus, almost defeated as it seemed, turn my brother's head down and look up to heaven, his lips moving in urgent prayer; we saw the strain and sorrow in his face, and his shoulders heaved with a deep sigh. Then he looked back into my brother's eyes and said, "Open now."

Joset's hands twitched, one jerkily began to move; he was raising it, raising them both, they were on Jesus' shoulders, he was clutching at him and crying out hoarsely, "God my saviour! God my saviour!" He was weeping, something I had never seen, and fell suddenly on his knees with his hands still raised as though he would cling to heaven itself, praying aloud through sobs, the same words again and again, "God my saviour! O God my saviour!" Yeshua, Yeshua, Jesus' own name. Then Joset was weeping and kissing Jesus' feet, but Jesus raised him up and spoke softly to him; and I knew suddenly that my twin was hearing him as I never had.

The release, the breaking, had burst through all the village. People were pressing up behind us now, their eyes alight with wonder, exclaiming in voices of awe, treading on each other to see better. I heard my mother burst into noisy sobs of joy. But then I looked back at Jesus, and remembered how he had sighed. He was still standing speaking to my brother as though they two were alone in the world. And I understood that we had all shouted at my brother in hate and fear, but Jesus had spoken to him in love, and in that same moment I understood that he loved his people, he loved Israel, that was all his urgency and his gentleness. He had come out from Nazareth to cry to them and to suffer their rejection because he loved them, as I did not. For he was a man in the image of God, full of mercy and pity, and his silence was the silence of listening. When he stood before my brother while he dangled his hands, he had been listening. When he let his message seem to die away, and went uncomprehended among the people, he was listening. And so God listens in silence and love to his own and lets them reject him.

It was in vain that I understood that this was the strongest word of all in the end, that this very silence and suffering is God's word to us after all, that he too is ceaselessly saying, "Ephphatha. Open." I was weeping as freely as my brother because I knew now that Jesus must die. He will break his heart to break ours open. I saw it happen, already, that day, in my village of stony ground.

26

ITCHING

OSIAS THE MEANSTER was asking to be lynched. Of all
the tax-collectors in Judaea he was the worst, and that's saying
a lot. Once he'd got his claws in he just went on digging till
you either gave up the fight or gave up the ghost. Who knows
how many families he's ruined? He went too far when he
cheated me and Samson my brother on the eve of a festival.
He should have known better. He was asking for it, I tell you.
He knew we were a rough family. It's as though in a way he had
his claws into himself by then—even when he saw danger he
couldn't draw back. He must have known we'd kill him if he
squeezed us any more, yet he went on squeezing; as though he
were frightened to stop. What do you make of a man like that?
He was less afraid of dying than of easing off his victims. Or
maybe he just couldn't, he was past it. I don't know. There have
been tax-collectors—"leeches" is the name we use—there have
been leeches who came off it. Jesus the Nazarene used to convert
them. He liked them. He was always their buddy. He was
buddies with Osias the Meanster too; used to go to his house
when he came up to Jersualem. But there was no biting there.
It would have killed Osias to do what Zacchaeus of Jericho did.
Well, he kept on doing the opposite, so we killed him instead,
or nearly. Tabernacles time it was. It's easier to lose your temper
to murder point on a festival. He should've known not to black-
mail on the eve of a festival. . . .

I thought we'd killed him. Day and a half he lay there in the
street. Nobody comes up our street except who has business to,
you know. We all just watched him and the dogs—they'd take
care of the body. Come to think of it, that should have warned us
that he wasn't dead, that they left him alone. Or maybe he would
have poisoned them. But it was good to see him just lying there
is his own blood. Did me good to stand on the roof and watch.

That's what I was doing, when late in the second evening a man in a pale cloak comes along—somebody from outside our circle. I took care not to look interested, but I got my sling ready in my pocket (oh, David would be proud of us boys of the Lower City!). Then I realized that someone had tipped someone off, because here he was making straight for the body. Well, there was nothing on it, so if it was a relative, he might as well have it, mightn't he? But then I thought, well, who'd have thought Osias would have had any relative so fond of him, or friend either?

Because while I watched, the stranger bent down and clasped him tightly in his arms as though his heart would break; like a mother cuddling her baby boy! I was amazed, till he turned slightly and I saw it was you-know-who, as I might have guessed, though even so it was funny, because he hadn't converted Osias, nor was likely to. Osias couldn't change, not even for the Leeches' Friend. Yet there you are, I saw him hugging the old man, doubled up with grief.

I did, then, sling a pebble down, not to hit him, but just gently to touch the wall beside him, to warn him off. I wasn't in a mood to kill really, not again so soon. But he looked up at me with such a look of sorrow and anger I couldn't have slung again if I'd tried. I couldn't move! And he picks up old Mean Osias, slings him over his shoulder, and carries him off—while I pulled myself together and ran down to the street, in time to follow and see him turn into the stables of the inn we call the Dungheap because it's right by the Dung Gate. So then I knew that the dogs and I had lost Osias for the time being.

I was beginning to get angry by now. I went to find my brother Samson, and he was angrier. We stood outside the Dungheap shouting threats, but no good. The people in that inn were a hundred per cent under the Nazarene's thumb. They kept Osias and nursed him—nursed him! At their expense, too, or the Nazarene's, since we'd left him clean. They smuggled him out of Jerusalem eventually. Last we heard of him, he was up in Galilee—extorting. Jesus could have brought him back from the dead, and he'd have gone on extorting.

So then why didn't he leave him to us? Eh? Who had suffered by him, who'd been bled by him? Didn't we have a right to repay in kind? In fact, it was cheating us to send him up to Galilee. And the more I thought about it the more I regretted that warning stone I'd slung. I wished I'd simply stolen down and put a knife into that pale-cloaked back bent so agonizedly over Mean Osias. Really, it was asking for a knife, that back. Asking. He was asking for it. I itched to have done it. All winter, I was itching. Anyone so good is asking for it, he's going to make somebody itch.

So what was there for me to decide when the oily-haired fellow from the priests came down our street calling out a silver piece for anyone who'd shout "Crucify the Nazarene"? And it was festival time, too: itching time. Jesus should have known. He was asking for it.

27

THE FALLING OF THE DARK

HE TALKED AGAIN about the coming night that evening. A sombreness seemed to have fallen over him ever since they nearly stoned him in the Temple. "Twelve hours of daylight," he would sigh, "and then the night; I must work while there is light; and how short the time is, how little achieved. . . . " It was to my sister Mary he would mostly say things like that; nothing frightened her, she understood him too well. But to me he would say, "There is nothing hidden, Lazarus, that shall not be made known, and nothing buried, that shall not be uncovered. Don't be afraid." For he knew that I felt the darkness coming as well as he.

But I think he forgot that we had not all his strength. He could go calmly forward in face of anything, it seemed. But I felt the shadows falling and was overwhelmed. The powers of evil could not crush him, but they could crush us, they were crushing me.

That last evening before he escaped into hiding up north, we held a subdued little farewell feast, but I could scarcely eat. It was winter, too cold to sit in the courtyard. I cannot rid myself even now of the image of him in the light of the brazier, which made his eyes flash strangely as he talked, though his face was sad; and the Twelve, and the rest of us, sitting round in the flickering shadows, so puzzled, so uneasy. And as for me, the pain had come unmistakably, grinding and eating at my heart; no hopeful blaming of Martha's over-generous garlic was possible this time. I was afraid. Yet it was not that fear, or the pain, which was causing me anguish of spirit, but fear and pain for him; a black and nameless terror of the dark. I slipped out in the end into the cold wind, thankful for it in a way, and sat on the steps looking out towards Jerusalem, praying that neither he nor Mary would follow me: I could not hide things from them.

Martha, at least, would believe me if I said I was wanting a breath of air.

I could see the lights of Jerusalem across the flank of the Mount of Olives, and below me, the white glimmer of the chalky road. I have been watching this road all my life, I was sitting on the steps as I had sat since I was a child; all my boyhood was around me, yet now it seemed strange and frightening, the road twisting away into doom, and the dark hanging over Jerusalem. The Master's words kept coming into my mind, and they all seemed sinister now: "Keep awake, I say; I am warning you; keep your lamp burning. Don't let sleep overtake you, for you never know when the hour will be. And keep your eyes clear; for if the light in you is darkness, how great that darkness will be. . . ."

I remembered the time I had said to him, "Nothing can ever be the same now again. Either Israel will be saved for ever, and you will be king, or destroyed for ever, and you with it." And he had smiled, and said, "I have not lit a lamp to put it under a tub; what man would? And shall my heavenly Father's word come back to him void?" But I thought now, watching the first lights of the city go out, it may come back to him having destroyed; for his anger will be against us if the lamp is smothered after all; and we are smothering it.

I groaned aloud, partly with pain, whose gnawing was increasing, and was startled as an arm was flung over my shoulders and a voice beside me said, "Is it that bad, then?" It took me a minute to recognize the friendly, gap-toothed grin I could just see in the light from the house. It was Reuben, the old beggar whose sight had been restored by the Master, who was now inseparable from him and followed him everywhere. I could not help smiling at the sight of him, and also a little, disloyally, at the memory of Martha's perpetual discomfiture as the Master brings in one after another of these filthy, stinking protégés of his. She's given up complaining now. Reuben pulled her leg too often. She says he has no respect for God or man. This makes him and Jesus smile broadly at one another, and the little old fellow's eyes dance like black flies with mirth.

I said to him now, "I've got a bit of a pain, that's all."

"You what?" he said. "Remember I came outer that pool with eyes that I could see wiv! Don't you try to fool me."

So I admitted, "Yes, I'm depressed. It just feels like darkness falling everywhere. I simply can't see how we'll win. I suppose he can last a little while living in hiding . . . just another Galilean outlaw . . ."

"And what else did King David do, and isn't he a chip and a half off the old block?"

"And it's true, of course," I said, sitting up, "that God made all things out of nothing, and the task of the Messiah is to bring to light the hidden things of darkness . . ." But as I said that, the words seemed to close in on me, burying me: darkness, darkness. There would never be any light. It was like a stone slab falling on me, shutting out the sky, shutting out hope. I found myself shuddering and burying my face in my hands.

Straight away old Reuben was gently slapping my shoulders and saying, "But he'll do it, sonny. He is doing it. You're forgetting I've been in worser dark than what you can think of. Fifty years, I didn't know what seeing was. 'Light?' I used to say. 'Can you eat it? Can you drink it? Then you can keep it!' I couldn't imagine it, see. But now, Martha gives me a plate of victuals and I mutter 'Doesn't exactly shine, does it?' You take my word for it, there ain't nothin' comin' that he hasn't got taped."

I laughed. "I'd love to take your word for it, Reuben!"

The tease suddenly went out of those merry black eyes; they became intense, fixed on mine; Reuben said, "Don't you remember what the prophet says? I don't suppose you even notice what's read in synagogue—but a blind man remembers what he hears." He broke into Hebrew, in a high, nasal singsong, strangely impressive. "It is too little that you should be my servant to raise up the tribes of Jacob; I will also give you for a light to the Gentiles, to the end of the earth; you shall say to the prisoners, Go forth; to them that are in darkness, Show yourselves." He lapsed into his normal speech, yet still with that dreamy excitement, as though his new sight were indeed visionary. "That's him, don't you know it? The light of the world. And opener of the prisons. That's for you, p'raps."

"What prison? What do you mean?" I cried, alarmed.

He ignored me. "And you know what else he said? That the only reason I'd ever been blind was so's I'd see the glory of God all the better. Punishment for sin, indeed! I was the luckiest man in Jerusalem, though I grant you I didn't know it then. I *seen* him. I seen him better than you ever have. That's what he said. Well, we was sorter pulling each other's leg, you know how we do. We been at it right from the start. When he first comes up—'Do you believe in the son of God?' he says. 'Well,' says I, 'who's he then?'—knowing well enough of course, but I couldn't say it right away like that. 'You can see 'im,' he says, larking back. Well, you know all that story. I'm trying to say that I think only a blind man, someone who's been blind, can really see him. None of you lot can properly at all yet. Lumme, you're so dead worried about him! But you will, though. You will. Oi, I'm as stiff as an old shutter. Come on in out of this wind, sonny. You won't do yourself no good sittin' here looking at them lights go out."

He may have been right. But I did not follow him. I sat on, watching, as he said, the city lights go out, unable by any stretch of the mind to think how the triumph of darkness could be to the glory of God. The wind ate into me, and the pain.

Death came up the road that night with both his hands held out, one to Jesus, and one to me.

28

IN THE WAY

IT HAS BECOME such a strange, strange journey. We set out cheerfully enough on what seemed like just another of our tramps to preach the Good News. True, we did realize, I suppose, the risk of bringing it to Jerusalem, with all we had met there so recently and with Passover so close. But Jesus had gone up there twice now in danger of his life and got away with it—the last time was at the end of this past winter when Lazarus died—and I'd come to believe that the Jerusalemites had no power to harm him really. I thought we'd shaken off the gloom that hung over us that last winter at Bethany, before we were forced into hiding, when it had been so cold and the Master had seemed so sad, and Lazarus—well, Lazarus was dying, as we know now. He was a few weeks from his death, or from his life if you like. So that's all right, I was saying to myself. That's all it was, and Lazarus is raised now, so that's all right, isn't it?

We were in good spirits, setting out now for Jerusalem, except Gloomy Thomas of course. There was the usual larking around at the start. I said I wouldn't walk with Simon any more because he sings loud psalms out of tune, and Bartholomew thanked God he hadn't a brother with him, so Simon and I and the sons of Zebedee knocked the heads of the rest of them together. And then when we looked up there was the Master ahead of us already, ignoring us, striding on along the white dusty road, and somehow all the laughter went. I don't know what there was about him then, but somehow I can't get the picture out of mind—that tiny, striding figure, as white as the road with many days' dust, going forward with the mass of barren, jutting hills seeming to hang above him, burnt rock under that terrible Judaean sky: fiery blue it seemed against those mountains, and it was only the morning. If I were a man of Judah I could scarcely believe that God's throne is up there;

nor yet that those cruel mountains could be his footstool. I was suddenly frightened to be going into them; they were too harsh, too inhuman, without pity or place for man. I remembered how the Master had spent a long time of fasting among them once, and then seeing him dwindling against them as he strode on I was all at once afraid of him too. It seemed to me that I had never known him, that he was utterly a stranger among us.

All twelve of us, I think we were caught in the same fear. We hurried on together, forgetting our pairings, in a ragged, stumbling group, half-way to panic. Yet we did not catch up with the Master until nightfall. I don't know when he stopped to eat—perhaps he did not. When we halted and camped at last he went away into the darkness while we prepared supper, to pray alone. We scarcely spoke, let alone sang. The tougher of our camp-followers began to creep up in the shadows, those amazing women grimly hanging on, marching like men, and they too had caught the atmosphere: not one of them called out the greeting of peace to us as they arrived, but their eyes fearfully searched the darkness around for Jesus.

When he came back at last he said: "You know we are going up to Jerusalem. But you don't understand what is going to happen there. The Son of Man must be given up to the elders and scribes."

"Oh, Master, don't get involved with them! You'll never persuade them! You know the Pharisees hate you!" burst out Simon.

"Yes, and little do you know how much. The Son of Man is going to be rejected by his people. But God shall vindicate his suffering." He said the last words thoughtfully, looking into the fire, but they were no comfort to us; everything he said made him seem more and more strange, alien, a man of God, alone and far from us.

James and John were the only ones who talked about it. "See his kingship on him!" they were saying in low voices. "See the power already on him! It can only mean that he's going to Jerusalem to receive his kingdom. That's what he meant." And as though to assert their familiarity with him, they chose that night of all nights to ask for the seats at his right and left hand in his kingdom: as though daring his lonely reserve, wanting to prove that they at least were not afraid of him. I didn't in fact hear them do it. I was lost in my own thoughts, gazing at the cliffs around us against the stars, thinking about the patriarchs who had journeyed here, Rachel who had died not far from here, David who had come up in war here to take Jerusalem, and then later come bringing the ark in festivity; thinking of our many journeys with Jesus, till it seemed as though our whole life with him, and his life come to that, were one great journey. And I thought of Israel in the wilderness, and how we are supposed to consider ourselves still wanderers in it; we have to live in huts and shelters at Tabernacles to remind ourselves that we are still on our journey. That's what I was thinking about when the Master's voice interrupted my thoughts, and I became aware that there was a buzz of annoyance going on, and James and John were standing very upright, looking bright-eyed and angry in the firelight, while their mother—that marvellous old battle-axe—shrank away beside them with her arm up to cover her face. But the Master was saying, "You do not understand what you are asking. Can you drink the cup that I must drink, or be baptized with the baptism I must be baptized with?"

"We can," they answered doggedly.

"You shall indeed drink my cup, and share my baptism," he said, grimly, "but as for seats at my right and left hand—that's not for me to grant, but for my Father to give to whomever he's chosen."

Before we could break out in indignation against James and John, the Master had turned to us and was speaking to us all: "The Gentiles have lordship and power over each other, but that's not how it is to be with you. Among you the greatest must be the lowest servant, and your leader must be the willing slave of all. For the Son of Man did not come to be served, either, but to serve, and to give his life as a ransom for many."

Then he turned away from us, and we lay down in silence round the fire, but for a long time I saw wide-eyed faces turned upwards staring into the night.

I had journeys on the brain. All night, every time I woke, I thought I was late to harness the camels, that the tribes had gone on and left me, that I was seeing gallopers vanishing into mirage and sun. Distance, distance, the great hills swimming; the fear of leaving the water. The fear of going on beyond the last well; who knew what lay ahead? Barren plains and mountains swimming, and always the water left behind; there was never any real question; the distance was the call, the water must be left behind. . . . What did the Master dream of? Of Jerusalem perhaps, of the end of the journey for him? I know it was constantly in his mind.

We had left most of the rest of the party far behind, except for the few women who had managed to keep up with us. When I suggested we leave some message for them at one of the villages along the Jordan valley, he seemed to sigh, and said almost reluctantly, "We will wait for them at Jericho. But how I long to reach Jerusalem! For that is my real goal. Where else could a prophet end?"

He more and more often spoke like that: so that I didn't understand, and was afraid to understand.

So we went on down the hot valley, with the arid highlands rising sheer on each side of us, not knowing what we were going into, except that it would be a Passover like none other in our lives; and I thought back beyond Moses and Jacob to Abraham, our first father, who had gone out from his home and his kindred into a life of wandering at God's call. Perhaps he, too, had sometimes thought it more a land of threat than a land of promise, perhaps he had been afraid. Did he ever guess how much wandering he and his children would have to do, how long the journey would be? A long, long journey up to Jerusalem. And at Jerusalem what?

We had travelled too fast for crowds of the usual size to collect, though word began to go ahead of us now, and as we came to the towns and villages the sick would be already laid out, so that the Master could touch them as he passed. But there's only one incident that really came through into my dazed mind. It was outside Jericho, when as we were entering the gate, surrounded by now with a joyful procession, mostly of children, a great yelling arose from somewhere—we couldn't see where—in a cracked old voice.

He was bawling out, "Son of David, have pity on me! Son of David, have pity on me!"

Jesus stopped, half laughing and half not, and said, "Who's that? Tell him to come here!"

More hubbub, and then up came hobbling an old blind fellow, a grin splitting his face in two.

"Now, then, what do you want of me?" asked our Master.

"Son of David! Lantern of the Lord! Light of Israel!"

"Well?"

"Was it not said, 'His seed shall endure for ever, and his throne as the sun before me'? Sun of Judah and Jerusalem, give me sight!"

And Jesus was very pleased, though he didn't usually like to be called Son of David. "As you have believed, so it shall be done for you!" he said. And the man broke into cackling whoops of joy. "I see the light! I see the light!"

The people who had wanted to keep him quiet can have been no better pleased when he was healed. He followed us singing at the top of his broken voice and waving his cloak in the air, breaking out into praises and hosannas, all the way to Jerusalem. He's dropped behind a bit now out of sheer exhaustion, but I can still see him capering along, a mile or so behind. Whenever one of his yells reaches us, Jesus smiles, preoccupied as he is. He loves that old man.

Journeys and processions . . . A comical, raggle-taggle lot we are, to set us beside David or Abraham. But when I remember that crazy old chap's words, it makes me think. "They told me Jesus of Nazareth was passing by," he said. "So then I knew that my light was come."

And what was it said of Abraham? "In you shall all the nations of the earth be blessed."

Here come the children, though. Bethphage in sight. . . . It'll be good to see old Lazarus again. Wonder how he is. Stop woolgathering, Andrew. Get ready for another procession, no doubt. Master? yes? find you a donkey? you want to ride in on a donkey? right . . . Master—everything's been so strange—but it's all right now, isn't it? See how glad the children are to see you. It's going to be all right, isn't it?

29

THE LAME AND THE BLIND

Son of David indeed! Think I'd have yelled like that for any Son of David? We've had enough bad kings for one little country. Even David, mark you, was no friend to anyone north of Judah. He couldn't hold the country together even in his lifetime. No! The only king I'm shouting for is God on his throne, I can tell you that. One generation of my family was wiped out under the Maccabees; the next under old Herod; and I had a leg crushed by a fancy Greek pillar falling on me when I was slave-labourer to young Herod on the fancy palace he was putting up at our expense. Which incidentally meant I'd seen the inside of the Temple for the last time, since they don't let cripples in: not at all, theoretically, but in practice the priests let us come into the outer courts so as to make sure we buy their pigeons for sacrifice and don't have any excuse to bring our own. Because do you know what else we can thank good king David for? "The lame and the blind shall never come in here!" he declared when he captured Jerusalem, because, so they say, it used to belong to some race of people who were all lame and blind: the Jebusites, was it? And they put up such a good defence against old David that he lost his temper and made this rule against anyone who was handicapped. "He hated them in his soul," that's what Scripture says, and decreed that they must be cut off from the Lord. I believe he even got it put in the Law—not sure about that, though; but anyway, it's Temple law.

Mind you, the Temple itself was only put up by old Herod to ingratiate himself with the priests and Levites. No! I don't want no sons of David, neither usurping nor legitimate. Now I've got carried away. What I'm really angry about, it's the way the people's hopes in David have been exploited by the nationalists. All those poor cobs who faithfully follow any wild son of

David who turns up and get crucified on top of every hill for their pains. I used to think, when Messiah comes, a pretty kettle of fish he'll find to sort out. Three-quarters of the people shouting for the son of David, and the other quarter yelling "Not at any price!" But what about a real son of David who agreed with the second lot? Eh? How would that fit? Someone who put David in his place? I'll be chuckling at night for a long time over what the Prophet of Nazareth said in the Temple this morning. He just pointed out that in the Psalms David calls the Messiah "my Lord". Son of David, my foot! *Lord* of David! Hosanna to the Lord of David! And for anyone with old-fashioned ideas, he's son of David right enough, born in Bethlehem if it comes to that. But worth a hundred Davids. Ah! I knew it the minute I saw him.

I was sitting out by the Bethany road begging, next that unpleasant old so-and-so who says he was a paralytic up at Bethesda for thirty-eight years. Well, that's as may be, but he isn't a paralytic now, so why he can't get up and do a job of work beats me, but there you are, perhaps he only ever was darned lazy. There are too many of us who have to be beggars without the able-bodied sunbathing for alms on their mats beside them. Evenings, he used to pick up his mat and go home, but all day long he just sat on it. It certainly did look as though it had had forty years' wear, I will say that in support of his story, but if that's what a cure does for you, I'll keep my gammy leg, thanks. That's what I used to think, anyway.

Well, that Sunday, we were there begging as usual (it being the only shady spot for a quarter of a mile), when we heard such a din in the distance as made us both prick our ears. And when we heard what they were shouting (they were kids' voices, so they carried a good way), then we did sit up. It was "Hosanna to the Son of David". I may not have felt enthusiastic but I was quite curious. Then round the bend from Bethany come all these children dancing along, and the excitement was somehow catching. You found yourself thinking, "Well, supposing the Kingdom were really coming, just suppose, eh?" And I did let out a shout, not for no son of David but for God on his throne.

And then there came into view the Nazarene on an ass. "Daughter of Zion, see your king coming to you meekly on an ass", you know. It meant he saw himself as a peaceful king, which was a nice change; all the phoney Messiahs and sons of David so far have had one thing in mind—war with Rome—which is what lands their followers on crosses. So I liked the look of that ass and gave a Hosanna or so for the peaceful rule of God. But I wasn't taking any of it seriously, was I? No. But not so old Taddai next me on his mat. He stared as though the eyes were being pulled out of his head. Then up he jumps yelling Hosanna! fit to burst, and looks round at me to shout, "It's him! He who cured me! It's the real Messiah!" And there was that in his face, gave me a sort of shiver. I mean, he'd been such a disagreeable neighbour, and now he was all splitting and busting with joy. And he grabbed his mat, that disgusting object, and flung it down in the donkey's path for his hero to tread on.

Somehow that really touched me. I felt as though I were watching the un-paralysing of the rest of him. Well, that may have been what happened; I mean, if the first thing I ever saw of the Nazarene was a miracle, that would explain why I felt what I did about him. Which was sudden passionate joy. I caught it from old Taddai, who was running alongside the donkey now yelling "Hosanna!" as though he thought they were hard of hearing in heaven. I saw the Prophet of Nazareth give him such a grin, that suddenly I was laughing my head off and hopping alongside the donkey now bawling Hosanna to God on high and the king of peace!

Taddai had started something, because now everyone started flinging their cloaks and things down the way he had his mat, and the kids scaled the palms which provided our shady begging-pitch and threw branches down. Someone stuck a piece of palm into my hand, so then I had something to cheer properly with—it helped me keep my balance too, And on we went, a procession of beggars and children gone mad with joy because the Healing Prophet of Nazareth was coming to town. We didn't care what anyone thought. When some dressed-up Levites came barging through, shouting to the Prophet, "Don't you hear what they're singing? You mustn't allow it!" he answered, "I hear well enough. Have you never read the Scripture, 'Out of the mouth of babes and infants you have brought forth perfect praise'? I tell you, if these here keep silence, the very stones will cry aloud." And so they would have—we could have told them that! He didn't mind what noise we made, the Prophet didn't. Perfect praise he reckoned it was.

And yet in all that racket of welcome and hosannas I looked up as we came to the city, and there were tears running down his face; he was in tears over Jerusalem; I saw it plain as plain. And it touched something else in me to see that, something much deeper down. It was the beginning of realizing that this "Son of David" would have sympathy with the real sufferings of the people, and not just force them into war with Rome for his own glory. He was humble, that's what he was; and that's what gave away that here was a really great one.

I had to fall behind soon after that. I couldn't keep up, not hopping. (I'd lost my crutch along the road somewhere.) But just that short ride in triumph—some triumph!—and watching what had happened to old Taddai, and then seeing him in tears, was enough to make me decide. "He'll do as king," I remember thinking. "I'd trust him with the power." Because I saw he'd never make himself king—which is the mistake all the sons of David make, forgetting that even David never did that. It was God who made David king. And I believe he has made this one, the Nazarene, David's lord, our true king, our king in his sight: a king too wise to seize any regalia but the kids' palm branches and Taddai's mat.

And that won't please the other three-quarters—or it may be nearer nine-tenths—who want nothing better than a fighting great son of David. Eh, it might have been a sight safer if he had only let the stones sing hosanna. . . .

Well, we saw him in another mood today! And if I'd not seen the palm procession I'd have loved him for this. He and I are of a mind, it seems, not only over sons of David, but over Temples like sinks. When I say I loathe the sight of the Temple, that's not meant as disrespect to God's footstool. It's because it means old Herod to me, and money squeezed out of our blood, and a priesthood like filthy leeches on our people. Is God honoured by that, I ask? Is our Temple as it has been the sacred place of his coming, the pure sanctuary of his holiness? What used you to see there? Cherubim and Seraphim? Or mean-faced and fat-bellied Levites at their dirty little booths all round the Court of the Gentiles and filling the gate? The only acceptable sacrifice of praise? Or the only doves passed for sacrifice, selling at the price of a man's livelihood for a week? What did you hear as you got inside the outer gates? Holy, Holy, Holy? Or the yapping cries of the money-changers, the swearing and flattering of the sellers of the sacrificial animals?

Not, I suppose, that I need care. I'm cut off from the presence of the Lord, aren't I, since I was crippled. But I do care—for God's honour. That filthy blot in the middle of his holy people where his Name should be sanctified! I can't think of it without such bitterness that I can almost taste it. And I've prayed every day for the last thirty years that God would be quick with sending his angel to purify the sons of Levi, because, by my soul, they need it.

And I saw it! I saw him do it! The Lord came most suddenly to his Temple, and caught them right on the hop! I was laughing and crying for delight and bitterness—the same as he was feeling, I know that—when the Holy One from Nazareth purged the Temple courts just like the very angel of vengeance himself. I'll never forget him, single-handedly clearing the place with shouts of wrath, driving the cattle out, overturning the tables of the money-changers. "Take these things out!" he said. "My Father's house is meant to be a place of prayer for all nations, not a den of thieves." And he swept them all out! He did! No-one could stand up to him or answer him. He had the fire of God in him. I was hopping in the gate, cheering and weeping. That I should see the true son of David come to David's city and build the true Temple, which Solomon did not! Solomon's Temple must have been a wicked Temple too, or God would have not destroyed it. If David had built his own it would have been the same. But the Holy One who has come to us now will build a righteous one at last. I know he will. It is why he has been sent to us: to be our true David, our king of peace, to restore all that is fallen and cleanse all that is evil. It is written in his face. They saw it, they knew it, those filthy swindlers at their booths; they went and were glad to get out of his presence; I saw them running from the Temple as fast as their fat legs would carry them.

Then the Temple saw what must have been its first real sacrifice of praise since it was built. Jesus sealed off the entrances with his disciples, so that the precincts could no longer be used as a thoroughfare for goods traffic (which they had been constantly), and called in, instead—who do you think? The lame and the blind. God be praised, a greater than David had come to his own city to change David's warfare into peace, and to open the gates to the lame and the blind. God be praised for his blessed messenger, the prince of peace! And those poor devils of Gentiles, too, when they saw what they thought of as the Temple staff running away, they dared to come into the Temple, into their own Gentiles' Court, where they'd never been too welcome before. But they seemed to sense they were being welcomed now. A house of prayer for all nations! Yes, it might be, if Jesus were king and high priest too. Hosanna to the friend of cripples and outsiders! We came to him freely, fearlessly, all of us who had begged in the gates so long, and he healed us. We came in limping, we ended up dancing. We did indeed! You'd never believe it if you hadn't been there! Poor Misael, who has sat begging so long in the Gate Beautiful, he doesn't believe it at all. He's down with fever in the wine-seller's house by the Dung Gate. I went to see him to tell him that the Lord of David has come to Jerusalem, and show him my new leg, but he doesn't believe his own eyes, let alone my story. He says I must have fever too, because it sounds like delirium to him. The Temple empty of our task-masters, nobody there but the common people, the beggars and the cripples, dancing and praising God in all the courts to the singing of children! Have we ever seen anything like it? Shall we ever again before the Kingdom comes? I only know that it was true, and it was like being in the Kingdom already, on that blessed day when the Lord visited his Temple.

At the end of the afternoon the priests pulled themselves together, and came nervously to ask the Prophet who he was and what he was doing. "Would you destroy the worship that is offered here as God commanded us?" they asked. (For they were scared stiff.) And he answered very seriously, "I am not destroying the Temple: it is you yourselves who will do that. This Temple is doomed, because you are bent on pulling it down. I am the one who will raise it up, a new temple, not made with hands; yes, and in a very little while."

You should have seen their eyes gleam when he said that. "Blasphemy! Sorcery!" you could see them thinking, framing the charge in their minds already. So beginning to grow bolder they told him he must declare his authority to speak and act like this.

"I'll tell you if you tell me one thing first," he said. "The baptism of John: was it from heaven or men?" Now, you'll notice they did not even ask themselves what was the truth. They'd have liked to say, "From men", but they were too frightened of the people. So they said they couldn't answer, and Jesus said, "Then neither will I answer you."

Heaven is written all over him, same as it was over John! We—the common folk—shouted for glee at the way he'd caught them out; but those priests went away with murder in their hearts.

And yet there were those among the ordinary people, even then, who started muttering, "All right, let's see this power from heaven." There were those, even then, that best day in the Temple's existence, who were ready enough to turn against him if he didn't play their game. I wouldn't be surprised if one day we saw those professional troublemakers and the priests ganging up together against him. Ironic, it may seem; but I haven't begged in the streets and gates of Jerusalem for thirty years without learning something of the hate in the place, simmering. We're a proud people, that's our trouble, and we've been humiliated too long; we've seen our holy city stuffed with triumphant pagans too long; our own kings have ground us down, our harvests have failed, our summers are too hot, our little nation too helpless. And all that bitterness has got to explode somewhere. It could explode against the priests—it often enough has. But the priests themselves hate better than anybody. I think it may explode against a king who rides in on an ass and will not consent to be David's son, but purifies the filthy Temple. If he should find all the hate of Judaea levelled against him . . . all those different hates, concentrated, levelled. . . .

Then who will be left to be subjects of the king of righteousness? The lame and the blind! The lame and the blind! They're the only ones who will enter this kingdom, because they're the only ones poor enough to want it. The lame and the blind! The beggars and the children! Hosanna to the Lord of David from the lame and the blind; hosanna, hosanna!

30
THE WINGED HORSE

WHEN MY FRIEND Xanthippus, who had become a proselyte of the Jewish religion, told me he was going on a pilgrimage to Jerusalem for their great spring festival of Passover, I announced I would come with him. Always I had been interested in the Jews, in their tenacity and their "one true God" and their faith in him, and how could I, who was a seeker for none but God, afford to neglect them or regard them with contempt, as some do? I would go to Jerusalem, I said, and try to learn whether perhaps their God was indeed the Beautiful Itself, the True Itself, which is the quest of my life. "I can learn from their faith, if not their manners," I said.

The evening before I left my house to join Xanthippus at Piraeus, I sat long with Agathon's vase in my hands, brooding. I had loved him long ago and he gave it me before he died. It showed the monstrous chimaera threatening Lycia, with Pegasus in flight, poised above it, and on the other side the free, untamed Pegasus stamping on Mount Helicon where his stream Hippocrene gushed out. Pegasus in his fierceness and strength and Pegasus in his grace. I thought, "The beautiful must be the wholly free. Perfect form must be the freedom from any constraint. It is truth which shapes all things, it is not shaped by them. Is this what the Jews mean by God?"

In the temple of Athene in my home city of Apollonia there was a frieze again showing the winged horse, who was tamed and ridden at her command but afterwards threw and maimed his rider. Always, from my childhood, the winged horse on that frieze had moved me more than any of the gods or heroes. I could honour that horse as I could honour none of them, in the perfection of its form, the unity of air and earth, spirit and body, symbolized by the glorious raised wings. I think I have been seeking the winged horse ever since, as though I would ride it even if it killed me.

We came to the land of the Jews, harsh enough by any standard, and I talked to every wise man, teacher and priest whom I could meet. Still I came to no conclusion, though I went every day to their Temple with Xanthippus. "How can they be both so ignorant and so wise?" I thought. "Why do they slave to serve their God in a multitude of laws, and never ask if he is not the principle of all beauty, the form of utter truth, which is so far beyond food laws and prayer rites? How can they say that to serve him is enough for them, and they are not concerned to enquire into his nature?"

While we were there, there was much talk of a wandering teacher who seemed greatly to have shocked some of the Jewish leaders, though I could not tell why, except that he had broken the Sabbath. I was interested in the reports of his doing which I heard, for he sounded like a second Asclepius: said to have the power of healing, he was going about opening the eyes of the blind and driving sickness and death away. I could tell he was an enlightener. I spoke to a man who had followed him in the northern province of Galilee, and he told me, that if I would really learn about the God of Israel, I must watch and hear Jesus of Nazareth, for he was possessed by his spirit. I had in Greece heard of possession by a god, usually Dionysus, although I thought that the truth was rather perhaps that such men beheld the divine more clearly than others, so clearly that it was seen itself in them, making them seem strange and even mad to the earthbound. For men can be intoxicated by beauty; indeed they can. Jesus, then, perhaps beheld the ultimate truth and goodness, perhaps even showed it himself, and this was the secret of his healing power. "How can I meet him?" I asked my informant, and was told he would surely come to keep the feast at Jerusalem. A few days later, the same man came running up to me and Xanthippus in excitement at one of the Temple gates and cried, "There he is, Jesus of Nazareth, with his disciples!" and vanished.

It was impossible either to see or approach him through the crowd, but Xanthippus and I managed to speak to two of the disciples. Indeed, we would not have wanted to approach him directly. Instead we sent a message to him by these men (who spoke a barbaric Greek), asking to speak with him.

The two disciples came to our lodging in the evening with a carefully rehearsed answer, courteously phrased in a typical Greek metaphor.

"The seed must fall into the ground and die before it can bear fruit."

We bowed and thanked the Teacher through his messengers. We thought we understood. The time was not ripe for him, as a Jew, to give his teaching to us, as foreigners. No Greek could have excelled the courtesy and charm of his refusal, and I respected him the more. And yet a nagging doubt began to grow in my mind: had we indeed fully understood him?

"The seed must fall into the ground and die."

I could not stop wondering about him. And I thought of the winged horse, the beautiful one, tamed and rearing before the evil chimaera it had been harnessed to fight. I thought that he was the winged horse of his nation, in a way, and that who rode him might find themselves thrown to their laming. For those who look towards the truth do so at their peril; it is greater than the sight of man.

I asked a wise man in the Temple about him, mentioning my unease, and there I learnt—to its tenfold increase—that he was indeed in danger of his life. He had already forfeited it by Jewish law in the matter of Sabbath-breaking, and had further angered the authorities everywhere by the audacity of his teaching. It was certain, said this scribe, that he would very soon, perhaps at this Passover, be either stoned or handed over to the Romans for crucifixion: this last because many of the people regarded him as uncrowned king.

I was deeply shaken and distressed, I did not know whether more for him or for this people of his which I had come to love and respect. The same had happened to Socrates in our land. Were the Jews about to follow the example of the Athenians? Was there no place for truth in a city, even in a holy city?

". . . before it can bear fruit." I understood his reply now. It was not so much that the time was not ripe, as that for him there was no more time.

But what fruit can come of the persecution of truth, what? That night I dreamt. I was in a great theatre with Xanthippus, watching a tragedy he had written. It was the story of Pegasus and the chimaera, Pegasus defeated. The theatre was full both of Jews and Greeks. A deep sense of doom was hanging over us. The audience and chorus alike were muttering in terror. Then the air was filled with flashing wings and hooves: Pegasus was flying down towards us. At that we all rose, we had all become the chorus, and catching him by his tail we pulled him down and set upon him, kicking, dragging, slashing, binding, twisting his limbs apart, pulling his wings to pieces. At last we left him, splayed out like a carcase, rolling in agony in the midst of the theatre, screaming a horse's scream. "He will roll on us and kill us," I thought, and in the horror of it nearly awoke.

But instead, the dream seemed to start again. Once more we were seated, waiting, and I heard the first beat of wings over me. I looked up and saw the great horse feathered with light, all wisdom in his eyes, all perfect knowledge, poised to plummet down to us and his death, and I knew suddenly that the Pegasus story was false, he would not kill us, but the truth and beauty of him were lifegiving even in his death. This flight of his, more than all the flights of his freedom, was the perfection of his grace and movement, where he plunged into accepted constriction, arrowed down on his chosen arc and fell. And in this second dream I saw now that the spring of Helicon had bubbled out where his hoof touched the ground, where, as he plunged, the winged horse tamed and broken by his own will, all truth and all beauty went flying in the zenith of freedom.

31

BITTERSWEET OILS

I *Mary of Bethany*

I THINK THERE'LL be no more talk of my betrothal now for awhile, at least. When Martha said significantly this evening, "You know, Cleophas of Emmaus has inherited thirty acres of vineyard? And he has no wife—" Lazarus stood up at the table, in all his new authority and manhood he seems to have gained since . . . his raising, brought his fist down and thundered at her, "Is this a time for marrying? 'With the Kingdom of God on our very doorstep?" Martha shrank away, amazed at our new brother, while I was full of glee and relief. How can she expect me to think of marriage now, at such a time? It's true she has been worrying about betrothing me ever since she was widowed. Though she tells everyone else I am a child, she is always telling me I am almost a woman and must behave like one. She would keep me out of the courtyard while the Twelve are there if she could, and even at first tried to stop me going there when the Master was there—one would think she invented jobs in the kitchen she suddenly needed me for. But it soon changed. Neither the proprieties, nor the purifying laws, exist at all in his presence. There is no such thing as impropriety or impurity. It is the life of the Kingdom. She knows it now.

And when he came, my betrothal was forgotten altogether, because our hearts were simply too full. There was no room for anything more or any other love. Only those who didn't know him failed to understand, like Barsaeus, Martha's father-in-law, who comes to stay with us each Passover. Last year he had heard that the Rabbi of Nazareth comes to our house whenever he visits Judaea, and as they waited for their meal I heard him asking Lazarus questions of the kind I dreaded about our distinguished visitor. Martha and I looked at each other, aghast; then before she knew what I was doing, I had burst in on them, shouting out, "He will never marry any woman!"

They were all shocked: I didn't care. Barsaeus asked, "Why not?"

"Because—because he is lord of all the earth."

Then I was shocked at my own words: not at their immodesty but at their apparent blasphemy. Yet it's true. He loves as God loves, each single one wholly, but there's no claiming him, no possessing him. He is the king, but he'll never have a wife. All women know it; that's why they aren't afraid to follow him, leaving their husbands and families in Galilee, to look after the Twelve on their journeys. He needs to be totally free to give himself so totally to us all; as God is free, and as God gives himself.

The sovereignty on him has grown since that day when I blushed and ran from the room to hear my own words to Barsaeus. I wouldn't be afraid of such words now. Perhaps the Kingdom is closer now, perhaps we only see it more clearly. We have watched the powers of evil ranging themselves against him, Satan fighting a pitched battle for the possession of the earth, driven back step by step. There are no half-shadows where Jesus is, no room for grey. Against the blazing light of the lordship that is in him everything must stand out in starkest contrast. Nothing has ever been so dark as the black entrance to Lazarus' tomb, when the Master stood before it and cried out, and the body came out in obedience—white . . .

People like Barsaeus say to us, "I should think you couldn't believe your own happiness to have your brother back from the dead," or "How wonderful it must have been . . . what a thing to remember." No, there was no happiness. It was not happy. It was not, in that sense, wonderful, and I remember it with fear and worship. It was terrible, not joyful; terrible to see the glory and the evil so close, to see the struggle so bitter. The Master may have wept for us, but it was for himself he was groaning, and if Martha and I were weeping at first for our brother, it was for Jesus I was weeping at the end, I can tell you. For I saw that he was going deeper into the evil yet, that this was so far from being the final victory that it was scarcely the beginning of the conflict. When he stood before that black doorway—I was afraid he would go in. . . .

And perhaps, in a sense, when he stood and called Lazarus out with that great shout, perhaps he did go in. For I can still feel the lordship and authority on him, yes, the kingship, which we all felt in that moment of his greatest power, but I can feel the darkness too, as though the grave had spilt its blackness round him, drawing him in, in revenge for its loss.

I think only Lazarus, and among the Twelve, John and maybe Judas, know what battle he's fighting now, and that his is a kingship over death, wrested from death. We call him God's Chosen One and his Anointed; but who knows how bitter the oils of his anointing are?

II   *Mary the mother of Jesus*

I had offered to help my hostess Martha with the preparations for the party they were giving for us that night, but I was still so tired from the long journey on foot from Galilee that after a while I had to excuse myself and withdraw. It seemed like the thousandth party in Jesus' honour I had been at, or helped at; everywhere he goes, people want to welcome him with cele-bration. Only at home there is never any, but hard looks and suspicious whisperings; I'm sorry, I can't help it, he understands; it's one more thing I have no power to give him. I found myself saying bitterly to him once, "Even if it were true you were out of your mind, do they think I would love you less?" Yet the estrangement has crept between me and him, a little; fear and weariness in me, and a kind of strangeness on him, a loneliness, so that sometimes he hardly seems like my son at all.

I went into the cool inner room, and there I found the younger sister, my namesake, sitting on the floor by an open chest, her dower-chest I guessed, lifting clothes out of it and sighing; I smiled as I watched. Then she gently took out a flask from the bottom, delicately made of alabaster. It was clearly what she had been looking for. She threw the other things back in the chest and sat caressing the flask. I said to her jokingly, "You will truly be Solomon's bride one day, dripping myrrh on the doorhandles of your wedding-chamber!

She lifted brooding dark eyes to me, but said nothing.

"Do you know who your husband is to be?"

"Perhaps they will marry me to Cleophas of Emmaus." She shrugged and then burst out, "I don't care! I don't care! Perhaps the Kingdom will come soon and I shall never marry!"

"So that's where your heart's set," I said, and went and sat beside her. "I've watched how you listen to the Rabbi."

"He's never sent me away," she said defensively. "Martha thinks I'm wasting his time. She says I'm too young to understand the ways of God and it's not for a young girl to occupy her head with such things."

"Well, that's not true!" I said warmly. "Believe me, God is not ashamed to send down the whole of his salvation on a very young and ignorant girl." I stopped, but too late; she understood well enough that I had spoken of myself.

"Was that—when you knew you were going to be his mother?"

"I don't know what I knew. Only perhaps that God had laid his hand on me and covered me with the shadow of his power." I found myself adding, "From first to last, it was the work of God. . . ."

"Did you see the Glory?" she asked shyly, her great gazelle's eyes glowing.

"Perhaps I did . . . I was younger than you—rather like you. Our Lord God is too great not to be humble. It's the little ones he loves best of all and lifts up the fallen." I took her flask and examined it, not so much from interest as to stem the flood of memories, of joy and grief, that this Mary, the shadow of my girlhood self, was waking in me. I was afraid I should cry and I felt I had not the strength for any more crying. "It's a lovely flask," I said. "I had one like it once; not that it was mine. A stranger from the lands of the East gave it as an offering of honour when I had your Rabbi in the cradle. I never knew who they were, those strange dark men, perhaps they were princes. . . .

They spoke words of prophecy I could not understand over him, and gave gifts of homage, and went away. Strange, strange."

"What became of the flask? Has he got it now?"

"My dear child, do you think a poor family like ours could keep treasures such as those intact for long? When the Lord summoned us back out of Egypt, where we'd gone to hide from Herod, we were so nearly destitute that we could not have made the journey as the Lord commanded if I had not sold the strangers' gifts. My husband was living as a hired labourer, and I was a wool-washer for the Jews of that place. I was very unwilling to sell them, I promise you. I did open the myrrh—it wasn't a sealed flask like this—and rubbed a little on his chest. He didn't like it—he cried; so did I. It was all I could give him, then or ever since, just our poverty."

"But it was a token for all you couldn't give, so it was everything," cried the girl, her eyes brilliant.

I began to realize that I was not going to succeed in keeping back tears. "He's done all the giving, all of it," I said. "I've been able to give him nothing, not even what was his own."

"I know what you mean, oh, I know what you mean," she said so fervently that I was amazed. "But you're wrong. I'm the one who has nothing to give him—I mean," she stammered, "we are. But you have! You gave him his life, and surely you are the luckiest woman in the world."

"It was God who gave him his life," I said. "I gave him only our poverty."

She suddenly buried her face in my lap, sobbing, "It was everything, everything," and my own tears ran off her young black hair. I could not tell her that sometimes it seems as though he will not even let me give him my motherhood.

III *Mary Magdalene*

It was grand to be in his train when he rode into Jerusalem. Oh, what a king he is! And it was grand to be at that party in Bethany as his guest. It's the first time I've been anyone's guest at a party; not, I mean, there professionally, or completely an intruder like the famous occasion! When, I may say, I didn't even notice there was a party going on. I'd been following him half a street behind, wondering if I'd ever dare to speak to him, and it didn't exactly help that the other men who noticed me assumed they knew what I was after and let me know what they thought about it. Still, I was hanging on when he turned into that house. I must've known it was Simon the Pharisee's house, but I didn't even think of it. Which shows you how desperate I was.

In fact, actually, desperate's not the word. I was half crazy with *hope*. He'd been preaching in a square in the bottom end of town, you see, the night before, when I was there on business with some of my colleagues. We thought at first he didn't know his way around; what was a Rabbi like him doing in a place like that? But he knew all right, and he started telling us that the good news of God was not a kingdom far off but a kingdom very near, near to all, near to us, as near as he was. That's what he said. Not a word about our sins. Just that he had come to heal the broken-hearted. Well, that was us all right. You know, I just collapsed in a corner of that square and wept my eyes out. I'd almost forgotten that I had a heart, there was no-one who wanted me to have one, it's better not to in our life. But of course I did and it was broken so bad there was no-one but him who could mend it.

He must have begun that night, in fact, without my knowing it; he left me with awful heartache, though! Heartache, that's the word. That's what I came with to the Pharisee's house. Heartache so bad I couldn't see straight. And heart's longing. And finally, well, you know, I was just so happy, let's face it. He knew that (in spite of his wet feet!). That's why he said to the Pharisee that mine was the love of someone who had been forgiven. Well, I hadn't thought of it exactly that way till he said so; I was just—happy, and in floods! But he was right enough about the loving, though it's a good thing he said it for me!

You've got to understand. It was God I wanted, it was God I had given up hope of, years before. I was sure I was condemned in his presence. I knew the devil had me. In fact I was more accursed than any of the other women. The devil was living in me: seven times over, the scribe said, when he told me I could never pray again until I had been exorcized—or if I did, God wouldn't listen—and who was going to exorcize a practising whore? And how could I stop practising, and why should I anyway since I was so damned? You've got to have been where I was to know what it's like. You've seen what becomes of the devil-possessed, maybe, you've seen them running naked among the tombs, the last wreck of what a human can be. You know that madness is beginning in you, you see those tombs coming nearer and nearer. You cry to God although you've been told he won't hear you, and sure enough, he doesn't (or so you think at the time; now, I don't know). Maybe you try to repent and go to John the Baptist, and the devils in you lash out and throw you out of the water, the river refuses you, the water burns you. That's where I was when Jesus came down our way. And he knew devils when he saw them. He knew how it was with me. I mean, I realized afterwards that he'd known. And he told us that God never stopped loving his lost ones, that he sent his messengers out to pull them into the feast they might never have dared to come to otherwise.

But you know, it was himself, Jesus, even more than what he said. Because he was kind to us, we began to guess that God was kind—was being kind, was turned to us here and now. When Jesus was welcoming you, you just couldn't believe that you were condemned. I don't know how it was, how the religious bods explain it. You just knew and that was that. Because he was the messenger of his story, of course, sent by God to pull us into the feast, poor beggars off the streets who couldn't read their invitations and thought they were warnings to keep out. That's how it was. And he can pull hard!

So here I am a lady, and he a proper king. I've never got used to it, you know. That he's glad to have me following him. That he liked what I did that day when I poured my scented oil over his feet (some men would have died rather). That he liked my hair. It was the only beautiful thing I had left, that

I hadn't spoilt. All my life was ruined. I just had left my hair, and my scent, and my kisses (my real ones, I mean). And he was glad of them all. I guess I never will get used to it. That he wants me to love him. He does, you know. With my heart, not my body. Well, it's been his heart from the start, hasn't it, ever since that evening in the lower market square.

I'm not the only one! There was ever such a lot of us this time, this journey up. It was like we felt instinctively that we must go with him, that he'd need us. We weren't all off the streets. There were his mother and his aunt Mariamne, for a start, his mother's sister that is. There was Salome, the wife of Zebedee, the mother of James and John. And there was poor old Joanna, the wife of Chuza Herod's steward, who I had such a feud with once; oh dear me! And we were all the best of friends. I've never had such a good time. But we only had half an eye for each other really. It was *him* we were watching, and worrying over too, because we all saw what most of the men apparently missed, that there was something terribly wrong. He was so sad. And he got sadder and more kingly all the way and somehow out of our reach. We could cook for him and look after him but how could we tell him we understood? And anyway we didn't understand.

This party, it felt so serious, you'd think not even the men could have missed it. Partly it was having Lazarus there, who he'd raised from the dead. Well, you can't be just ordinary gay, like, in the face of someone back from four days among the dead, can you? He'd seen Abraham, hadn't he? And God himself? And yet obeyed the voice of Jesus calling him back? I mean, it makes you think.

It was Lazarus' little sister who did what astonished me, though. And shook me right to the bottom. She stood up in the middle of those guests and broke a flask of spikenard oil on Jesus' head; like she was crowning him. So close to what I did long ago, and yet so different! There she was, this young girl, pure and innocent, all the things I wasn't, not pouring out her scent and her heart on her own account on his feet, but in all seriousness doing for him what suddenly seemed the only thing appropriate. That was what we women had been longing to tell him! That we knew he was the Lord's Anointed, and that we knew it was terrible. That he must carry the lordship of the last days. But we couldn't have told him, because we didn't realize properly, did we? Until that lovely girl upped and did it. And she's a Mary too.

And you know what the men said? Not, "Oh! Now we see". Not "Hail to the Lord's Anointed". They said—or perhaps only one of them said, I was that mad, I don't remember—"What a waste! She could have sold that and given the money to the poor." As though she were likely to have sold her dowry! It was offering it to the Master or nothing. The Master was as indignant as I was. "Why must you make trouble for her? It's a fine thing she's done for me. You'll have the poor with you always, and you can help them whenever you want; but you will not always have me." And then he said something I only understood later. "She is beforehand with anointing my body for burial. She'll be remembered for what she's done. Beware what you are remembered for."

But in spite of his defence of her she was standing at the side absolutely white, stricken, her great black eyes on the man who had groused at her. I was so moved, I just couldn't help myself. I went rushing over to her, threw my arm round her and pulled her to a seat, "Never you mind him!" I said. "He's an old so-and-so. I know what you were doing, because I did something like it myself once, only I didn't have half as much understanding as you. Forget what those old meanies said, the Master was ever so pleased, I could tell."

But she threw her arms round my neck and burst into tears. "It was Judas," she sobbed, "didn't you see his face? He hates him! I thought he loved him, but look at his face!"

I looked around, but Judas was gone. "Never mind him," I said again.

"I thought it was just death he's fighting, but it's hate. . . . You knew he was fighting death, didn't you? Martha doesn't believe me."

I hadn't known it till that moment actually. I said "Mary! Can you be right? What do you mean?"

"When he raised my brother from the dead he groaned so. It was terrible. No-one realized what it was costing him. It's the struggle of the last days. And didn't you hear what he said just now? I was anointing him for his burial?"

"Well, yes, but—Mary, love, you don't think he's not in charge of it all, do you? If you knew what I know of his power over evil!"

She smiled at that in her tears, a quick wry smile, then she was sobbing again, inconsolable: "How can he hate him? Why do so many people hate him? Why do the Pharisees want to kill him? What'll they do to him? What's going to happen? Oh, Mary, aren't you frightened? What's going to happen?"

"He'll be made really king, perhaps. Cheer up. I'm sure Judas doesn't really hate him. He was just in a mood. He's all right."

"No, that was hate. It was absolute hate. I saw it. Haven't you ever met hate? Oh, Mary, I know he has power over evil. But why must he fight evil? I don't want him to have to! I don't want him to have to!"

I couldn't do anything but squeeze her. She wept and wept, crying out passionately, almost hysterically, again and again: "I don't want him to have to fight evil! I don't want him to have to!"

All the evening seemed sinister, full of foreboding. There was nothing I could say but "Mary, love, don't cry, he'll be all right." She had me scared too now.

32

THE LAST PASSOVER

I

THE YEAR WAS ending, and all the old order. We knew it; I felt it. "This month shall be the beginning of months for you, it shall be the first month of the year to you." Surely this was a prophecy of the last redemption, as well as the Lord's commandment concerning the first, and surely its fulfilment was upon us. Never, even when I was called Simon the Zealot, and prayed at each Passover that it would be the last, the great deliverance indeed, never have I felt the coming of Passover as I felt this one. For the Master had been as Moses in the days beforehand, speaking doom over the world of our bondage; great was he in those days, and a terrible fire in his eyes! He would lead us on to the Mount of Olives, and there, gazing over Jerusalem, he spoke his terrible warnings of the great tribulation that was upon us and that should last till the final Day. But again and again he promised us that we who believed to the end should be saved. Even so was Israel led out long ago into her great testing. How I longed for it, for that leading-out, for any testing! We would not fail, as our forefathers did; we would not need to be told, "Stand fast, fear not, for the Lord is fighting for you," as Moses told the fainthearted Israelites of old. So when our Master said to us, "When you see these things beginning, lift up your heads, for your redemption is near," I burst out, "Lord, my head is lifted up, my shoots are breaking into leaf!" Though he warned us of persecution and of evils, of the wicked world that should vent its fury on us, I was not afraid; thus had Pharaoh hardened his heart also; and thus had Moses in his time brought on the unrepenting land darkness that could be felt. Truly the darkness could be felt in Jerusalem in those days, and a great fear was on many. But the power of the Lord was in Jesus and no-one could lay hold on him, neither Herod, nor the Pharisees and Sadducees, nor the priests and elders: no, nor Rome itself, as we saw when he drove the traders out of the Temple and purged the holy place, before the very eyes of the might of Rome, and they quaked and suffered him. Under the terribleness of his eye and the brightness of his presence all wickedness was revealed and confounded; even in our midst, in our very midst, the son of darkness found his secret heart uncovered. For nothing that is evil can endure the countenance of the Anointed One.

At every Passover the pit of Sheol is shaken, with the remembrance of the deliverance that was and with the first tread of the coming Kingdom. For wherever it is kept, the doors that hold back the Kingdom are shaken, and the cry of all flesh comes into the ears of God: "O Lord, we have waited for thee!" So it is every time, but this Passover, truly I thought those doors could not stand. The greatness of the redemption was on our Master, his eyes burnt with such a might of love that God himself seemed to be looking out of them. The awe and holiness of that feast grew as the night fell. I felt all the generations of Israel who had hoped, the patriarchs and prophets and kings, and all his forgotten people, their eyes fixed on us from their place far in the earth. They had desired it, but it was ours to see it. The Master said, his voice deep with emotion, as we sat down, "How I have longed to eat this Passover with you before I suffer! For amen, I tell you, I shall never eat it again until it is fulfilled in the Kingdom of God." And later, as the solemnity increased, he said, "Truly I shall never drink again of the fruit of the vine until I drink it new with you in the kingdom of my Father." And when he said that I was so unmade with joy and longing and grief—for he spoke of his suffering as though it were certain now—that I hardly knew what happened after. He told us he was giving us his power and kingship, that as we had borne his trials with him so far, we must stand fast now, and he was setting his own authority in us; I know now that he was strengthening us for the weakness he saw was in us, which we did not see. He promised us thrones in his kingdom. Yet that seemed not to matter so much now. There was much else that he said and did. I don't remember. I was unmade by his glory that night, unmanned. If he had not soon hidden it I think he might have broken all hearts and destroyed the world with joy. But for such excess of brightness he became dark (as Habakkuk prophesied, "There was the hiding of his power"), and no eye saw how God was glorified in Jesus in his suffering, no eye saw the redemption. For no mortal could have seen it and lived, and now too, exalted to God's right hand, his glory hides itself lest it should blind us. But when our eyes and hearts are ready we shall eat and drink with him anew in the kingdom of his Father.

II

If there is one thing I remember it is the face of my marching-partner, Simon, worn and haggard with the intensity of his expectation over so many years when he was one of the Zealot party, that grim face all softened and the tears running down into his beard as he looked at the Master and heard nothing that any of us said, nor even remembered to eat. For all hearts were open that night, the Master's too. He spoke as he had never spoken before. "You are the men who have been with me always in all my trials," he told us. "You have stood by me and loved me, and now the Father is standing by you and loves you. . . . Love one another, as I have loved you." I think most of us were nearly as dazed and uplifted as Simon, but it was only at the end of supper that the meaning of the whole evening began to come clear. For Jesus took and blessed bread and wine and gave it to us to share, saying over the cup, "This is the cup of the new covenant in my blood. . . ." Then I found my flesh trembling with fear and joy, for I began to guess what was happening in me and in all of us. It was not merely the warmth of feeling which any Passover gathering will generate. This was more; this was the creation and the covenant promised by the prophets: "I will take away the stony heart from out of you, and I will make you a new heart, a heart of flesh; and a new spirit within you . . . and I will make a new covenant with the house of Israel and Judah, and will write it in their heart, and I will be their God, and they shall be my people. And they shall all know me, from the greatest to the least of them, and I will remember their sins no more. . . ."

I tell you, I felt that new heart being planted within me that night as Jesus spoke, and it seemed to me he was writing in my very heart. And what was he writing but the burning words that God has spoken for ever to us, "Love me, O my people, for I have loved you, and if you love me, obey me"? And were they his own words indeed or . . .?

Had the Glorious and Eternal One come as close as this at last? Had the desire of Israel come, had her lover and maker taken her to him at last? He whom Abraham had worshipped, whom Moses had spoken with in thunder, coming closer and closer in covenant after covenant, hallowed with the blood of animals; what was this covenant in Jesus' own blood if not the last taking, the last forgiving, the last uniting, for the sake of Jesus, God's holy servant, dearer to him than Moses or Abraham? Who were we that God should love us so?

But then I remembered how earlier in the evening Jesus had washed our feet, to try to make us understand how he was our servant, and knew that he at least did love us so. I never saw the authority and kingliness in him so great as when he acted the slave to us, and by the time he was speaking his final prayer for us and blessing over us there was no doubting any more that if he chose us and loved us, that choosing and loving were God's.

There was much more that happened. There was sorrow as well as joy. It's hard to remember it all that evening. Only somehow, by what he said or did, by his manner, by (in another way) each other's presence too, we began to know a little how the love and mercy of God had touched us through this man. And afterwards, not at once afterwards, but when his Spirit came to us to teach us, we knew that God had indeed made his covenant with us, the new covenant of the heart.

But that night the memory of the supper was eclipsed by the darkness and horror of what followed. Then the only cup it seemed we had to drink was the cup of the Lord's wrath, as we stopped in our terrified flight from Gethsemane and looked at each other, those of us who were still together, and knew what we had done. But Jesus drank it and called it the cup of his Father's good pleasure, and we call it now, not the cup of wrath, but the cup of fellowship and blessing. Bread for strength, and wine for joy: God's miracles of life out of the dust of the earth; and both of them now for resurrection.

III

But it was an evening of grief and terror, of sickening dismay, creeping up the flesh and into the heart. You call me Gloomy Thomas, but could none of you feel the anguish in him? Was the taste of death not in every mouthful we ate? The angel of the Lord was brooding over our houses once again, and this time his hand was raised against Israel; and our Master was the first-born.

All through his ministry I had felt the shadows of death pressing in on him, hounding him. At the very start he was nearly killed by the outraged crowd at Nazareth. Again and again he walked with clear and open eyes into traps set him by his enemies: as that time in the synagogue when a man with a withered arm had been "planted" there by the elders to induce him to break the Sabbath. Do you think he didn't know? Do you forget how he looked round on those malicious men with anger and sorrow at their hardness of heart—and then cured the cripple? And do you think he did not see death at the end of the road in Jerusalem for him, while you laughed and sang and talked of the Kingdom, and mocked me for my long face? You thought that because he had walked unharmed twice through a mob in Jerusalem with stones in their hands, he would never let himself be taken. You never listened or understood when he said, "My hour has not yet come", or to his words before he entered Jerusalem this last time: "My hour is at hand." You danced and sang hosanna, but my heart was sick within me; and can you forget how when he came in sight of the city he wept, and said, "Oh, Jerusalem, Jerusalem, will you always stone and murder those God sends to you?" Or did you think he meant only the prophets of old?

Then as we sat down to eat he said, "How I have longed for this; for I shall never eat it again with you. . . ." Do you think there was joy in his words, "I shall never drink of the fruit of the vine till I drink it new with you in the Kingdom of God"? It was the joy of grief, or joy and grief so intense that they were the same. And were you not dismayed by the bitter sadness with which he warned Judas? You were, of course you were. Don't forget it all now in the joy of the "new wine". Don't forget his suffering. And indeed he will not let us. Why do you think it is through the breaking of bread that he would have us remember him?

Those affirmations of his love for us, and the promise of his Spirit to comfort us, they overwhelmed us all; but did you not taste the grief even there—did you not understand that they were his farewell? It is true that God has turned the bitterness of that parting into life with him for ever; but that is life from the dead; you know it was death for him and for us, to be parted, "smitten and scattered".

He didn't want to die! There was never any man so alive as he. He taught us what it was to live. He gave life wherever he went, to all who came to him. Yet even that perhaps had the shadow of death in it for him. He took their sickness on him and gave them his own life. But he didn't want to die! He was killed along with the Passover lambs when his life was as fresh as theirs.

As he had given us his life while he was with us, so he gave us his death at the end. "Take this bread and eat it," he said, "it is my body given for you," and "Drink this cup, all of you, for it is my blood poured out for you and for many, for their forgiveness." So he tried to strengthen us beforehand by making us understand that all he was to suffer was for us, that what we had tasted was the pledge that he was making atonement for us and all the sinners whom in his life he had loved. Yes, and for all Israel. So the servant of the Lord had to pour out his soul unto death, for he was bearing the sins of many. But which of us was comforted? I was not.

True, of course, I sang praise with the rest and blessed the

Lord. He had called me to follow him, far away in Galilee, and if that meant following him to a joyful feast for his death, well. Nothing, I thought, could separate me from him, however bitter. But the worst bitterness was to come when the great fear seized us all and I knew, when I stopped running, that I, too, had forsaken him. Then it was that I truly tasted death.

IV

I tell you, Thomas, I think of his suffering every moment of my waking life, and you know why, you know I swore denial of him for fear of it. It was judgment, that night, make no mistake about that. The others tell me that it was there they learnt for the first time how much the Master loved us, or that he invested us with his own authority, or that he gave us the cup of the covenant of the new creation, or I don't know what else. But as for me, he broke my heart that night. The trial came we had been waiting for so long, and what happened? All the treachery, cowardice, faithlessness, lovelessness of our hearts rose to the surface and swamped us. And if they think back, they may remember that early in the meal he said in deep distress, "One of you, eating here with me, is going to betray me." And they all said then, "Is it I?" Those sorrowful words of his cut us to the bone and we all knew just for a moment that we could have been his betrayer. That was what the meal was about, believe me; it was a warning to us of what would happen that night, that evil was at home as well as abroad. He knew what was coming, he knew what was in us, that before another cockcrow one would have betrayed him, the rest all have scattered and left him, and the one who believed he loved him most would have denied before God that he knew him. He tried to tell us that he knew and that in spite of it, it was for us he was laying down his life. So he held the joyful feast of love in the very face of it all, and it was judgment, I tell you, worse than if he had come on the clouds with a sword in his hand.

I didn't want to understand. I was uneasy with his strange performance of washing our feet. I told him he should never wash mine, but he looked up at me with that look of his and said, "If I don't wash you, Peter, you will never be in fellowship with me." Even then I didn't understand.

He tried to warn me again later, when I was asserting that I was ready to follow him to prison and to death (and the others joined in heartily). "Peter," says he, "before cockcrow you'll have denied me three times." I said, "Never! I would lay down my life for you." Who'd have dreamt it wasn't true? Not I. But: "Will you indeed?" he says. "Be careful, Peter! Satan is at work among you. He has been given leave to do his worst. But I've been praying for you, Peter, that your faith may not fail, and when you've come to yourself, you must strengthen your brethren." It was only later that his words sank in, and I knew he had been praying for me all the time. There and then, I hardly even listened.

He meant us to remember the whole feast, you know. He meant us to think back and understand later. Because it's in the remembering that it hurts, breaks and heals your heart. And why? Because you know then that it was forgiveness all along, that the forsaking and betraying and denying were in that cup he blessed and gave to us. It was his own body and life, that bread and wine, which we were quick enough to swap for a safe getaway. Little did we care for his life then. But he knew we'd be sorry, that we did love him, and that's when we'd remember what he did and know that it was all given back, the love, the fellowship, his life with us, even before we'd given it away. And that's when a body broke down and wept outside the High Priest's house.

There's nothing that hurts worse than forgiveness, there's no burning and purging to equal it. Judas couldn't bear it. He escaped from it through a hanging noose into a place where he thought Jesus could not look at him any more. It's the looking, you know, more than anything.

Believe me, that's what it all meant, the bread and cup and all, and the keeping Passover ahead of time, so that he was killed along with the lambs. He was telling us that this coming death of his was his forgiveness of us and all his other enemies too. He was letting all the worst that was in us come out and have its way on him, so that he could forgive it. I said breaks and heals, didn't I? John has a name for him: he calls him the Bread of Life. So he knows it too.

Was it only for us that that bread was broken? Or did God remember too those kept prisoners so long in their disobedience, from the days of the Flood until now, and all Israel's long, long faithlessness? Surely that precious blood of forgiveness was ready from the foundation of the world and until the foundations are shaken at the last. Surely all the sinful world must pass through the fire of God's mercy, that I first knew in a cold Jerusalem street as the look of forgiveness from a condemned, betrayed and rejected man.

V

Even as late as that last Passover I had not realized how great the change was in my brother John. I assumed that he was thinking as I was, as we always had thought together, and there was such deep fire in his eyes—more than ever seeming to have caught it from the Master's—that I felt sure it was the kingdom and the glory in his mind. He says it was glory indeed, the very glory of God overshadowing that upper room as once the camp of Israel, that he was seeing, and then I know our minds are sadly far apart. For I saw the glory on the mountain that time as much as he did and there was no such vision tonight. Instead, there was a different solemnity, a blood-stirring, ancient solemnity, a martial holiness. As we renewed the pledge of our forefathers at the sacred meal, I felt certain that the Master had gathered us together now as the Lord used to gather the tribes of old. Yes, the camp of Israel! But preparing to march! This was the assembly of the hosts of the Lord, sworn in brotherhood to each other and in covenant with the Holy One. So Jesus had gathered us together to consecrate us for our sending-out now and band us together. (And John says I don't know how truly I speak.) So he made a covenant meal with us in the name of his Father, and I saw the darkness sheering away before the face of the light, the kingdom given into our hands. Did Jesus not say so? "I appoint you thrones over the twelve tribes of Israel," he said, that very night. And at the end he warned us that we would need to learn to use the sword; though it's true that when I found two dirks in the corner, belonging to the people of the house, he brushed me impatiently aside, but surely that was only because he had much else to teach us and the time was running out.

I don't care about invisible glory, and neither did John once. I want to *see* the glory of the Lord, I want all flesh to see it and worship in amazement. I want Jesus to take on his heavenly power. I knew that he was going forth from here into the woes of Messiah, but how could I doubt that his heavenly Father would vindicate him and give him the kingdom? The others tell me he spoke in very thinly veiled terms of his immediate death. I missed them, then. I thought it was just such another solemn commissioning, on a greater scale, as when he called us together to send us out two by two bringing the good news of the imminent Reign of God. And did we not have power in those days—power that was seen? Did we not drive out devils like lightning?

I know something else: Jesus was thinking as I was, too. He was longing for the revelation of his Father's glory and his own, as I was. Perhaps it is true that he refused to take the kingdom in that way, in the end. Perhaps he saw that he must go through bottomless humiliation first. Maybe that was why he prayed so long in the garden on the Mount of Olives. But even when he was arrested, and he said himself that this was the hour of the power of darkness, those powers fell back before his face, just as I had dreamed, so that when he said, "I am he—Jesus of Nazareth", some of the soldiers reeled and fell. And further, he showed how close his thoughts were to mine, when he told Peter not to fight because he could at any time call on his Father, who would at once send twelve legions of angels to his help. But he did not. He chose another obedience instead, the fulfilment of the scripture: "He was numbered among the transgressors." And yet will not the Father honour him doubly for that obedience—don't we know how high he has honoured and exalted him? And has he therefore forfeited the power of the

Kingdom? No, never! And has the promise been cancelled that all flesh shall see it together? No!

Our hopes and longings that night were no dishonour to him. He accepted them as he let Hosanna be sung to him when he rode into the city. Perhaps I am one with John after all, and we merely did not know how truly we were thinking. If we had known the whole of what was coming, with how much more joy and worship would we have sung the Hymn of the Hallel as we went out?

It stirs me almost more than the memory of the Passover meal itself to recall how we went singing through the trees up the slope of the Mount of Olives, with a hundred thousand festal lights burning in Jerusalem below, knowing that we were his chosen, covenanted ones, the possessors of the promise of his Spirit, knit together into one by that meal more closely than ever the tribes were united at Shechem; for the Master himself was our unity; the bread, he had said, was his body, the wine his blood. We sang the great triumph song, and he sang with us: "The Lord is on my side: I will not fear what man may do unto me.... The Lord is my strength and my song, and is become my salvation . . . the right hand of the Lord has the mastery, the right hand of the Lord brings mighty things to pass; I shall not die, but live, and declare the works of the Lord...." A thousand times more we would have sung it if we had known all that was coming. He knew, and he did sing it; I can still hear his voice ringing over ours: "I will thank thee, for thou hast heard me, and art become my salvation; the stone which the builders rejected is become the chief cornerstone; this is the Lord's doing, and it is marvellous in our eyes." He did not need the legions of angels; the Father himself was with him, he was glorious in his accursed death; and till the Kingdom comes or my flesh fails I shall hunger and thirst for the showing forth of his glory, for the splendour of God to cover the whole earth.

VI

But I can see it, James my brother, you old son of thunder, and so can you, or how could you speak so?

His glory was revealed that night, the glory that was his on the cross, as it never shall be again till the end of time. He knew all that was coming on him, he knew full well. As he had always obeyed his Father, so now in the last extremity he still obeyed him, and obeying him, he gave thanks. We saw it; we heard it; and it was for us he gave thanks, because even in that hour of our imminent forsaking we were his own, whom the Father had given him. He knew that he had kept us and would keep us still, safe as the flock when the shepherd is with it, because after the smiting of the shepherd and the scattering of the sheep, he would be raised up to go before us, our true keeper still. For in all the evil that was coming he knew the Father was keeping him and us in his hand and we could never fall out of it, no, not by any forsaking. Only the one whose love had grown cold could fall, the one in whom the sap of the vine no longer ran, the one who had in the end loved darkness rather than light: that darkness into whose power Jesus was delivered, that he might break it.

He knew that he must go into it, that through that very darkness the Father's glory must shine. It was his own glory, that he lived in from the beginning, abiding for ever in the Father's love. He had come from God and was going back to God, but he took on himself the darkness of this world, that we might see and know the love that was between him and the Father. So he stripped himself of his visible glory and became our slave, washing our feet, bearing our sins. So when the traitor went out into the night he knew that the hour of his glorifying on earth was come, when he should honour his Father still through torture and death on a gibbet. So he took bread, the bread of his life as well as ours, bread that he had shared with Judas, and gave thanks. All that he said and did that night was thanksgiving. He blessed his Father for the glory that was at hand and the glory that was for ever theirs, for his life in the flesh and his life in eternity, for us and for all who should ever be his own; he gave thanks for his death. And because we could not see his glory on the cross, for the weakness of our sight, he asked that we might see it then in his great thanksgiving, and know him truly for ever in the breaking of bread.

He asked not only that we should see his glory, he asked that we should share it, and that by his spirit in us, the love between him and his Father should be in us too. So he gave us the wine of his blood, not only so that we should know it was shed for us, but so that we might know ourselves of one blood with him; he the vine and we the branches. But it had to be shed first. It is because we were with him in his death—because he had us in his heart—that we are alive in his life now. It was through his suffering that he became so close to us, and yet again he suffered only because he was so close to us, for the glory and the love that he entered into were always his, and so, before we existed, were we.

As the vine bears its branches, so he bore and bears us, and as its sap runs through the veins of every twig and leaf, so his spirit is in us, and so that we might know what he had done for us, he gave us the bread and wine of his blessing to eat. They were his self, his life, laid freely down, and they were his own thanksgiving. We have no life outside his life, we have no prayer outside his thanksgiving. For his suffering was his greatest prayer, and he told us beforehand that it was for us, so that his own joy might be in us and our joy complete. And the darkness has no more power any more; it is only the place of his glory; but we have his joy and his prayer for ever; his self and his life. He told us that prayer long before, and we eagerly prayed it after him: "Our Father, may your Name be hallowed!" But we did not know what we were asking. It was Jesus who had to pray it for us, covering our weakness: "Father, glorify your Name"— through his death.

That was all he ever desired, the glory of his Father, the one God of truth; and for us too, what can life ever be but knowing him and Jesus whom he sent? Whether we understand what we are asking or not, still you and I, James, want nothing but to drink Jesus' cup, to pray his prayer, "Father, glorify your Name"—and it has been glorified, and shall be again!

But when the Master said these things, I understood none of them, no more than the rest of us. Only afterwards, when he had been lifted up, I remembered and believed.

33

TREES

I *Mary of Bethany*

WE HAD BEEN warned not to expect either Jesus or any of
the Twelve that night. They were keeping Passover on their
own in the city. There was some doubt over the date this year,
since the Sabbath intervened; the Pharisees gave one ruling, the
Sadducees another; the Judaeans and Galileans were divided too.
Martha would have preferred to keep it the next day, when most
of Jerusalem did, but Lazarus insisted we keep it when the Master
was doing so.

On the Thursday, then, we ate our Passover in the house of
Baruch the flax merchant, within the city walls, knowing that
somewhere close Jesus and the Twelve were doing the same. As
we left Baruch's house we heard the lamb for his own family
bleating in the courtyard: it would not be killed till next day.
"It's *not* Passover night," said Martha obstinately. "I only hope
we have kept it lawfully," and loyal as Lazarus was to Jesus, he
could not find any reply but "Be silent, woman." None of us
really knew—then—why Jesus was insisting on anticipating
Passover.

But to me, as we walked home under the stars, it was more
like the first Passover of all than any other I had known. Somehow the sense of having done our part and yet of the full festival
still to come fitted with the ominousness of everything, which
was growing as the days passed. I was shivering with excitement
and apprehension, and ran and skipped on the starlit road when
Martha was not looking. I thought, surely the Israelites must
have felt like this on the night of the slaying of the firstborn in
Egypt: wondering if it were true that this time deliverance would
really come to pass; in trust and in doubt of Moses; hearing the
cries of death all round and fearfully wondering if the other

Hebrew households were safe. . . . It was impossible to want to sleep when we got in. We had never felt so wide-awake, so on tiptoe with suspense—so ready, if you like, for the exodus. Long after the houses around us were in darkness, we were still up and at prayers, Lazarus leading in the heartfelt prayers of old for redemption, for the kingdom, for the deliverance of all Israelites.

We were still gathered there—the three of us and Barsaeus, Mary the mother of Jesus and her sister, Reuben the former blind beggar, and several others who had followed Jesus from Galilee—when there came a din of wildly pounding feet outside.

Lazarus leapt to the door, and John son of Zebedee burst in on us, seeming half demented, his clothes torn and his hair dishevelled. He cried out, "The judgment of the world has come! It has pulled darkness down on itself, darkness!" Then he fell on the floor, doubled up with hysterical laughter, mad laughter. "They came with swords and torches to take him alone! A cohort of soldiers! All the High Priest's guard! Pikes and swords and torches! They came with lights for fear of the dark. They came with flares and lights to take the light of Israel captive. And all their light was darkness, darkness!"

"But what's happened? In the name of God, tell us!" "Is he safe?"

"Now is the judgment of the world! The prince of darkness has prevailed!" was all he could say.

Then Lazarus saw someone else standing in the courtyard entrance, swaying, seeming dazed. He went out, and called back, "It's Simon Peter." We saw him trying to speak to Peter, but he only panted and gulped and stared wildly round. In the end John calmed enough to tell us, "Judas betrayed him. He brought soldiers from Pilate and the High Priest's guard to take him captive when he was praying in Gethsemane after supper. As though Jesus were a thing of evil, a thing of the night! Like a thief or a robber or a foul thing in the night! And night has fallen on Israel!" He was shouting again; then suddenly he froze. "Where am I?" he said. "What have I done? Did I leave him? What have I done?"

For a moment he seemed as dazed as Peter; then he ran out of the house, seized Peter by the arm, and dragged him away, crying, "Let's see the end, at least let's see the end. Peter, don't you understand? This is the end."

His words hung in the air after they were gone. We looked at one another and knew it was the end. Lazarus raised his hands and began again in prayer: "Stretch forth thy might as of old, O God of Israel, our Saviour, for thou alone art our helper, thou alone art our Holy One . . ." But his words fell into silence and trailed away, his voice was drowned by the night. Martha tried to respond: "In thee have we trusted . . . we trusted. . . ." The words went round and round, empty, mocking, the sound of our own voices rebounding from the black iron plate of the night. "He trusted . . . he trusted. . . ."

I could not bear it. Suddenly I was the wild child again, the sister whom Martha could never tame. I broke out of that house before anyone knew what I was doing, and ran up the road and into the trees. Already it was better to be out in the dark, breathing the same night as he. I plunged and stumbled through the olive groves. On the lower slope of the hill, below me, were the pilgrim fires; Jerusalem was ringed with them. But I was alone, above them here, where so short a while ago, he had been. I could see better now as my eyes grew used to the moonlight. I could not pray Lazarus' prayers. This was all I could do, to follow, to breathe, to taste the darkness he had tasted—was tasting still.

I had lived on this hill all my life. I had played with Martha in Gethsemane at pressing olives between two bits of wood, every summer of my childhood. I knew every stone and goat-track. And now I stopped suddenly, seeing the oleanders beaten and battered, stones knocked off the oil-presses, as though a whole company of stamping men had forced their way over here, unseeing and uncaring what they kicked aside. Then I saw the charred end of a torch, and another, and another, and I went down on my knees and kissed the bruised earth and laid my forehead on it. In spite of myself, Martha's words were echoing in my mind, though not in prayer, I can tell you, unless desperate reproach can be prayer. "He trusted in thee, he trusted . . ."

Judas. I remembered the look I had seen on his face when Jesus rebuked him for being indignant against my anointing. Could I have warned Jesus? Could I have done anything? If he had done nothing was it because there was never any way out, never any other way? Or because he still meant to save himself somehow?

When I looked up I saw over my head an ancient olive tree, gnarled and silver in the moonlight, strangely distorted; twisted as though wrenched against itself. I could almost fancy I heard the wood groaning. Of course I did not; it had hung there silently suffering longer than I had been born. Somehow it was strangely comforting, that old, misshapen thing, as though it had waited there with a tree's sympathy for all who had come with tortured hearts to this place; for it's had a long history of them, Mount Olivet, from King David who had gone weeping over it in flight from his own son Absalom, to the heroes of almost our own time who had had to watch their holy city trampled underfoot by Gentiles, the brave and doomed Maccabees. And always the gnarled olives were there.

I stood up and looked down the hill to the harvest-floor where I have danced with the other girls at the vintage so often, picturing the guard and the prisoner tramping across it, their weapons shining in the moon, their torches alight, and the true light of them all quenched in their midst. Then I noticed on the way down how the old vine growing up the stone wall where the terrace started, the oldest and still richest vine of all that vineyard, seemed to have a branch broken, its tendrils trailing crookedly across the moonlit patch. I forgot soldiers, prisoner and all and ran down to it. I have loved that vine all my life. Shammai, the vineyard-owner, lets the children eat freely of it; he says it's too old to belong to anyone but God and the children. Now I saw that someone had slashed at it—it was cut, not broken— someone passing had struck at it with a knife, or a sword. It was dripping sap on to the earth; the stones were dark under it. I was on my knees trying to bind it up before I knew what I was doing, feverishly, clumsily, trying to tie it together with my hair-ribbon. I had forgotten Judas, Jesus, God and all. It only seemed desperately important to stop that wounded vine from bleeding away into the earth, to save every drop I could of its oozing life.

II *Mary the mother of Jesus*

"I couldn't bear to see my son crucified," said Martha, almost reproachfully. I made no answer. John took one arm, Mary of Magdala the other, and the three of us set out on the white dusty road to Jerusalem; it was high morning already and the ground shimmered and swam. Mary could not speak for crying, but I had wept myself dry. The youngest Mary I had not seen since she came in so late last night and would not say where she had been. She had shut herself up ever since in the room she shared with Martha. I was a little afraid of such passionate grief in the girl, and because it seemed to have no outlet. But the other Mary's warm heart was holding me up.

Since John came back this morning with the news of Barabbas' release and Jesus' final condemnation we had scarcely spoken. He was no longer last night's hysterical runaway, but a man whose life had ended and who wondered to find himself still alive. None of us had any comfort to give the others except his or her mere physical presence, and somehow that did comfort.

I could not go fast; the darkness was coming and going behind my eyes. I stopped presently, too exhausted for a moment to go on, and would have sunk down by the low wall on one side of the road, but John tugged urgently at me: "Not there, mother. Not under that tree. There is better shade under this one."

I looked up at the other and said, "What's happened to it?" It was covered with leaves that seemed to have shrivelled as they opened. It was a frightening sight, that picture of death in the spring. John said in a low voice, "The Master found it barren, and he prophesied of it, that it should never bear fruit again. When we came by the next day, it had withered like that."

The darkness came in my eyes and I had to lower my head till the faintness passed. "So," I said, "it is really the end. The Lord has cast off his pleasant vineyard Israel."

He had loved it and tended it so long, so long. Why was its wood so bitter, its heart so hard? John said, "When Peter exclaimed in distress when he saw it, the Master answered him, 'Yet have faith in God, even now'."

"Then," I said, "we must have it. But let's not sit here all the same."

He helped me up and we went on, leaving the terrible sign of forsakenness, of the Lord's rejection of that which was ever dearest his heart, his own chosen people that had rejected him.

There was seething tumult in Jerusalem, as we passed below the Roman garrison tower, the Fortress Antonia, in the narrow streets between it and the Temple. It took me a little while to understand that this was not only the noise and crowding of Passover, there was real disquiet: agitated figures rushed hither and thither, anxious faces craned out, every Roman who passed seemed to be angrily fending off knots of beseeching, weeping women. I overheard one, running alongside an officer pulling at his cloak, crying: "In the name of the justice of your law . . . In the name of Caesar . . . He has done nothing. . . ." It was a shock to realize at last that it was for Jesus the city was so troubled. But there were other groups, blocking the streets, hard-faced men jeering and chanting, "No King of the Jews! No King of the Jews!" They could afford to jeer. They were the ones who were having their way.

Somebody pulled John's sleeve and said, "They have left the guardhouse. You'll meet them if you don't get swept too far up." He was gone before I saw who it was. John put his arm round me and said, "Shall we go round the walls straight to the place of crucifixion? There's so much noise in the city."

"No," I said, "no, let's go with him."

"Let's try to get through here, then."

We were in a quiet side street opening into the busy stall-lined market street along which he must come. There were gardens and fine old houses in this part of the upper city, belonging to the priests and ruling families. Over my head was an apricot tree in blossom, reaching over a wall. I gazed at it and was taken back thirty years or more, to the months I had spent with Elisabeth when we were both with child, in her hilltop village where the sweet wind blew, the quiet, happy, happy months of that long-ago spring and summer. For there was an apricot tree then growing outside her door; it was in full song of blossom when I came there that blessed evening and fell into Elisabeth's arms crying for joy. Every morning I was there I went out to see how its leaves were unfolding, how far its fruit had got; all things in that time were full of hidden life. . . . My little apricot tree, I used to call him, when he was born, and sing to him Shulamith's song: "Like the apricot among the trees of the wood, so is my beloved among men; I sat down in his shadow with great delight and his fruit was sweet to my taste. . . ."

For a moment the grief and horror gave way. I was glad that there was an apricot tree out for his death too. Then John called, "Here they come!" and we were forcing our way out into the thick-packed bazaar street. We could hear the tramp and shouts of the soldiers, their route about to converge with ours, a little distance ahead. The crowd began to make haphazard way. As I stood looking up that long street waiting, all I could see was bustling humanity pressed together. Everywhere pilgrims were squatting, hastily erected stalls were selling Passover sweetmeats, goats and lambs, chickens and children ran, bleated and shouted. Most of the Passover sacrifices were not to be killed till that evening, and meanwhile every family had a lamb or kid even if they were sleeping in the street. The wine-sellers went up and down calling, the water-carriers toiled by, laden mules forced their reluctant way through, and now everyone was gathering here to see the crucifixion party pass. Here came the women from the houses, the rich and pious ladies of Jerusalem whose custom it was to console the condemned men as they passed and offer them drugged wine. And I stood and looked over it all, stretching as far as the eye could see, and it was as though I were standing in the camp of Israel of old, on the eve of the first Passover, that whole people preparing to march with their young and their old, their flocks and their herds. It must have been just so: the feverish expectation and preparation, the baggage, the column stretching out of sight, the long, long road ahead, the long years of wandering. The whole people seemed to be gathered there in front of me; as indeed to a large extent it was.

Then over the milling heads we saw the Roman lances appear, and pressed urgently forward. But so did every soul there, and the rich women were in front. We could see nothing but the lances and crests, until as we peered and pushed, I caught a glimpse of what seemed to be an ungainly, broken tree falling forwards in the street, a leafless, blighted branch. The next second I knew it was a man's body doubled under a crooked stake bound across his shoulders, his arms twisted back over it, but the image remained of that blasted, falling thing, like a dead tree.

Mary of Magdala let out a shriek when she saw him, John groaned, but I was silent in a greater pain than either of them can have known, for something was happening now which had not happened since the tranquil days of our life together at Nazareth, when it used to happen often: we thought each other's words before they were spoken. He was looking up at the ministering ladies and my ear caught his voice through the din: "Daughters of Jerusalem, don't weep for me; no, weep for yourselves and your children. The days are coming when you will say to the mountains, 'Fall on us', and to the hills, 'Cover us'. For if they do these things when the tree is green, what shall happen when it is dry?"

Then he was being driven on again with a curse, up that long, long street, and we lost sight of him again. And I was weeping at last, not only for him, but for all Jerusalem and all her children, who had pulled down on herself the curse of a dry tree; the green was withering, hanging in shreds of dead young leaves, death in the spring. And I was mother to all those cursed ones because my own son was treading that way ahead of them all under the sign of a stricken, hideous tree, no longer my little apricot tree but the terribly blasted one, flayed and bent, dragging

his stake up the hill to his accursed death. And as I followed
behind along that interminable road it seemed that this was
Israel's journey too, the lost wandering through the years that
that proud-hearted, hard-hearted people must fulfil, desolate,
rejected, cast off, God's own dearest banished from him. I saw
no end to that journey; I was Rachel weeping for her children,
because they were forsaken. Yet it was he who had cursed the
fig tree who had taken death on a tree for himself, it was he
whom Israel had rejected who was walking Israel's road, and
perhaps even then he was showing us the ways of God as he
always had: that God will not curse without himself bearing
the curse. For Israel had disobeyed a thousand times, rejected
and been rejected a thousand times, and yet is for ever God's
dearest and beloved, forsaken only to be more deeply found. And
though I saw nothing but death, perhaps I knew then in a way,
more than I had ever known, that my child was the Holy One;
and perhaps too he was more the Holy One in his forsakenness
than in all his apricot prime. But I thought no thoughts then
of holiness or forgiveness. There was nothing to see or think
of but death by blasting in the spring.

III *Mary Magdalene*

It was over at last, that waking nightmare, the shouting and
the sobbing, the catcalls and the harsh voices of the soldiers,
and the final terrible dying cry. I thought a lifetime must have
passed as we stood there; already some memories seemed like
things remembered from one's childhood—the slow fright of the
darkening sky, when we all looked up one by one to see why
the light was becoming so lurid; old Joanna standing at the
bottom of the hill bolt upright, her hands by her side, tears
streaming unheeded down her lined face; young Mary, Lazarus'
sister, who had come in the end, shouting into my shoulder,
"Why is hate always stronger than love? Why?"; John cowering
under the fearful sky crying through his hands. "It is darkness
over the whole world—not Israel only—there is darkness over
the whole world!" And hearing in the end those long-drawn-out

sobs and realizing they were my own, that had not paused since we came here. . . . Then it was over. They were taking the body down, we hardly knew why, or realized what a friend we had in that rich councillor. There was only the amazement, even now, that he let himself be carried off like that on a stretcher between two servants to a place he had not chosen and didn't know he was going to, he who had moved in such freedom and authority always and none of us had been able to hold. When I and the other women, following behind, came to the cave where Joseph meant to bury him, we saw him lying helpless on the rock slab and even then I know we all stopped in shock. Then we went in to help with the embalming.

And we were not so wrong. He had the same power as always, even now. It was the power of silence. Our sobs died away, and the desperate anguish, as though he had let himself down from the cross to give us peace. His presence was peace as it always had been. Perhaps I knew more than any how he had power to still, but it was as though he laid his hand on all of us grieving women and said, "Don't".

Joseph's servants were unwrapping a great bundle of myrrh and aloes, more than I had ever seen in my life. No-one was watching, so I laid my head down on his dirty, bloody chest and said in his ear, "Don't leave me. If you let go, the devils will come back, like they did to that poor man in your story, you know they will." There was no answer but the silence, the strong stillness, and it came to me that even the devils were dead. There was nothing to fear as there was nothing to hope for.

The youngest Mary was lamenting softly, "Must he lie in bitter aloes, oh must he lie in bitterness?"

"He must," said Mary his mother. But I said, "No! He was all life, all strength! Give him something fresh and sweet!"

"There are oils of cedarwood and sandalwood at home," said the other Mary, "I saw them when we anointed Lazarus. . . . Let's take some of these aloes and dress them."

And his mother seemed to change her mind. "Yes, it's right that all the trees should give their oil. Yes, for the blasted fig is lord of them all." But I did not know what she meant.

We cleaned the blood off as well as we could and laid him out in silence. The quiet and peace were growing, evening was falling. The Sabbath was beginning. We had to leave him as he was, wrapped in myrrh and aloes. We came out of the cave into the soft grey dusk. I was surprised by the smell of sweetness, by the greenness; I had not noticed when we went in that the tomb was in a garden.

"I believe this was the tomb Councillor Joseph had meant for himself," I said. "See, it's new-cut."

And whether at my words, or whether at the scent of the evening, the other two Maries fell suddenly weeping in each other's arms; the little one was sobbing, "He has to let us give him things now; burial, that's all he's ever taken from us, that's all he's ever let us give him"; and his mother, much calmer, was saying into her ear, "But nothing is a lot to give. It's what he's giving back to God now. He's the one with only his poverty to offer. My dear child, don't you understand he took all you so wanted to give?"

I was astonished. "That was the most characteristic thing about him! That he was so glad to be given things, even spoilt worn-out old things! He accepted everything!"

They smiled when I said that, smiling at me, I don't know why, but it was the first smile there had been for a long time. It was part of the spring evening and that fresh garden, the peace of life surrounding the greater peace of death, all new and young things growing around him, the way he was in his life; it made me remember him surrounded by children. There was a tree in blossom right over the cave, an apricot I think, and I was comforted somehow; that quiet stillness and strength of him were spreading over the garden. I didn't want to go away. I could bear it here. I didn't want the Sabbath and an enforced day in the house. I wanted to come back here and wrap him in sandalwood oils. Close to him here in this place of new life, I knew that I need not fear an empty heart, that his love lay undying in the tomb.

But we had to leave, and to hasten, if we were to be home by nightfall. Joseph's men were rolling a boulder against the cave mouth to keep out beasts of prey and tomb robbers. And the youngest Mary cried out again when she saw them at it.

"But Lazarus can't call him out! There's no-one, no-one to call him out!"

She was tormented all the time by the thought that Jesus had in a way changed places with her brother.

I took her arm as we hurried back down the hill carrying swathes of fragrant aloes, and said to her, "It's not true that hate is stronger than love. He still loves us even in death. Isn't it written in Scripture somewhere that love is strong as death?"

But she only laughed bitterly. "'Love is strong as death, jealousy cruel as the grave'! It was for jealousy they killed him. Love may be strong as death; it's not stronger. It's the cruelty wins."

Away from that garden, the peace was ebbing. I had no answer. We were coming down into festive Jerusalem, celebrating Passover. Sounds of glad voices and hymns came out of every window. All the people were rejoicing in God's redemption, both those who yesterday had shouted for crucifixion and those who today had seen their light go out, and the many more who knew nothing, cared nothing. They were one people again now: redemption must go on though hearts break.

I understood at last that he was dead.

34

THE LAST SABBATH

MARTHA WAS SETTING lights at a festive table when we came in, and we halted, scarcely believing what we saw, in the doorway. Her sister behind me exclaimed "Martha! What are you doing?" Martha turned round to us, her face swollen and crimson; I saw that her hand was so unsteady she had not succeeded in lighting the floating wick. She said in dogged defiance, "It's the Sabbath. It's dishonour to God not to keep it in delight." She looked at me and said, "Mary, you're his mother. Wouldn't he have wanted us to honour God on the Sabbath?"

"I'm sure he would," I said. The youngest Mary choked and fled from the room, but the rest of us came in in a kind of thankfulness. It was something we knew, something to come back to, Sabbath celebrations, and the lights were nice; we were so tired. We had never needed rest so much. I seemed to feel the thankfulness even of the body lying in its quiet tomb at last. But the rest we kept that evening and the next day was a quiet, deepening grief, and we needed that too. The youngest Mary, however, refused to keep it: "Why obey the commandment? Why obey any commandment? Why is God still keeping on his commandments? What's he doing now? Is he resting and contemplating his works?" And she spent her time running wild on the Mount of Olives, in the places she loved. We did not try to hold her in. Every one of us was tasting that bitterness which was swamping her.

"How can this have happened? Why did God not save him? Why did God withhold the kingdom? Did he not serve God faithfully? Is it true what they said, that he was deluded all along? Why did God do nothing?" Always that question, the bewilderment that was worse than the grief: "Why did God do nothing?"

"Perhaps he failed at the end. Perhaps God was no longer pleased with him."

"Or perhaps he was mistaken and it was never time for the Kingdom."

And little Mary's agonized phrase, repeated again and again: "Did it have to happen? Did he have to face death if God knew death would win? Did it have to happen?"

Joanna was out of her right mind. There was a strange scene the night before as we came down from the sepulchre, through Jerusalem. As we came to the Sheep Gate heading homewards she was there, her clothes rent, in the middle of the gate, prophesying. She was shouting that the earth had quaked and given up her dead when Jesus came among them. "I saw them, the holy ones, rising from their graves," she was shouting, "as it is written: All flesh shall arise and worship before the glory of the Lord. Behold them in the city, behold them in the Temple, they that dwelt in darkness! For how shall they lie in the dust whom God has visited with his glory?" She would not come back with us to Bethany, saying that she must cry aloud in the streets and Temple, telling Jerusalem to look up and see the children whom God had given her, the hosts of her own dead, for the holy city was given up to them and living flesh should live there no more. "This is the word of the Lord," she cried: "on this day the dead are more blessed than the living." And truly it may have been so.

But no visions came to the others of us, we had no word from the Lord except the Sabbath command to rest. We obeyed it humbly now as we had always obeyed it, without understanding, without hope, our trust in him refused and thrown back at us; there was still only obedience left to us. So we rested, that terrible rest, and blessed him for his handiwork and his everlasting law.

For me, at any rate, the bitterness was gone now. The deep Sabbath had overtaken us. I knew God was not mocking us, nor was he displeased with Jesus. It was not understanding, but it was something a little like it on another level than that of the mind: a profound quietness of knowing that indeed this had had to be. It came to seem with hindsight that I had known it for a long time, that all through his life I had been reading my baby's death. I could tell Mary now, "Yes, my dear, it did have to happen"; though no more than anyone could I tell her why. And yet again perhaps we did both know why, when she retorted to me, "Yes, because there's nothing but suffering for anyone who loves in this world," so that tears came into my eyes for her now, and I could say only, "Oh, my poor little one."

The deep Sabbath had overtaken us, God's silence on the last day of creation, himself the beginning and end of all things. It was John who said to me that day to comfort me, "He came from God, and went back to God, and knew that he would," and I answered, "I knew too." This was the silence and darkness of end and of beginning, the Sabbath of God himself. When it is said that "God ceased from all his works", what can it mean but that his unchanging self was seen once more, and he rested in his own eternity? Now we too saw his unchanging being, revealed to us in the end, but revealed as that which always was, his unfailing love. In the stillness of his own Sabbath he had borne the rejection of it by men, their rejection of his very stillness, of his eternity. In his creation he had sent out his love and in his Sabbath he endured the world's hate, taking it away and healing it in his own perpetual bliss. In his silence he is evermore rejected by men, by his own people, and is evermore forgiving them, and that is the meaning of death, it is the Sabbath of forgiveness as the waiting womb is the silence before his first word. For the angel spoke to me, but God was silent, and that was the beginning of creation. Then the word rang out, for six days it rang out, and rang with both joy and premonition. And now came the Sabbath of blessed, merciful rest, and all things were at peace in God's silent, unconquerable love.

35

THE NEW TOMB

So he had forsaken his three Maries at last, left us to comfort one another as best we could. And what was there for us to live for now? For me, was there betrothal and marriage. that famous betrothal? I'll never marry now, I thought. They can't make me. Mary his mother had courage of her own. I don't know where she got it from. Mary of Magdala was living for the morning, when she could go and finish anointing his body. What would she do when that was over?

I thought I would not sleep at all the night after that interminable Sabbath, but in fact I did half-sleep, half-awaken and half-sleep again all night, hearing the breathing, dream-moans and stifled weeping of all the others crowded into the room. We had clung together by instinct, and all the women who up to now had been camping under the olives were with us tonight; I was sharing my bed with Mary of Magdala. And I dreamt of her. I dreamt of that moment in the tomb when she exclaimed that this must be Joseph's own tomb, because it was so newly hewn. I had not really listened, but now in my dream she was telling me with such urgency that I couldn't ignore her: "It's a new tomb, Mary, it's a new tomb, no-one has ever died here before." I awoke and thought sleepily, though oddly shaken, "How silly, no-one dies in the tomb," and drifted away again. I don't know what else I dreamt, until at nearly the end of the night, after a long wakeful pause, there came into my mind on the brink of sleep an image of darkness, but not the darkness around me but as it were the night sky shot with fire. And sudden as the image, words came into my mind: "All creation issues from darkness and the hand of God." The fire was turning, falling and leaping in a single movement of shattering the blackness, spun flame soaring clear, and I knew that I was watching another creation, that God was again saying "Let there be light"—

but not the same light, not the same letting-be, it was not repetition but something as new as new creation itself, something none of us had ever guessed or seen. It was only the split second of the threshold of dreaming, and then I was fully awake again, lying in amazement saying to myself, "All creation issues from darkness and the hand of God." There were figures stealing about by shielded lamplight; Mary was gone from beside me. I got up, finding myself trembling as I did so for excitement at I scarcely knew what. Mary of Magdala, Joanna, who had come in late last night, Susanna and a couple of others were dressed for going out and had the sweet spices we had been making. "It's nearly dawn," whispered Mary, "we're going to the tomb. Are you coming?"

"Yes, of course, what about the other Mary?"

"Ah, don't wake her, or Martha, they've only just slept."

So we went softly out together, just the five of us. I was still shivering uncontrollably, from cold and from suspense. It was still dark. But the dawn breeze had begun to come up from the eastern hills. There was a freshness I had not felt since before these sombre days of unleavened bread had begun, indeed not since I could remember at all. It had all been darkness and heaviness so long. But the jubilation of that dream, if it was a dream, was ringing in my mind now, mixing with the soft crunching of the dust under our feet and the sweetness of the cold breeze. I could see the olives and pines all misty, the high skyline faintly traced where the great wilderness began, the heights of Judaea. There was a deep hush over everything: only far away a cock was crowing. We skirted the city walls in silence, passed under the Temple (I could not see it, but felt it hanging over me) and so up the hill towards the burial-garden. The deep waiting was growing more intense all the time, and the remembrance of who it was lying there at our destination was forcing itself into my mind almost with something of his own power. I said suddenly, "I'm frightened."

"Not of *him*?" Mary of Magdala said reproachfully, squeezing my hand.

"I'm just frightened, that's all. Yes, of him, if you like." I stopped and said aloud, almost involuntarily, "What can it mean for *him* to be dead?" In the quietness my voice sounded as loud as shouting. We all stopped, struck, I think, as I was struck, possessed, by the impossibility of him being dead. He and death were two things that could never go together. Yet he had died. Susanna broke the moment by saying, "What I'm afraid of is that we shan't be able to move the stone."

"There may be somebody to help us," another of us said, and we went on. But the power of the remembrance of him was growing, just as though he were there listening to us in the darkness, as he so often used to sit and listen unobserved with quiet laughter in him. I was really afraid now of seeing his body again. "But perhaps it will kill me too," I thought. And still the ringing joy of my dream went on and on, greater all the time, and the sense of the hidden power of him, but I had forgotten the words about creation; the charged silence seemed ready to break out into new words. The trees of the garden rustled softly. There was no-one to challenge us (we had heard a guard had been mounted). And then the fire and exultation broke and I knew them as terror, my own unrecognized terror, a second before we saw the gaping blackness of the open tomb, and became words indeed: "He is not here!" Someone was shouting them, perhaps I was, perhaps the terror was shouting itself. "He is not here! How can the living be among the dead?" It was my own question shattering the morning, taken up and echoed round and round: what could *his* death be? "He is not here!" But we were running already: only Mary of Magdala lingering, hesitant a moment, then she too running with the rest of us as fast as we could, in a fear like no other fear we had known, away from that death like no other death, away from the empty tomb.

36

THE PILLAR

THEY LAID HIM in a grave hewn in the rock, but none of them knew then how deep that grave was. He lay in the very heart of the earth, a guest in the pit of Sheol. And all men accounted him a thing of scorn, as since from the beginning the Holy One of Israel has been mocked of the peoples of the earth. But that was the night whose darkness became as the light. That was the night when the Lord blew the waters back with a strong east wind all night and laid the path of Sheol bare for his own passing. For with a mighty hand and stretched out arm God called his holy servant out of the pit of destruction, the one on whom he had set his love, his son, his beloved, and the earth was shaken and the graves opened at the power of his rising. In fire and in glory he arose and all who were slaves of their own wickedness followed him, for every enemy was overthrown in the sea before him. And what was it overthrew them? What but the brightness of his own presence and his triumphant love? For has God ever ceased to love his own? Is he not the Faithful One? And was that love not in Jesus? Did we who had followed him not see it? How then did we ever think that he could be silent in death? But his glory came from afar, from the depths of the land of slavery, in a pillar of fire to shelter and guide all whom he had brought with him, his redeemed ones.

But the thunder of his power who can understand? As Israel of old, so did we: we wept and lamented on the sea-shore when we were already saved and did not know it. Word spread that he had risen and been seen, but it seemed to us like folly and cruel jesting. We did not guess how the Lord had been fighting for us, how in the depths of the earth he had exerted his might. We had still not learnt to trust the faithfulness of God and of Jesus. But it was in the very darkness of our hearts that he arose, from the furthest caverns of the grave of our grief, alone and without our help, he came travelling in the greatness of his strength, in the victorious purple of his own blood, shattering the deepest darkness of our unbelief. Look, look how his glory comes speeding through the night, out from Egypt, up from the bottomless pit, see it coming nearer and nearer, to the mouth of the cave, bursting aside the futile stone, see it rising into the heavens, our Lord and God glorious in his triumph! And in the end even we knew it, the faint-hearted ones, we knew how his love had prevailed over all evil and over us, when we saw him on the mountain, a great concourse of us, just as Israel knew their God and Saviour when they saw his glory on the mountain of old. And as he led them then, so he leads us now: Christ Jesus going before us in a pillar of new fire.

37

THE SLEEPERS

THE BURDEN OF Joanna the prophetess, the wife of Chuza, Herod's steward.

On the day that the Lord Jesus died in Jerusalem, the word of the Lord came to me, "Woman, go down and lie among the dead." So I went and lay among the dead outside the city walls below the Gate of the Condemned; and there was great darkness; and I lay there until the sixth hour. Then one of the shadows arose and called to another above him, "Watchman, what of the night?" And he was answered, "Night has fallen, night without end, for the day has been turned into night and there is darkness at noon over all the earth!" Then all those shades that lay with me groaned and said, "We have hoped in vain, like men that trust in a mirage, and lo, it vanishes; there shall never any light dawn on us now!" And that place was fearful to me, for the darkness, and for the groaning.

Then the Lord God asked me, "Woman, what do you hear?" So I answered, "I hear footsteps far off, Lord, as of someone running down from Jerusalem." He asked me, "Whose do you think they are?" I said, "Lord, you know, not I." He said to me, "Ask among those who lie with you." So I cried aloud to the shades there, "Who can tell me whose are the footsteps which I hear running towards us?"

Then all those shapes began to stir and to rise, and looked on one another with amazed faces, and one cried, "Listen to the steps of the messenger that brings us the summons to battle! The Lord our God is sending to call us, as he promised long ago, when it was said by his prophet, 'The Lord shall surely come, and all his saints with him, and shall bring to light the hidden things of darkness.' O Jerusalem, look and see where your children are rising, that we may fight once more for the Lord before we sleep here for ever; O inhabitants of the land, fear greatly, for the doors of darkness shall be opened and the foundations of the earth are shaking!"

Then one who seemed to me older than Abraham rose and prayed, "I bless the Lord who this day has sent his messenger to bring me out of the pit, that I may see my children living on earth and bless them." But another stood up and cried more terribly, "No, old father of mankind, for this is no angel, but the Branch of David has been cut off. Howl, O people of the pit, and be horribly afraid, for never shall there be hope, never any more, for he whom the earth awaited is cut off into darkness, and the prince of life is slain."

Then a crying went up from all that multitude as of men that despair in battle, saying, "Woe is us! Have you also become as weak as we? Are you brought down to us? Is your splendour brought down to hell, and your glory made into food for worms? How are you fallen from heaven, O daystar, son of the morning! How are you cut down to the ground, when men looked for you to ascend into heaven! You of whom we said, His throne shall be exalted above the stars of God: you are laid in hell, in the uttermost part of the pit! And men shall shake their heads and say, 'Is this the man that made the earth tremble? Is this he that shook the kingdom of death, who is become its slave?' And great shall be the desolation, nor shall it ever have an end; nor will the Lord ever any more comfort his people."

Then the Lord God said to me, "Woman, do you know now whose steps those are?" I said, "Yes, Lord," and wept bitterly. But he said, "Do not weep, but listen now and tell me what you hear." I answered, "I hear a great knocking, and all the people of Sheol are in terror." He said, "Ask them what it means." So I cried out, "Which of you can tell me what this knocking is?" And they answered, "Beware, beware, for the earth must split and shake to receive him whom the heavens cannot contain; for death is too small for him, hell too narrow, yet he is knocking to come in as one of us!"

Then one whom I knew as the prophet John arose, with his garment of camel-hair about him, and cried, "He that is mightier than I is coming after me, on the road that I have prepared for him, even unto death! O foolish people, do you not know that this is his realm also, even from the time that he was baptized into our death, just as many shall be baptized into his?" Then he went swiftly to the gates of rock and called, "Lord, what of the night?" And a great voice answered him, "The night is ended, and day is at hand; and never again shall there be darkness, for the night of sorrow is past!" Then John commanded and said, "Open, you everlasting gates, lift up your heads, for the King of Glory to come in!" And at his words the gates fell to the ground and the earth shook; the rocks split and the grave was opened.

And I Joanna saw one like the Son of Man, clothed in greater brightness than the noonday sun, standing between the portals of the cavern of death, with as it were a rod like a cross in his hand, and a great light shone through that cave so that all the dwellers there fell down stunned; and he cried, "Peace be with you!" Now the old father who had spoken first had fallen on his face before him; so the Son of Man reached out his hand to him and raised him up, saying, "Arise, sleeper, arise from the dead, and I will give you light. I am your Lord, and I am your son. Arise, sleeper, for you were not created to lie fettered in Sheol. Arise from the dead, for I am the life of the dead." And as he raised him he breathed on him; and I saw that old man become young again and his chains fell from him, and he leapt for joy. And next he who had entered came to John the Baptist, who had opened the gates to him, and to him he said, "Well done, good and faithful servant! Enter into the joy of your Lord, and receive the Holy Spirit." So he breathed on him also, and the Holy Spirit came on him in fire, so that he exulted in gladness and praised God, saying, "This is what I always desired, to be baptized by you." Then the Son of Man came to a third, and took him in his arms, and kissed him, and said, "Peace be with you, abba, Joseph son of Heli." And he answered, "Is it truly you, my son, Jesus?" And he said, "It is I."

And now all that multitude of shades began to awake from their trance, into which they had fallen when the brightness of his presence struck them; and they cried aloud: "Thou art come, O our Redeemer, to us who dwelt in the pains of darkness; blessed is he who comes in the name of the Lord!" Then I saw where he entered in among them, and the splendour of the Lord filled that place of gloom, and he cried, "Come, you blessed of my Father, and inherit the kingdom prepared for you from the foundation of the world." And the chains fell from every one of them. Then he went to and fro among them with the song of the Lord on his lips, calling those who had been long forgotten out of the farthest depth, and those who had no hope out of the kingdom of sorrow; and as he went he reached out his hand to those who could not rise, and drove away the shadows from the eyes of those that could not see.

At last I saw where he came to the bottom-most vault, and in the farthest corner one lay with his face to the wall; and the Son of Man went to him calling, "Friend, what are you doing here?" And the other answered, "I am keeping my own place; for I am twice guilty, of your blood and of mine." Then the Son of Man said to him, "Yet you must arise; for did I not say to you that no man was taking my life from me, but I should lay it down of myself? And did I not tell you further that no sin against the Son of Man should be beyond forgiveness, but only to call his Spirit evil? And have I not made intercession for the transgressors?" But the other answered, "I can never arise; I am chained more than any of the inhabitants of the pit; I cannot move, nor turn towards you, for I am accursed in God's sight and in yours." Then it seemed to me that the Son of Man took hold of his chains and broke them, and raised him up, saying, "Yet see now, I have set you free." Then he that had lain in darkness cried, "Rabboni! Hail, my Master!" and kissed him.

Then the Son of Man took the broken chains that were still about the wrists of the other, and bound them to his own wrist, and said, "Was it not written of old, I have drawn you with bands of love?" And the other said, "I sought my own place, but you prevented me; I went down to hell, but you were there also; nor have you turned your mercy from me!" So he led him forth, and there was rejoicing among the shades. And the Lord God said to me, "Woman, do you understand what you have seen?" I answered, "How can I, unless someone explain it to me?" And the Lord God said, "Tell the dwellers on earth that captivity itself is led captive."

Now I saw where he who was like the Son of Man opened the prison-house and led out his own, whom he had redeemed; and they followed him singing, "Hosanna to the King of Israel! This is our God; we have waited for him, and he will save us; this is the Lord; we have waited for him; we will be glad and rejoice in his salvation." Then in his light they followed where he went before, and I followed after; the eyes of the blind were opened, and they saw him, and he led them out; so they were delivered from the land of death, and he freed the hosts of the dead.

Then the Lord God said to me, "Woman, where are you now?" And I answered, "In Jerusalem, and there is rain falling." He said, "Do you know what it is?" I said, "No, but it seems like a rain of blood and water, and the streets are running with it, and those who came with me from the lands of the dead are scooping it up in their hands." Then the Lord God said, "Was it not written that dew should fall on the dwellers in the dust? Taste it." So I scooped up some in my hands and drank it, and it was red wine and white; and I wept with joy to taste it. "Is it good?" the Lord God asked me, and I answered, "It is good, for he who gave it is good." Then the Lord God said to me, "This is the feast I promised to make for all people on Mount Zion, a feast of wine on the lees and of fat things full of marrow, of precious wines on the lees; and there shall never be an end to it, but this wine shall fall for ever and be poured out from heaven." Now the wine was sweeter than honey in the mouth, but it burnt like fire in the heart, and all who had been redeemed from death sang to the Lord and said, "We will praise and glorify thee, for thou hast been a stronghold to the poor and to the needy in his distress, a refuge from the storm and a shadow from the heat; O that men would praise the Lord for his goodness, for he has opened the gates of brass and burst the bars of iron!"

Then I asked, "Lord God, where is he who led us out?" And

he said, "Look there." And I saw him standing on the Mount of Olives, and from his side the dew of wine was springing out; and it fell on the Temple and the whole city of Jerusalem, and it shall never be exhausted.

Then the Lord God said to me, "Go now, woman, and cry to the inhabitants of Jerusalem to come out and see the delivered prisoners feasting in their streets, and bid them join. Cry in the Temple and in every thoroughfare that the Lord is raining dew from heaven and for three days there must be rejoicing, for the dead are redeemed; I am the Lord! And know this, woman, that they will not hear nor believe you; but afterwards they will; yet none of the living shall taste this wine until the empty grave be sealed again. And you must bear witness to them in that day that it was poured out on the dead also and they have drunk of it, for I am he who gives life to the dead. And at the end of three days my Son and Beloved shall lead them into the holy city, the heavenly Jerusalem, and Sheol shall be empty; and this too you must tell to them who live on earth, saying to them, 'Sheol is empty, and death is robbed of his prey, and you are the dead now, for they whom you think are dead are more living than you.' And know this, woman, that they will not believe you; yet for all who will believe, the red wine and the white shall be poured out, and they shall never know what it is to die, nor shall hell's chains ever bite on them; I am the Lord!"

So I ran through Jerusalem for three days, and cried as the Lord God had bidden me, and on the third day he said, "It is enough. The saints have entered the heavenly city in glory. Now cry again and tell them, that my holy servant Jesus was dead and is alive for evermore, and holds the keys of death and hell; I the Lord have spoken it. Cry, and rouse them, for they are all asleep, and mean to re-people Sheol if they can. Waken this people, woman, and tell them that if they choose the grave they shall have no companions there, for my righteous servant humbled himself to death and death is destroyed."

And so I run, and cry to Jew and foreigner:

"Awake, sleeper, arise from the dead, and Christ shall give you light."

And the wine in my mouth is grief and sweetness to me, the wine that is the joy of the dead; and it burns in my heart like fire, like burning coals amid kindling. For the Lord has poured out his glory, and we have drunk of it; we have tasted, and known his grace.

38

THE VAGABOND'S BREAKFAST

HE HAD TOLD us to follow him to Galilee. And I was thankful to leave the tension and tumult of Jerusalem and join the caravans of returning pilgrims, as though it had been an ordinary Passover, just one more completed Passover. We sang our slow way back to Galilee; there were few of us who could bear to stay in the city for the whole interval between Passover and Pentecost; better two arduous pilgrimages, for us slow men of the lake, than half the summer in Judaea. And I was choked with emotion, I could not take any more. It was not so much, now, the arrest and death of our Rabbi; not the burning in my mind of the fire where I denied him; but it was the cold dawn meeting with a stranger in a street of Jerusalem, it was the sudden knowing of him, it was the searing, speechless grief and the still more searing forgiveness, it was the command almost too hard to take to "Go back to your brethren and strengthen them." The word ran round the brotherhood, "The Lord is really risen! He has appeared to Simon!" but I could not tell them how it had been: the grey stone, the seeing him, the falling in the doorway, that doorway. . . .

No, it was not now the clamour and flicker of torchlight under the olives when they arrested him; it was that doorway, and it was the sweet, sweet joy of bread and honeycomb in the evening; the locked room, the stranger in our midst, the terror and the hope, the slaying sweetness of bread and fish and honeycomb, the peace and gladness. I was choked and dazed, I needed Galilee, I needed the water and the boats and the nets. The others were in little better case. When I announced that I was going fishing, James, John, Andrew and the other fishers wanted to come too. It was a still, apricot evening; we launched off without words, and the blessed darkness overtook us. There was no moon.

The lantern in the bows sent its soft glow in a circle round the boat; Andrew steered, and I worked the nets with the others. The peace of the work took us into itself—the casting, the drawing, the turning the boat, casting, drawing. Only late in the night did it occur to me that the fish were being uncommonly slow in rising. I asked James, "Zebedee say anything to you about scarcity of fish?" James shrugged, and we worked on. It was not really fish we had come out for. But now none of us could help thinking of that first morning when we had caught nothing all night, and then our Master used the *Rose of Sharon* to preach from, and afterwards we split the nets when we drew them in.

We rowed slowly in at the first lightening of the eastern horizon: not to Capernaum itself, but to the cove outside where we used to dry our nets on the beach. John said, "Do you remember Acumenos of Caesarea telling us how the Greeks say the sea is made of wine?"

Acumenos was a strolling philosopher, who made his living by amusing idle Romans, undertaking to defend or attack any proposition they cared to put to him. He used to look at our catch and say sadly, "Anything from Greece today?" and I would pick out something and swear it had swum in from the seas of Greece, and many other jokes we had with him. "I thought he was only quoting poetry," I said.

"It looks just like wine now," said John. "Inexhaustible wine." I understood suddenly what he was thinking and it hurt like a spasm of cramp. "Don't, John," I said.

As we came through the gentle dark ripples (that were, indeed, just like wine), with the sky still night above us, one by one we grunted with surprise as we saw an orange point of fire on the beach. "Someone's put in already. But who? Were any of the other boats out? Oh, some wanderer." We gave it no more thought, yet there was something about the fullness and emptiness of that night—the fullness of the richness and darkness, the peace, the inexhaustible wine, and yet the loneliness, the towering firmament, the failure of the fish, the absence of him who was filling all our thoughts—it was like a sign. The silence that had been with us all night seemed a waiting, as though all things about us, the water, the fish in the depths, the fresh smell of dawn, the night itself, knew what was coming and who was there and were hushed in his honour, and only we did not (or did we not?).

We could see the lonely watcher by his fire now, a pale figure in the half-light of the very early dawn, standing and watching us come in. There was no sound but the soft splashing of our oars, till he hailed us: "Had any luck?"

"No," I called back, "not a tiddler."

"Try on the other side," he said. We looked at each other; then we drew the net round the stern and cast it on the other side, and straight away felt it dragging, tugging, jumping, and the *Rose* keeled over with the sudden weight—the fullness. John and I stared at each other; John's mouth tried to frame the words "It's . . ." but he could not speak. And I suddenly grabbed my cloak and plunged into the shallows, wading, paddling, trying to run through the soft sand and waist-high water, to get there, to get to him, and I threw myself on my face before the stranger and his fire.

The others came up presently towing the nets behind the boat. "Bring some of your catch and join me at breakfast," he invited; still playing at being the unknown vagabond, teasing us as ever. I thought of Cleophas' comic chagrin, as he told us, "Ten miles he walked with us, and he was laughing at us the whole time—he never let on—and pretending that he didn't know a thing about it—I thought he was laughing, I even told him there was nothing to laugh about, and all the time it was himself." But we knew him now, though none of us dared to challenge him by name, and we knew that his casual invitation was nothing other than the solemn bidding of God who calls his children to feast with him, and gives his own fullness, as he gave us then fish cooked on charcoal on a Galilean beach in the dawn.

It was something he had so often done with us: the taking of bread or fish, the blessing, breaking and giving, and each time it seemed to mean more, he seemed to be giving more. This time it was all the hidden glory and bounty behind the arching night and the rising sun, all the presence of that creating and saving love which was focused in him now, all the fullness of God himself. The wanderer by the fire on the stones, spearing fish on a stake to offer to us, was host at God's very banquet that he made once for Adam in Paradise (so the rabbis tell us) and will make again at the end of time for his own. For he lives in festivity always on his blissful throne, and Jesus now with the grave joy and silent laughter in his face was sharing it with us.

And the teasing at the end that broke and healed my heart ("Simon son of Jonas, do you love me?"—again and again, till that denial that haunted my thoughts was purged out and undone)—did it not mean the same? That I should do what he was doing now, and take his place at the table of God's mercy and welcome: make my poor tramp's fire of coals on a fishermen's beach and so call his own to the feast of his joy? "Do you love me? Then feed my sheep." The glory, the fullness, pouring down into a single point of giving? I began to tremble and sweat as understanding gradually came, and he looked at me and said, "Yes, it will mean for you, too, what it did for me: to be bound and delivered up, the final giving; but don't you remember what I said to you at first? Follow me."

Who knows what it costs God to give himself? We saw giving unto death in Jesus; yet neither was that the end for him, nor shall it be for us.

As the sun came up over the hills beyond the lake, a golden shaft struck his face; the fresh wind lifted our hair and stirred the water. I remember the smells: smell of the lake, smell of smoke, smell of grilling fish. I remember his firelit hand giving us the fish and his sunlit face. Smells of all new things, the new, young light, the joy growing beyond belief, yet gently enough to bear. It is these he has left for us to remember, not the thudding grief of denial and desertion, not the inexorable crushing of his life, but all things restored. For we drew up the nets full at last, and we ate and drank with him after he rose from the dead.

39

SEEN BY ANGELS

As I came back through the thronged streets of the Upper City after offering the evening sacrifice of praise in the Temple, my heart was overflowing with such joy that I sang softly under my breath, and the meaning, though not the words, was, "O praise the Lord, for he is good, and his mercy endures for ever." The children squatting over their games by the doorways called up at me, "The Lord prosper you, old Abba Hananiah," and I blessed them in the name of Jesus, his holy servant, who was put to death in this city and raised for our forgiveness, to pardon us in God's name for all our transgressions from of old. For so the Lord has never ceased to deal with his chosen people Israel, and now in these last days he has shown us the fullness of his mercy. Ever since I entered manhood at twelve years of age I have walked these streets to the Temple and back, twice daily, and blessed the children as I passed, but I bless them in the power of his Anointed One now, though I would also like to say, "Not Abba, my little ones; don't call me Abba", since the Lord Jesus gave us that name for our Father in heaven alone. But they would not have understood, and they had been calling me Abba Hananiah all their lives.

We had broken bread earlier, in the house of Mary and her son John Mark, in memory of the Lord's suffering and the glorious power which raised him from the dead. And as we were praying and blessing the Lord, the Spirit moved our hearts, and we sang a new song:

"He who was shown to us in the body
    was shown triumphant in the Spirit
    and was seen by angels;

he it is whom we proclaim,
  the hope of all the earth,
    glorified in highest heaven."

At that, Peter leapt to his feet. "Brethren," he cried, "how blessed are we, who saw him thus exalted! For we were with him when he bade us farewell. He led us out towards Bethany, to the Mount of Olives, where we had so often gone with him, and there he gave us his last commission to tell to all the world the good news of the Kingdom in his name; and he told us never to fear, for he would be with us. And then as he blessed us, for very brightness we saw him no more; yet I tell you, brethren, that once before, we had seen him overshadowed by the Splendour of God, so that we quaked and fell as dead men, and thought we would have been destroyed for the revealing of that Glory. Yet how glad I would have been for that Glory to remain, unveiled, and fill the whole earth! But it was not to be: not then. It departed and hid itself once more. But surely when it shone again on Olivet, it had come to rest on the Lord Jesus for ever, no longer only transfigured, but glorified; for he was raised to God's right hand, and all heaven made way for him, and we saw his passing, but no more; for God had as it were hidden us in a cleft in the rock that we should not be destroyed by seeing more than we could bear. And you all know that it is from his place next to the Father that he has sent us his Spirit; to him be the praise!" And we all cried "Amen!" to Peter's words, and the Spirit sang again in us a new song:

"Made as a man,
  humble as a slave,
    he was not ashamed to die as a transgressor.

Therefore God exalted him
  and gave him the name above all names;
    yes, at the name of Jesus every knee shall bow!"

And the whole house rocked with the power of the Spirit. I was passing below the Antonia garrison fortress now, the little streets under the Temple walls left behind, but I was thinking of all these things and scarcely saw the proud monstrosity of it. All my life, as I've passed it, I've raised my fist against it, but I don't care about it now, for we have a greater king than Caesar: Caesar was never exalted to heaven, or given power over death and hell. But today, as I hastened on, a rough voice I knew called: "Well, old Hananiah! Done your duty in the Temple? How was it? See anything of your God?"

I stopped, ready to weep, laugh and be angry, all at once. It was Gaius Nonus, chiliarch of the cohort, who from the time he was first stationed here had been amused by my grey Jewish beard hurrying past his guardroom, morning and evening, and had early on taken to hailing me in this way in order to tease me. He was no fearer of the true God, yet in a way we were friends.

I told him now, "I have seen more glory than you can dream of."

He was standing arms akimbo in the side entrance, while the sentries stood to attention. "You're very easily pleased," he said.

"On the contrary," I answered, "it is you who are content with pieces of carved wood and stone, which you say show you what your gods are like."

He laughed heartily. "Hark at him! What a Jew! If you had ever seen the Jupiter of Phidias, you would know then whom to call the father of gods and men. If you had seen the Minerva that stood over the harbour of the town where I lived when I was a boy, you would know what divine beauty is. But your God has shown no face at all. If he has chosen you for his own people, why doesn't he show himself to you?"

"No man can see God and live," I quoted God's own words to Moses. "Yet he has shown himself: in his deeds and glory. To us—not to you—he has shown himself."

"But not with a face to him! And why not to us? I'm sure we'd honour him if we'd ever seen him. Can it be that he fears he is not so handsome as Jupiter? Or is he there at all?"

"Enough!" I cried. "Don't blaspheme, you ignorant dog!"

He looked at me slyly. "After so many years of an absentee

God, I suppose an absentee Messiah seems natural to you."
For he knew that I honoured Jesus as God's Holy One, we had
spoken about him before. "In Rome, we think a king should
reign!" He believed that his soldiers had ended Jesus' reign
before it began by crucifying him. The truth was impossible to
tell to him.

"Ah, no, enough, Chiliarch," I said. "Don't blaspheme.
When he comes in his glory, so that even you can see it, do you
want to be counted among his persecutors?"

At that, to my surprise, he turned away as though uneasy.
"We arrested him," he muttered, "we had to. We had good
reason. But it was your own people who forced us to execute
him. They were rioting for his death."

"Ah! Hard is the heart and blind are the eyes of Israel!"
I cried, "Yes, when God revealed himself at last, and sent us
his own Son, who knew him? It is too true! But now God has
vindicated him by raising him in his own might and covering
him with his own splendour, so that all men may know him and
repent, and accept forgiveness in his name."

But Gaius Nonus had lost interest. "A thousand years of
awaiting the Messiah, and then whoops! he's back into heaven
like a spent arrow, because he found the power of Rome hotter
than he thought!" He chuckled, and went inside. I went on, but
I was sad at heart now. "O Lord, why do the heathen mock us
yet?" I prayed. "Why are we who believe so few? Truly, you
have not chosen us because we are many or great!" I thought of
Peter the fisherman; James the Lord's brother, the carpenter;
Mary the poor widow, and the other Mary, the one of ill fame;
and I thought, "Yet we have seen his glory. We have seen it."
Then I remembered the priests who had engineered his death,
the lawyers who had counselled it, the Pharisees who had desired
it, and the patriots who had rioted for it, and I cried aloud,
"Who is blind and deaf as the Lord's servant Israel?" And there
was bitterness in my soul. "O Lord Jesus," I prayed, "come soon,
and let them all see. How long will you hold back? Why do
you not show yourself? Is it not true, what the Roman said
just now?" So I thought in the folly of my heart, never guessing

into what unbelief I myself was falling. "Why did you have to leave us and go into heaven, Lord? Why could you not have set up your reign on earth then? O Lord God Almighty, why is thy glory hidden?"

I had no time to think further on these things that night, for ten poor men, my brothers in the Lord, were lodged with me, and my daughter and I were hard at work serving them until late; and then we sang psalms until the lamp ran out of oil. I had no more until someone paid me for his shoes, or until one of the brethren gave me some oil. What then was my consternation when much later that night, a light shone on me, awaking me?

A man in white was standing by my bed. I knew the moment I saw him that he was one of the four angels who hold back the winds, which on the Day of the Lord shall be let loose. "Hananiah!" he said. I was in terror at the sight of this figure from the end of time, yet I managed to answer, "Here am I." "Why are you grieving because the Lord has entered heaven?" the angel asked me. "What is it you would see, that you do not see? Or why do you sorrow for losing that which is your own? But go now to Peter and John and tell them all that is in your heart." Then I was sweating and shaking alone in the darkness.

I rose at once, put on my sandals, wrapped my cloak round me and hastened to Mary's house, where Peter, John, and several of the other apostles were staying, with Mary the mother of Jesus and James his brother. Rhoda the maid opened to me, late as it was, and I found Peter and John within, still awake, praying together, for Peter (I learnt later) had been greatly troubled in a dream.

When I told them, incoherently enough, of the heavenly apparition, they looked at each other and nodded. "It was he, and another of those Four," Peter said to me, "who told the women not to look in the sepulchre for the body of the Lord. And they stood beside us again when the Lord was received into his Father's glory, and told us not to stand there staring into the sky, where we would never see him; but he would come again in the bright splendour of God, that we had seen take him."

"And now?" I asked, and with a dragging heart I added,

"I had been grieving that after all his suffering, and after the Father has raised him in glory, we still do not see him king of Israel, and Jerusalem is still trodden down."

There was silence before Peter said, "The Lord has sent to tell us that for us Jerusalem is in heaven. Oh, Jerusalem!" He covered his face with his hands, and I said, suddenly guessing, "Is great woe coming to Jerusalem? Did the Lord Jesus prophesy it?" He nodded without looking up, and I was afraid. Then he said, "For a little while yet the angels are with us to protect us and deliver us. But sooner or later we must shed our blood and Jerusalem must shed hers."

Now John spoke for the first time, not directly answering Peter but me.

"He is king of Israel, and we saw him crowned, when he was lifted up on the cross with the title 'King of the Jews' written above his head. He is king already, and we saw his glory. It never did depart on the mountain where we saw him transfigured. Peter was afraid that it would leave us, and he tried to capture it in tabernacles—oh, Peter, I heard you! But it had been shining all along, and it shone afterwards too. The glory remained, it was we who wavered. It never departed, but it did hide itself, in the one true tabernacle, the one true temple." His eyes glowed, and I understood that he meant the body of the Lord.

He leant forwards and placed his hand on my shoulders. "Don't grieve for the passing of any of the old tabernacles!" he insisted, and looked sideways at Peter. "On the night before he died the Lord commanded it. He told us to rejoice for his going away. Peter, don't you remember? He said it was good for us that he should leave us, because otherwise he could not come to us in the Spirit. Would you have those days back again, and lose his Spirit from your heart? Go back to being servants instead of sons? And the same for his holy city, his holy people. If the time should ever come when God is no longer worshipped on Mount Zion, it will be because he is receiving the worship he truly wants, worship in spirit and truth."

Peter looked up at last, and I saw tears in his eyes. He said,

"It is kept in heaven—the glory! It is laid up for us there all safe, an inheritance that nothing can destroy, but it's not for us now." He stood up as though he could see it better that way, and words began to pour out of him in his eagerness, yet tears were running down his face too. "Yes, that's our treasure, God's keeping it for us, the glory that shall be revealed at the end, the salvation there shall be. He's testing our faith now by waiting and hiding himself, but we'll see him at last, and Jesus Christ in his kingdom. We don't see him now, yet we love him, we trust in him without seeing him, and that's already joy too great for words—" and it was true, he broke down for a moment. When he went on it was no longer to us that he was speaking.

"So it is, O Lord God, you have called us out of darkness into your marvellous light; you have said 'Come here, my people!' to us who had made ourselves your strangers and enemies. O blessed be our God and Father, and the God and Father of our Lord Jesus Christ!"

And there we stood praising God in the night for his unseen glory, and for all the suffering and desolation we had begun to guess were coming, praising him with joy too great for words; blessing the God of Israel who had never shown us his face, and Jesus his Son who had hidden his face from us. And in a little while the Spirit himself gave us words, and we knew then by the love and power in our hearts that Christ Jesus himself was present there with us; we knew it more surely than by any seeing.

40

THE TRAVELLER

WAITING WHILE THE brethren come, in ones and twos, stealing through the Jerusalem streets with baskets of bread or fruit under their cloaks, the suspense, the uneasiness come again; the stirring, hushed hope. We who know each other so well, men who have been through so much with each other, we sit silent in the lamplight and exchange shining-eyed looks with one another, needing to say nothing, while on the table the bread and wine lie in their own silence and Peter or James is a dark, upright shape at the table's head, waiting to preside. Everything is full of waiting, while at the door there are fresh steps and knocks and whispers, happy exclamations.

And we know what is going to happen, and yet we never know. It will be just as it was when the Lord broke bread for Cleophas and me at Emmaus—the sudden recognition, the leaping-up of the fire in the heart—and yet it never happens twice the same. Or perhaps it is the one time always new.

He goes on surprising us; and yet each time too, there's the same sense that there was at Emmaus: "He was there all the time." The breaking of the bread only showed him who had been walking with us, laughing in his hiddenness, all that long footsore journey from Jerusalem. And the uneasiness: "Who is that there with us? Who is it? When did he come?"

Yes, it was just like that, on our sorrowful tramp: when he spoke to us, the stranger beside us, and suddenly we were both wondering, "Who is this? How long has he been walking with us?" And we didn't know.

And yet we did know. There's that too, the same now as then: at the breaking, the recognizing, there comes the sureness, "We knew him all along." Yet never knowing when he joined us, when his journey with us began.

The uneasiness before. The shadows, the flames, the glowing

eyes, the waiting. It's the waiting of hope now, but I remember that first waiting of fear. There had been peace at his burial. But then there came fear, a strange fear, fear of women's visions and perhaps—even then—fear of him, when we heard that the grave had been robbed and the tomb was empty.

I remember wondering at the time if I had felt it coming. For the news struck me with such a sense of inevitability, a thud of rightness. It was like him, to leave his tomb. It was how he might have acted if he had been living. That much we might know of him, that he could not be held down. And there were the words he had spoken to Cleophas and myself when we became his disciples on the same day. "Master, I will follow you wherever you go!" I had cried, and he answered sombrely, "Foxes have holes, the birds of the air have their nests, but the Son of Man has nowhere to lay his head." A little further on, we met Cleophas, his clothes torn, kneeling in the road. "My father died today," he said. "When I have buried him, will you be my new father, and make me your disciple?" But Jesus answered him: "Leave the dead to bury their dead. You must go and announce the kingdom of God." As though to say, "Not 'when'. Now!" There was always that ruthlessness and urgency in him, and you might say the refusal of anywhere to lay his head. We could have known he would not lie for long in any tomb of ours. The fate of a lost body, the prey of grave robbers, seemed right for him. There was no real resting-place for him on the earth. And still we were afraid, thinking of his homelessness, afraid of his wandering in death as we had stood in awe of his comings and goings in life.

He journeyed endlessly, walking always, never riding, except on his last solemn entry into Jerusalem. He had chosen that way, God's will for him, the way of a poor man, a wandering vagabond. He travelled the country in poverty and freedom and shed awe wherever he went. I only made a short journey with him, a trifle compared with the distances the Eleven must have gone, yet that one hard march has eaten its way into my bones, my very body remembers it, so that even sleeping in my bed, I wake up sometimes with my legs kicking and my feet aching.

Walking along any sunny, dusty road, I catch myself looking up all the time, expecting to see him striding on ahead, deep in dispute with someone, or calling out his greeting to the workers in the fields. But when we did see him, it was not like that. He was there when we were not looking for him, not striding ahead but at our elbow, unrecognized and most deeply known.

Who was he? Which of us ever really knew? Which of us knows now? There is old Taddai, whom he healed from paralysis, who claims that for close on forty years he had come and stood behind him where he lay at Bethesda pool, behind him, where Taddai could never see him, but truly stood there (Taddai believes) and looked at him every day to see if he was ready to accept healing yet. We smile a little at his story. Forty years! The Lord did not live forty years on earth. Yet we know well enough what Taddai means and none of us argues with him. We don't know when the stranger joined us on the road. For he walked in the mystery of God, and how long has God journeyed with us? Since he hid his presence in the ark of the covenant and sent his angel before us in the wilderness, to be as it were his face towards us? Since he moved before and behind us in a pillar of cloud and fire to shelter and save us? Or before that, did he go with Abraham, to be his shield and exceeding great reward? Was it to Moses only that he said, "Certainly I shall be with you"? Surely this is the truth: that when man was cast out of paradise to wander on the face of the earth, God came also, unseen, and man did not know it, nor guess for many generations who was with him, had not cast him off but was with him.

For he who cannot be commanded is the faithful and true, and his mystery is his goodness. His comings frighten us, we don't understand. When Jesus left his grave we were frightened, not understanding that it meant that he was living and had come back to us, had kept faith with us. And though we pray for it we are afraid of his last and greatest coming, God's final visitation, his last appearing in our midst to startle and terrify us. But it will only be the vindication of our trust in him and he will only come as he who was there always.

How can we think of the humility of God? Which of us understands his presence and his journeying with us? Which of us understands how he came to us in Jesus? There is no getting used to him, there is no getting used to Jesus; he will meet and amaze us as long as he is walking with us, and that is all the way, the whole weary way. But at the end, at the table of his kingdom, we shall know him in the new breaking of bread, know at last who it was with us, who was there always.